MORANT

MORANT

Roy Goddard

ERRATUM PRESS

ISBN: 978-1-7397708-3-9

First edition.

First published in 2022 by Erratum Press
Sheffield, UK
www.erratumpress.com

Design and typesetting by Ansgar Allen

A year or two before steam traction was abandoned in Great Britain a diesel train pulled into Stafford station, a train from which David Morant, who had been troubled by excitement and dread, descended. During the journey from London he had been beset by diarrhoea and vomiting. It started here and would reoccur for much of his life so that whenever he travelled he had to take care to plan his journeys in order to avoid embarrassment, as far as this was possible. The broken sleep that afflicted him began at a later date. As he carried his suitcase along the platform, he noticed that there were a few others, mostly a little younger than himself, similarly burdened and heading towards the bridge across to the platform on the other side of the track. As he crossed the bridge, as he descended to the other platform, he finally yielded to what seemed to him a recognition that his life was about to blaze and the world to appear to him for the first time, as he had always known it would, in its full, ungoverned possibility. He was to remember little about that day, except that it was perhaps overcast, the sky pale grey, unaccommodating, and not at all like another station in France, Lyons perhaps, the sun so bright that it seemed to bleach the colour out of the scene, so that there was just the dark shade created by the roof above the platform and a blinding whiteness beyond. This was how he remembered it, how he remembered the whole of the south of France in those few weeks of that earlier summer when he and his friend Tommy had hitched across France. On the platform they had observed a group of young men mock a very tall young woman who had dressed oddly, as her mother might have, one of them following her on tiptoe, imitating her walk and speaking in a high, piping voice which amused his friends. Later that evening, they were still waiting for their train—he couldn't remember why they had to wait so long—and a young man, older than themselves, walked past with a rucksack. They noticed that he wore what later became known as desert boots and that he must therefore be English as this kind of footwear did not appear to exist in France. When the train arrived he boarded the same carriage as them and they spoke. He was Welsh, an art student and bearded as Morant was to be in a couple of years' time, and he had hitch-hiked to and from Turkey, now using the last of his money to finish the journey by train. It was his opinion that the French knew how to live better than the British, but were heartless, as evidenced by the incident, which he too had observed, with the tall young woman. The train was nearly full, but there was a compartment with three or four men who looked North African. The art student had spoken to them in French and he said to Morant and his friend that they could sit in the empty seats. The North Africans looked angry and started to protest. The student said that they were saying that their mates were coming back. David and Tommy thought perhaps they should move. The Welshman said that it would be OK and to ignore them. When the other Algerians returned two of them were left unseated. They started to shout and one of them drew a knife. The student said not to move, that they would back down. They always did. They did back down, appearing to appeal noisily to their seated friends to witness the injustice of what had happened, before leaving, presumably to look for seats elsewhere on the train. Morant had felt embarrassed and a little ashamed, but he also felt exhilarated. The student was from Usk and was at the Slade. Tommy went to the Slade three years later. On this later day, this North Midlands day, Morant knew that he would, again but more purposefully, be unfaithful to his wife, that he was embarking upon a phase of his life that would lead to him abandoning her, and he knew that he was going to behave cruelly and selfishly, but that this knowledge was not going to inhibit him. Later in life he would turn over the idea that his generation had been driven by two commandments: to enjoy this life and to change the world. In forty years' time one of his students was to ask him, with a look that combined amused scepticism and prurience, what the sixties had really been like, and he had said that it was a time when you felt that things were about to change or that you could make them change, that entrenched hierarchies, fossilised authorities could be overthrown and new, freer and more just ways of being could be brought about. It was a time when it was exciting to be young. He had hedged his answer with what he had hoped would be a consoling, conciliatory recognition— he did not want to appear to be suggesting that the young man's experience of youth, his time of efflorescence, of hope and possibility, was a necessarily inferior episode, although he thought that in some ways that was likely to be the case; and he was keen too not to come across as a sixties bore—that it was always, or should always be, exciting to be young, but that those years were a fortunate moment in time to be young, for which, of course, his generation could claim no credit. There had been other such times, no doubt historically more significant moments. And, of course, he said to his student, the great liberalising reforms of the sixties, ending capital punishment, decriminalising homosexuality and legalising abortion and so on, were the work of an older generation. He added the standard admissions that it had been a period marked by what had turned out to be political naivety and that the sixties, as they had come to be understood, were only experienced by a fragment of society, a small minority of the generations clustered around the decade that began some years after 1960 and ended in the early seventies. He forbore to say that this had been a time of infinite possibility, an opening into difference, a moment in which everything was questioned for its naturalness; the time—time—was replete with a variousness that was now unimaginable, almost impossible to communicate in the obliteratingly monolithic, the crushed and glitteringly sterile present, this congealed world, where passage into another possibility, the choice of exile, is all but sealed off. The nice young man—for some reason his students had seemed to become increasingly pleasant and amusing as he grew older—had looked a little disappointed so he added that there had been drugs and some sexual abandon, but not, for most, on the scale that, he had gathered, might well exist amongst some young people today. The student smiled and Morant knew that he was responding within the conventions of a game he and his students had evolved, in which he played the part of an older person who was surprised and perhaps regretful at the respectability he appeared to have attained and at the distance that separated him from them, whilst the students' role was to be amused by and to gently deride his dotarded condition even as they recognised, but never stated, that their tutor was, or at least, had been in the past, a little more rascally than he was letting on. A game of power in which he was in control, but one which, he hoped, was about the pleasures involved in tweaking the boundaries of authority rather than flattering his vanity, although he did enjoy being viewed as someone who had possibly enjoyed a lively earlier life. It was also part of a broader pedagogical strategy involving the kind of authority he wanted to lay claim to. Once, in a teaching session, one of his students had started a discussion about teacher and pupil relationships being based on familial relations—parent-child, older sibling-younger sibling and so on—and someone had asked him how, in family terms, he saw his relationship with them. He had demurred, but when pressed had said that he'd be the faintly disreputable uncle who'd been off somewhere, doing something the family disapproved of, like joining the merchant marine or living with someone foreign, and who told his nephews and nieces things their parents wouldn't. And none of this had been planned; it was how, between them, things had been unfolded, a patterning within the network of possibilities. Even here, perhaps, as he stepped onto the station platform in this North Midlands town he recognised that the twin injunctions—to live freely and fully, without stale and customary constraints, and to do good in the world—were not free of contradiction. He would change his world and enjoy it and he would wreck someone else's.

Morant would recall a coach outside the station meeting the arriving students, a meticulously paternalistic provision that would perhaps not be offered to students in later decades, although he had no knowledge of these things outside of the city university in which he worked or those to which his wife's and his friends' children had gone. On board he noticed a young man whose face was arranged in what seemed a carefully composed expression of cynicism, a ludicrously disdainful contempt. Some months later this student was to accuse Morant of being too intelligent when he pointed out the logical inconsistencies in an argument the student had made about class and academic achievement. Although he was never part of the groups Morant moved amongst at college the accuracy of this initial impression was confirmed by the unremitting sarcasm and pessimism that this student, whose name he would forget, although it was probably something like Roger or Tim, directed at any notion of education as a transformative or emancipatory endeavour, indeed at any intellectual effort at all. Morant could find cynicism amusing, but Roger's was charmless, humourless, unrelieved by the energetic irony or self-parody that might make it entertaining. It seemed to be the dominant and defining component of his personality, a grim monologism of selfhood. Several years later in a London pub, a pub in Richmond with a beautifully unsettling view of the Thames, Morant ran into Roger who talked at length about the pleasure he derived from teaching, his involvement with the work of his subject association and his conviction that he was involved in a vitally important enterprise. At that time Morant's feelings about their profession had been very different. Many years afterwards, remembering this encounter, he would wonder if, and in what form, Roger's faith had survived. The coach took Morant and the other students to what he discovered later had been war-time accommodation for workers at an ordinance factory, although at that time Morant had been told that this collection of buildings was an ex-RAF base, which had made it fitting that on his way to the day's induction meeting he encountered a young man with a neatly trimmed moustache who might have come from the forties, carrying a heavy suitcase and an instrument case. Inexplicably, he was wearing a dark grey suit. He smiled at Morant and said, in that curious home counties whine whose aspiration to received pronunciation is disarmed by cockney vowels and tantalising residues of a pre-industrial accent, I should have brought my batman. This was, he was to find out, Capel, John Capel, whose knowledge of every aspect of the counter-culture—music, politics, style—sat alongside a rigorous abstention from any actual participation in the dress, the behaviours or the cultural preferences of those times. The moustache was to become an equally kempt goatee. Decades later, Morant would wonder whether the beard was an experiment, a cautious move towards sixties unruliness—Capel's only one, since he always wore pressed trousers, polished leather shoes and the sorts of shirt that demanded, and often got, a sports jacket—or whether it was a nod towards a high-tone bohemianism to go with the classical music and jazz that he played and studied. Morant's only other clear recollection from a day that included an introductory session in a hall was sitting in the common room of a men's block—these were Nissan huts, four for male students and seven for female—listening to exchanges that were dominated by a rangy young man who offered, with extraordinary confidence, cynical, entertaining observations on the organisation of the day, the campus and the probable (poor) quality of the course they had embarked upon. Morant was immediately attracted to this student and knew that they would become friends. In this, he was correct, although after a few months the friendship declined into a more or less amicable acquaintance. Like many people Morant was to meet in his life, Tam Brown seemed to feel that nothing mattered, that all endeavour was worthless, pointless, that humanity was incapable of ordering itself peaceably and justly. In some this was a fear or suspicion which nestled uncomfortably in some hollowed part of them, a terror to be conciliated, to be placated by not questioning its residence in their being, a presence not to be disturbed, but which from time to time invaded everyday life. For Tam it seemed to be a deep conviction of the meaninglessness of things, a truth it was always best to keep in view but whose annihilating horror was to be held at bay by a mocking and vigilant recognition of the shitness of everything. Later it seemed to Morant that such people were, in one way or another, fearful of the world, believing that they themselves were worthless, unvalued, unlovable, and, as he imagined it, their nihilism nourished in a destitute inner space, a void that harboured the truth of the insubstantiality, the precarious contrivance of all human relations. In the first term Tam and Morant agreed to write a novel together, a satirical account of life in their unregarded corner of higher education, to be modelled on Terry Southern's The Magic Christian, which, as far as Morant knew, neither of them had read. Morant wrote the first chapter and passed it on to Tam, but Tam never wrote anything. After Christmas in that first year Morant visited Tam at his parents' home in Halifax. He was amazed and excited by the Pennines, which he crossed in his A35 van, their convulsive depths and heights. Morant went to the lavatory before the Sunday dinner and when he came down Tam said that he knew that Morant had been brought up in London, but in this part of the world it was manners to aim for the porcelain when you had a slash. His mother, a Swedish woman, served pickles with the meal, and when her prison officer husband, a huge man who looked like a Hollywood Red Indian, arrived and sat down, Tam said, this is Dave,

Dad, he's an existentialist. Three years later at the same time of year, Morant and Liz visited Tam and his wife, Kim, in their house on a modern estate in Barnsley. Kim did not appear that evening and the following day she told Liz that they had been decorating an upstairs room when she had pointed out that Tam had not matched up the wallpaper properly; he had pulled the sheet off the wall, wrapped her in it along with amounts of the unused paper, and punched her several times. Morant met Kim a few years later in Marks and Spencer in Sheffield and she said that she was glad they'd separated because life with Tam was endlessly dull and that the wallpaper incident, which she said she'd forgotten about, was the most exciting thing that had happened in their marriage. She was also surprised that Morant was still with Liz and thought that he would have had a string of mistresses by now. Morant said how do you know I haven't. Many years later, Morant, visiting a school in Barnsley, came across Tam who asked what his field of research was and when Morant explained and mentioned something about critiquing a major philosopher of education, Tam said, with familiar precision, that that was a contradiction in terms wasn't it, major and philosopher of education. The meeting was uneasy, overhung by too much past that they both knew would not be accounted for. The combative energy that Morant had known in the old, the young, Tam flared into laughter and denial just once when Morant reminded him that he still had the Bartok quartets he'd borrowed nearly forty years earlier. Later, in his car, he remembered how generously Tam had praised his performance—cast to type, he said—as Mick in a college production of The Caretaker. He had been told by the teacher he liaised with at the school that Tam was a keen pub quizzer and golfer. He had once been an energetic and creative head of department but was now, as Morant understood it, a miserable, deadening presence. A year or two afterwards, Morant learned that he had retired on grounds of ill-health— stress and depression. John Capel, who had once been beaten up by a drunken Tam and who had crazy parents, a mother who looked like a grandmother and who never spoke on the one occasion that Morant visited John's house and a father, a tax inspector, who spoke incessantly and screamed at John twice during a meal for infringements of dining etiquette, became, a friend had told him, a paranoid schizophrenic who believed that he was being pursued by a gypsy with a ponytail and who, after several walks late at night from his house to the top of the Ivinghoe Beacon, driven by who knew what terrors which he perhaps sought to confront or to appease by looking at the thrilling stars above and the comforting lights of the villages below, completed a successful suicide at the third attempt by jumping off a motorway bridge and smashing his skull. Morant later thought of the philosopher Gilles Deleuze who, leaping from the window of his flat, effected a similar death. Deleuze, a lifelong heavy smoker, had had a lung removed and then a tracheotomy. One can imagine the struggle that followed, the wrenching, unavailing effort at drawing the breath of life into the body and the failure, repeated in every attempted inhalation, to fill that one imperfect lung, that body, with the vital force that makes it possible to live freely. In order to survive he was, he said, chained to his respirator like a dog. Deleuze's work, which even at the time it was written was controversial and now, in more intellectually inflexible, intolerant times, may appear outrageous, immoderate, was committed to the notion that human desire had been co-opted, hobbled and corralled by the mode of repression we know as the bourgeois family, the institution within and by means of which an opportunistic capitalism regulates and reduces the explosive creativity of human energies to an infantile, sterilised consumerism. Desire, inherently fecund and multiple, is thus domesticated, channelled into a narrow focus on the homogenised pleasures of commodification. His philosophy, marked by what some have seen as a reckless proliferation of concepts that aim to identify lines of flight, of escape from this dead end, seeking always the unobstructed affirmation of life, offers the figure of the schizophrenic as the hero-victim of our age, the one who defies the repressive organisation of desire around sexuality, a nomad seeking the production of new desires, new ways of being. Suicide is often seen as a selfish act and a defeat, a weakening of life and an acceptance of death, a possibly sadistic bequeathing of the misery the suicide passes on to those who survive. Morant could see that the act was a passing on of pain even a cruelty, but was not disposed to pass judgement on individuals whose despair, confusion and terror were beyond his imagining. Deleuze, it has been suggested, chose his death as a last act of affirmation, of desiring-production, joining the air that had been denied him, his being filling with life's updraught. As for poor John Capel, all victim as far as he could understand, Morant would have liked to think that it wasn't just the moment's escape from horror, but something like joy, that it was some kind of fulfilment that he felt as he dropped to the obliterating tarmac. Decades after the suicide he had told his friend Matt about this and he'd said yes, and yet you couldn't forget that someone is left with the mess. Morant was to reflect later on these first encounters in a moment in time that was all optimism and possibility and when he was on a new path towards knowledge, understanding and freedom. They had had their flesh and their dreams, like him. On this first day at college Morant was wearing an army surplus khaki overcoat, cord trousers that were, perhaps intentionally—he couldn't remember—a little too short, possibly in order to expose more of the boxing boots he wore because he had not been able to afford new shoes he would have found acceptable and, anyway, they looked good, socks that were also from boxing, perhaps, indeed definitely, white, and almost certainly a cotton ivy league shirt, button-down with what he learnt he had mistakenly known as a fly, more properly perhaps a placket, front, a button at the back of the collar and below that just above a single pleat that you ironed in, just a few inches, no more, a loop, a tag, a tab perhaps, of cotton, for hanging the shirt . He might also have been wearing on and around hair that came down to his shoulders a kind of deer-stalker except it was square, not rounded to the skull. At other times in those days he eschewed this style of dress as too dramatic, a little vulgar, and he wore Lee Rider jeans, always an ivy-league shirt and a zipper. If he could have afforded it he would have worn a well-cut jacket like the one he had torn in a fight a few years earlier at the Majestic ballroom Finsbury Park when his friend John had been attacked for unknowingly dancing with someone else's girlfriend and when, disgracefully, the other people from school with whom they had gone to the dance hall had melted away and left them on their own. It was here that he found that if someone attacked him he was not frightened. He had, more recently, boxed there successfully in—what would be unknown to anyone who had never attended such an event—the hyper-real technicolour of a boxing show.

Morant had come to teacher training college for two reasons. Firstly, he had been unable to take up any of the university places he had been offered whilst at school because he had gained just the one A level, in English Literature, and, after four years of work he could cash in his one academic asset for a place at a college of education without the delay and tedium of studying for further qualifications; secondly, he had come to think that perhaps education was the key to creating a more just and exciting world. Although he would not at that time have expressed the matter in such terms, he believed that the recently founded comprehensive schools would blow away the hierarchies of class and thought that sustained a society characterised by ignorance, hypocrisy and unthinking conformity. When he had gained a place at grammar school his father had told him not to expect to be top of the class all the time as he was at his primary school; there would be boys cleverer than him. In the first few weeks he became aware that there were no boys cleverer than him and that most of them were less intelligent than the girl, Jeanette Moore, whom he remembered crying outside the gates of St Clement's Church of England primary school because she had failed her eleven plus. It was several decades later that he discovered that a system had operated for this examination that ensured that equal numbers of boys and girls gained entry to grammar school, and that girls, who were even then achieving more highly than boys, were often denied access whilst some boys who had done less well in the examination were allowed into these establishments—a personalised and precise application of cruelty amidst the generalised lumbering brutality of the system. When he thought of his grammar school, founded in 1583, he recalled teachers in gowns who conducted their lessons without, in the main, noticeable signs of enthusiasm and who communicated little of the intellectual excitement of their subjects. He recalled the disconcerting, eventually annoying, air of tribunal, the sense of obscure ethical and aesthetic codes that pervaded English lessons, the boundaries, sometimes breached, between the pupils from Hackney,

Islington and Holborn and those from the outer middle-class suburbs of London; he remembered arriving late on his first day because he had been to hospital for a check-up after an operation on his ear and realising that everyone had made friends and that, unlike primary school, he was on the outside of an already tightly drawn set of relations, except that that afternoon he sat next to a small Jewish boy, David, who was friendly and helpful and pleased that they shared a name, although he recognised soon that for all the boy's helpfulness there was a boundary here too, a barrier separating most gentile and Jewish boys, perhaps a little more porous than the class one, —much later he was to think of such dividing arrangements as like the walls and fences one met with in the countryside, which signalled and imposed exclusion but at intervals offered stiles and gates, a controlled access, a measured, wary politeness. He recalled high windows admitting streams of light into the Victorian classrooms, jacket-length gowns worn by prefects, a very small boy with a large forehead crying in the basement cloakrooms in the first week because his parents were divorcing, the same boy six years later, part of a group of prefects who, despicably, lobbied the head for permission to wear boaters—rituals and conventions that he later thought of as attempts to ape the traditions and institutionalised eccentricities of public schools. In each classroom a single, small, white-painted weight with a handle, called the white mark, that had to be taken from the teacher's desk if one wanted to go to the lavatory, the first year being called the second year so that after the third, actually second, year there needed to be a Remove year, small amounts of money being handed out to pupils at the end of each year by the school's trustees, on procession through the normally out-of-bounds, marble-floored, perhaps with a central mosaic, entrance hall, sixpence for each second year boy, progressing, it was said, to a guinea for the Head Boy who, it was also said, received any unclaimed amounts because of absences, Speech Days where old boys prolonged the last note of each verse of the school song so that it intruded into the next, prefects conducting detentions and the right they had, or so some of them claimed, to cane miscreant boys (one of them, a devout Methodist and a nice enough person, had given the twelve year old Morant the option of a caning rather than detention for some obscure misdemeanour, but Morant had sensed something in play other than an alternative version of justice and chose, despite the prefect's well-turned argument, half an hour's incarceration, thus denying the prefect a pleasure and an opportunity for repentance). At lunchtime and break there were vastly populated games of football, always segregated according to year, criss-crossing each other over the quadrangle in pursuit of tennis balls, and a game, up-the-wall, which involved kicking the ball against a delimited width so that you won a point if your partner couldn't return the ball within the defined area with his first kick, this game sometimes evolving into a repeated kicking of the ball against the wire grill covering the window of the prefects' common room. He remembered being surprised in early adolescence at the devout attention some boys gave to sex, talking about strange things like how many fingers they'd managed to insert, and how deeply, into their rectums, talk of masturbation competitions, a boy who claimed that another boy's father was known as twelve bob because he could line up twelve shilling pieces on his penis (how could you bear the thought of a father who would do such a thing?) and the strictness of the criteria applied to attractiveness in girls or, rather, criterion, since it only appeared to be breast size that mattered. In a history lesson the boy next to him drew his attention to the fact that in the row behind them two boys were attempting to bring one another to orgasm. He had been shocked and puzzled; the looks on their faces suggested that they were as much concerned with entertaining the rest of the class as with sexual gratification—and surely this was homosexuality. Before going to secondary school a girl up the road whose brother had gone to get a bat from his cousin a few streets away so that he and Morant could play cricket had allowed him to see her barely pubescent breasts and to touch her underneath, this last an opportunity he found exciting but not very informative, and he had once, aged about nine or ten, engaged one lunchtime in a bout of enjoyable and unsettling kissing in his bedroom with a girl in the year below his who was being given lunch by his mother because hers had had to visit hospital. He was aware that these episodes would be construed as shameful by adults and had been a little worried that they might be disclosed, to brother, to parents, and that this might get him into trouble, but until grammar school he had never encountered the idea of sex as what seemed to be a grim physiological inquiry into a region of excremental and transgressive desire, desire that was driven by contradictory impulses—furtiveness and display, competitiveness and a revelling in humiliation. Perhaps these were things he had to learn. When he was much older he saw the truth of the observation that sex was not the dominant human drive, just the most unruly, precisely because it operated under interdiction, under the shadow of taboo. What, above all, he retained from school—more than the pleasant lunchtimes as a sixth former spent in the art room with Tommy and their friend Brian, who was homosexual, more than his unsuccessful attempt to have an affair with a French assistante, Marie-Pierre, who told him that the psychological novel was dead because there was nothing new to discover about the inner lives of human beings, we were all made in the same, predictable ways, and that he should read Sartre and Camus, more than the enjoyable excursions on Saturday mornings to play football for the school teams and, in the summer, cricket, when he and his friend Steve would quietly mock the middle class boys—hello Gubby, mummy and daddy bring a picnic today?—who brought their families to watch the game, more than the rum babas eaten and coffees drunk after school at Cypriot cafés around the Angel with girls from the nearby girls' grammar school—was a sense of the real world, of literature, culture, politics and philosophy passing him by. He sensed the world as a problem, as an institutionalised, conventional rationing of what was possible, an ordering that needed to be broken if he was to get to grips with things as they were. He would remember that he was in part moved by a desire, not uncommon amongst his generation, to escape the stifling conformities of the period, which for him included the booming emptiness of its patriotism and its contempt for anything foreign, its obsession with respectability and its fascination with scandal, the lifetimes committed to dehumanising, repetitive toil, its ingrained, cheerful deference towards toffs and royalty, passionless Sundays spent in unquestioning submission to the notion that not finding anything better to do than doing nothing was recreational and—he saw later—the sense of being imprisoned in a faded moment of historical dying. None of this was acceptable; it had to change. But he felt as well that something was being kept from him which his educators might have revealed but instead they chose to fob him off with incoherently assembled knowledge— electro-magnetism, plant and human reproduction, the Peninsular War, Caesar's De Bello Gallico, declension and conjugation, French family life and the fables of La Fontaine, Sir Roger de Coverley, précis, poetic metre, the parsing of sentences, bits of Paradise Lost, erosion and deposition—a ramshackle and implausible representation of the world and an inadequate instrumentarium for its analysis. As an adult, he became aware that in some schools some pupils identified, had pointed out to them, a certain coherence in the disparate fragments of learning that were presented in different subjects, an overall curricular purpose that could even be presented as a heroic enterprise, the bold adventure of Western reason in its local, English variant, an assembly of interlinked forms and practices of knowledge, bound together in the endeavour of bringing order to the experience of reality, of explaining the world, and more, of offering the prospect of a rational and beneficent organisation of that world. Perhaps if this vision had been communicated to him he might have been recruited to this project. Then again, he knew that he would have felt hemmed in, oppressed by such a systematisation. Certainly, he was after answers and for a brief period in his middle teens he had thought that religion might relieve the aching puzzlement that afflicted him, but he soon saw that all it had to offer was consolation and, in any case, inclinations towards faith disappeared when he took up the suggestion of the befringed assistante Marie-Jean, who had, bewilderingly, told his friend Brian that he, David, looked as if he might be cruel, and read The Outsider and then The Plague and then The Fall. He had a memory which he knew to be true but which he could scarcely believe in later life. The assistante had invited him and Brian to a party, possibly in celebration of Bastille Day, in somewhere like Earls Court and Brian and he, the only English people present and younger than everyone else, had moved around a hall set out with trestle tables bearing food and bottles of wine, from which they sampled what they were told was rouge and blanc and also, he vaguely recalled, bread and cheese, hopeful, in Morant's case, but not for very long, of Marie-Jean admitting her attraction to him. It turned out that she had a boyfriend, tall and slim with the reptilian features which he later recognised French women seemed to admire, and when it became too late for Brian and him to travel home they went to a house in Earls Court occupied by French students and he shared a bed, chastely, with Marie-Jean, Brian and the assistante's boyfriend who was probably called Guy or Yves or fucking René or something. He found it frustrating and something of a wasteful injustice that Brian and not he slept next to Marie-Jean. It did not occur to him at the time that Brian might have derived some pleasure from sleeping next to him. Around about this time, perhaps a year or so earlier, he was converted to socialism by Michael Girner, whose father was a taxi-driver and whose scornful secularism required that Michael attend school on Jewish holidays so that, as Michael told it, he would leave their house in Hackney in full school uniform and slink past the street's tall Victorian buildings towards the bus-stop at the bottom of the road to the accompaniment of reprimands and abuse from more devout neighbours, and this new political perspective supported the conviction that had been taking root that what his school offered in the way of education was a kind of deception, that it was passing off as the truth what was just one way of looking at things and that it was, thereby, preventing him getting a clearer view of how the world was put together and how it might be changed. At that time this suspicion, this doubt, this at-oddsness with things as they were, seemed ordinary in that it was the way the fragment of his generation was, but extraordinary because he knew and others like him knew that this was the beginning of a vast abolition of the old and an inception of something new, something vital and beautiful, the making good of the full promise of life. If, when he was older, he was to wonder why he had been so susceptible to this moment of awakening he would recognise that it must have had something to do with his father dying. Also he could dramatise himself, no doubt sentimentally, as being stationed—placed by circumstance— at borders. He was working class but his father had been middle class, he was good at art and interested in ideas and feelings but he excelled at sports, he was compassionate but, apparently, cruel. He could never, even as an adult, sense fully the effect his father's death had had on him—not that he ever thought about it too hard—but it had been a terrible blow and he could see at an intellectual level its connection to what he became, how it had determined his attitudes, the decisions he made, his predisposition—but he could never feel the impact it had had on his life, could never trace a line between his devastated emotions and his rejection of school and authority. Clearly, however, it was an event that opened things up, acquainted him with the provisionality of things. Yet he was unwilling to reduce what he had experienced at that time to the level of personal need. History had stirred and something had got loose in society, something that wanted its way and not the way it had been directed to. In his first three years at grammar school he won at various times prizes for History, English, Geography and Latin. His father died near the beginning of his fourth year of school and he began to truant, eventually only attending those lessons in which his absence might be noted and those in which he thought he might not be bored—German because he had a new teacher whom he found likeable, French lessons because he and Peter Engel, for their own and some of their fellow pupils' amusement, used to terrorise Miss Fisher, a kindly woman in, he guessed, her fifties, who found his translations of poetry from French to English sensuous and who later became Dr Fisher; and he enjoyed P.E. and a few English lessons. He was occasionally caught out and spoken to by his form teacher or the deputy head, but never threatened with expulsion and his mother was never informed of his behaviour. At the time it did not occur to him that the school's leniency was connected to his father's death. After the third year he never figured again at speech days and by the time he reached the sixth form he was barely reading the texts set for examination in French, Latin and English. Instead he read Sartre, Camus, Kierkegaard, Faulkner, Hemingway, Scott Fitzgerald, Forster, Dostoevsky, Joyce, Woolf, Stendhal and impenetrable books of existential philosophy, a haphazard, restless search for significance, using books as maps, as someone later said. He enjoyed the pleasures that were on offer, the perspectives these books opened, the novel deployments of language, and like many young people before and since he thought that it was in literary fiction that he would find out how to live and think. At the same time he was uneasily aware that he wasn't perhaps reading these books in the way that some people thought they should be read, that there was a crudeness to this ferreting away at meaning, an overlooking of what literature really offered. Certainly, then and for ever afterwards his attention tended to slacken whenever he came to descriptions in fiction—rooms, towns, landscapes, the movements of characters in the spaces in which they were placed—and this, he thought, perhaps indicated an incorrigible coarseness of sensibility. This was not to be a self-doubt that persisted. Even then, at school, he had no time for the prevalent notion that books—literature— had a sanctity that must not be sullied, as if they carried a precious cultural load that could be damaged if they were roughly handled. He left school with his one A level in English, achieving a pass at C on three different occasions, writing about books more than half of which he'd not read. More than forty years later, a few months after his mother's death, he found a box of letters she'd kept and amongst them was one from the headmaster of his school saying that her son had been awarded a maintenance grant of £15 a term, to help towards him continuing at school during the sixth form, and asking her and her son to keep this matter confidential as it was impossible to help all boys in this way. He didn't know if he had forgotten or had never been told about this arrangement and he felt a little ashamed at his harsh judgement of the school. He had after all been an awkward pupil and yet the school, its head and governors, had acted with a humanity that he had either not known of or had not been grateful for.

About three weeks into the college course, Morant met Alison. She was a second year languages student whom he had observed as usually in the company of two boys in his year, one a fey blond Languages student called Michael and the other a large blond P.E. student, Ron, who was, he later found out, an Olympic swimmer. He guessed rightly that both these young men were privately educated and, seated opposite her one lunchtime at a table in the refectory, it was immediately apparent that Alison too came from that background. The presence of public school students at a teacher training college intrigued him, partly because he had only once that he knew of met anyone near his own age who had been educated outside the state system, but mainly because he thought it was odd that they were there at all. At that time there was, as far as he understood, no pressure to acquire a state-recognised teaching qualification to work in private schools. He later came to see that the few male graduates of private education at the college could be divided into four groups—the extreme academic failures who, even with the advantages (one might and would eventually say, cultural capital) that their schooling had conferred would not be accepted by any university;

missionaries, nearly always religious, who wanted to serve society; elite sportsmen who saw the facilities available at a P.E. Wing college as useful for their further development; and the pleasingly bonkers like Archie Thompson, a P.E. student who was on placement with Morant for his second school experience and who, whilst Morant was being visited and observed teaching by a lecturer who disapproved strongly of a previous lesson he had sat in on, in which Morant was teaching Auden's "The Shield of Achilles" to a group of fifteen year olds—too political, too depressing—so that he had felt it necessary to interrupt the lesson and conclude it himself, Archie, for no reason other than to see what would happen and to make things uncomfortable for the supervisor, had informed the staff room that Morant had been told that he was a disgrace to the college and had been suspended for inept teaching, so that after he had finished his debriefing meeting with Morant, the lecturer, who taught whatever technical studies was called at that point, was accosted in the school car park by the Head of English and asked to account for his mistaken judgement of his student's merits as a teacher. Morant didn't remember what followed, except that Archie, who shortly afterwards was escorted off a golf course near Crewe for throwing across the fairway the one club he and his partner, Evan, had between them, apart from a putter, this in full, unfortunate view of someone—Archie described her as the Lady Member—who was waiting to tee off behind them, seemed never to have been required to explain his exaggeration. Alison was interesting to Morant because of her exotic origins, because of her friendship with what looked like a homosexual male partnership and because she was attractive in a way that he was unfamiliar with, a face that was pretty but somehow bruised by life—years later he was to think she was like Ellen Barkin in The Big Easy. His first conversation with her was in the college bar where she was sitting with Michael and Ron and with Morant's friend, Jack, the only other Londoner he had met in the first months at college, the son of an Italian artist and a French doctor and brother to a heroin addict and an alcoholic, both of whom he met in a couple of years' time at Jack's marriage to Frankie, a languorous, pretty art student who was to bear two children before their divorce six years later. How efficient was the social sense that so quickly led these people to each other. We were all like this, he supposed, exercising finely tuned faculties of which we are largely unaware to sift through information about cultural preferences, style, class, taste, prejudices and whatever it is we mean by personality, to locate those whom we will find sympathetic. In his own case, he supposed that what he sought out in others was transgressiveness, a scepticism about authority, fairly unremitting and brutal humour, kindness, curiosity, restlessness, a lack of polish and finish to thought. This list, he knew, could quite rightly be viewed as self-indulgent, a catalogue of excuses for his weaknesses, and it clearly came out of anger and fears that he hardly understood, but it was, as a set of virtues, not unfitted to the times. Alison's group operated, he saw, according to another code which involved emotional restraint, an interest in what could perhaps be best described as fine things (Michael talked to Jack, a collector, about porcelain or Clarice Cliff or something else like that and it turned out on a later visit with Jack to Michael's room that he had some Armagnac and several nice objects) and a taste for kitsch (the two boys had recently given Alison, for her birthday, a fluffy bunny that squeaked something and a record by a popular singer who they seemed to consider cheesy but adorable). Why did Jack put up with these people? Alison had none of the qualities Morant valued except kindness and an uncomplicated interest in other people. She was gentle, modest, affectionately amused by others and amusing. He had never been in a relationship with anyone like her and never would be again. As always seemed to happen in the third and fourth decades of his life, the others drifted away and he was left with the girl, the woman, he wanted to be alone with. He always associated her with the song that played endlessly on the common room jukebox, Grace Slick singing White Rabbit. They didn't sleep together for two or three weeks. On one of the occasions when he had thought it was about to happen and she had said no, he asked her if it was because he was married. She said of course it wasn't. There were just some things she needed to get straight in her head. It wasn't about him. Later she told him that she'd had a relationship with an older man (I'm an older man, Morant said. Not that older, Alison said) that hadn't ended well. He had been her teacher. He asked which subject and she asked why he wanted to know. He said that he just wondered. He was her geography teacher. Her parents had found out, got him sacked and switched her to a sixth form college. He asked if she'd been in love with him. She said of course not, but that she'd been a bit besotted for a time. It was flattering. Morant asked how had she come to know Michael. He was a friend of her brother's and no, her brother wasn't queer and neither was Michael. He said that he hadn't been thinking about Michael or her brother's sexual inclination and she said yes you were. He asked how she put up with all that archness? What did that mean? Showing how sophisticated you were by pretending to like things that you despised. She said that it was just fun and had he felt threatened by it. He said that he was, perhaps a bit, but mainly incredibly irritated. It seemed like a defence against the world, a lack of faith in seriousness, a kind of despairing cynicism. He wondered why they couldn't occasionally be straightforward about what they liked. Did he mean her as well as Michael and Ron. No, not her. Alison said that she found it amusing, but perhaps he didn't like it because Michael and Ron, well, Michael at least, were camp. He said that she was right. He wouldn't have been bothered if they'd been homosexual, but he didn't like kitschy campness. He told her about his friend, Brian, who some might have seen as effeminate. In fact he had an oddly child-like way of holding himself, slightly clumsy; if he hurried he used short steps, his hands raised or looking as if they were ready to be raised, as if he were wary of bumping into things. Women could be like this but men preferred to look more confident, more in control of their bodies. Many years later he would be in a department store and ahead of him he would see a little boy, perhaps three years old, drop something, a round sweet perhaps, that rolled away from him and which he pursued, finally stopping it by crouching down, raising and lowering his arm in a movement that was extravagant and completely effective, trapping the object with his open hand, as if he were slowly, gently patting it. A man would have done all this with more precision, with a calculated action prescribed by an awareness of the possibilities for looking ridiculous and his disciplined body would lose all the innocent loveliness, the thoughtless grace of the child's movements. Brian, he said, had not been camp, either in sensibility or in personal style. And probably he was wary because he was short-sighted. Then Morant shut up. He didn't want to end up sounding pompous, a guardian of the rules, like the Marxist critics he read about much later whose attempts to engage with post-structuralism were compared to a policeman trying to arrest a particularly outrageous drag queen; perhaps there was something dissident about camp that he hadn't fathomed. One afternoon, as they sat together on her bed in her college room, which was, as he remembered it, quite bare except for a brush, a few bits of jewellery and some make-up on a dressing table and an Aubrey Beardsley poster, not the one of the woman masturbating the unicorn, he asked her if she loved her parents. She said of course. Why did he ask? He said because if he knew about her relationship with them, he would know more about her and he wanted to know about her. Why did he want to know about her? He couldn't say it was because he was possibly falling in love with her, because that wasn't really an answer to her question so much as an explanation of what made him want to know about her, and also because he knew that telling her he might be in love with her would be a kind of promise, a commitment that he knew he would break. He didn't want to do that again. He wondered why he wanted to know all about her, all about any woman he got this close to. Total knowledge about others was the fantasy of every tyrant. This was what he would enjoy more than anything else in life, holding a woman, a new woman, loving her giving herself, knowing her, as it seemed, naked in body and thought. He had a slightly embarrassing affection for women and a decidedly embarrassing impulse to protect them, which he knew many of them—at least the ones he liked—might find infantilising. And yet, they seemed to yield, to behave in ways that could only be described in terms that were clichéd: Alison was snuggling into him, sinking into his arms, giving herself, and as she rested her head between his left shoulder and the top of his chest he felt the shifts and adjustments of her small, vigorous body against his stronger body. These arms, these delicate, heart-piercingly braceleted wrists, the rib-cage that pressed against his arm; he could have crushed her. In this moment with this woman on this bed, her fair hair touching his cheek, in this moment drowsy with tenderness, he wondered, idly and guiltlessly, over these feelings. Alison said that her father bullied her mother, emotionally, not hitting her. She annoyed him all the time; she couldn't do anything right. Every day, in every hour they were together. It was relentless. She and her brother hated it. She left him last year. Her mother told her that he used to wake her in the middle of the night and ask her to admit that she looked at other men all the time, that she had been unfaithful to him with his friends or with some stranger they'd passed in the street that day, keeping her awake for hours, just quietly running through these fantasies. Morant said Jesus. Alison loved them both. She wished her mother hadn't told her all that. She thought her father knew that her mother had told her everything and she didn't know what to do. She said that her father was broken. He loved her mother so much. She didn't know what to do. Alison was crying, almost imperceptibly, a moist snuffliness dampening his shirt. What can I do, she asked. He said that he didn't know. He shifted his arm, lifted her head and kissed her. He wanted to help but all he could think was that holding her would help and then, as happened at other times in his life when a woman was sorrowing, he and she made love. It was suddenly easy to make love. He could never unpick the tangle of opportunism and tenderness that led him to believe that the best way to offer comfort was to fuck.

Although he had applied to college to do English and P.E. as joint main subjects, he had only been accepted for English. His interview had begun in a sports hall where he was required to undertake a number of tests of his physical fitness—a sergeant jump, sit-ups, press-ups, shuttle runs, pull-ups. Afterwards he showered and changed in the company of another interviewee, a Welsh boy with a flattened nose and Morant asked him if he did a bit. He said that he did. He'd had a dozen or so fights, but the nose was from rugby. He met the boy, Lenny, again, nearly two years later just after Morant had started to play rugby and they were both picked for the second XV. He was a diabetic and after the interview had had a bad few months so had had to defer for a year. Lenny was an exceptionally amiable person—not an unusual quality in boxers, Morant thought. Later that year when they were both playing for the first XV, Lenny at full-back and Morant in the second row, a freezing, horizontal rain had set in, limiting visibility to no more than ten or twenty yards and the referee had called the game off. Back in the warmth and steam of the showers, someone said where's Lenny. Most of the game had taken place in the outclassed opposition's half and Lenny, the rearmost player on his side, had not realised the game had been abandoned. Already cold from inactivity he had collapsed. Morant and he shared a house with four others for a few months. He was formally interviewed by Stan Holding, the head of P.E. and Dr Armstrong, an English lecturer who began by giving him a poem which she asked him to read and then inviting him to tell her what he thought of it. It was a poem of Hardy's and he told her he knew it and proceeded to tell her what he understood about it and how it worked. She asked him if he'd studied it for A level and he said, no, he'd read it for himself some time ago. Stan, who looked like, and was, an ex-army man, noted the exceptional performance displayed by Morant on chin-ups, sergeant jump and press-ups. Fifty press-ups before we stopped you. This is presumably from your training as a boxer. He said yes and that he did a bit of weight training as well. Stan asked which aspect of his training did he most enjoy and he said, probably running and that he did twenty to thirty miles a week, about half of it in one go at weekends, on Hampstead Heath. Stan said that he used to train on the Heath using the changing rooms at the running track near Parliament Hill and Morant remembered but did not say that when he and his cousin had started training for boxing they had got changed at the track where they met a professional boxer, Nick Casoli. They recognised him straight away and it turned out that their family knew his from the Caledonian Road. Nick was the number four lightweight contender in the Boxing Illustrated rankings, although he never got a title fight. They'd gone on several training runs together. Morant said to Stan that he sometimes trained from there, but these days more often went to the men's pond because there were weights there. Stan's part of the interview somehow never seemed to begin. There probably wasn't much you could ask a P.E. interviewee that would determine fitness for the course, since the letter of application and the physical test would give you most of what you needed to know. It was mainly, he supposed, about assessing what sort of an individual the candidate was, whether they had the personal qualities necessary for integrating with other course members and getting on with the lecturers. He thought he had a reasonably clear idea of what an ex-military head of P.E. would look for in the young people who would eventually be responsible for the physical development and athletic prowess of the nation's youth—single-mindedness in pursuit of excellence, clarity about goals and the means for achieving them, an absence of doubt about the value of the endeavours you engaged in and, this was possibly not unfair, a lack of imagination, and also what Morant thought of as a bluff and uncomplicated sense of humour. He had become aware during the interview that he was probably going to show himself incapable of composing such a self. This was the first of several interviews in his career which seemed to drift aimlessly, never really beginning and never achieving a distinct conclusion. Usually they led to rejection, but not always. The interview for his first teaching post was at a boy's secondary modern at half-term. The head of English, Jock, an elderly man, Morant thought, although he would later think that he was probably in his early fifties, seemed wrapped in an urbane cynicism, recognising but not entirely resigning himself to the futility of his work. He smoked throughout a tour of the school, asking Morant nothing of his views on teaching or his literary preferences, after a while simply inquiring if he wanted the job. Morant wasn't sure whether this was a question about whether he was interested in the post or a job offer. He said, well, yes, but presumably you're interviewing other candidates, and Jock replied that he'd interviewed the only other applicant, but he was a darky, so did he want it. A couple of months into the first term, he was called from the staffroom one lunchtime to a secretary's office to take a telephone call. It was from a head of English in Shropshire who had been one of two practising teachers seconded onto the B.Ed. in Morant's final year at college. Tim told him that there was a post going at his school and, if he was interested, he wanted him to have it. Two weeks later, Morant was on the train to Stoke-on-Trent from where Tim was to drive him for interview at the school. He had had to get off the bus taking him to Euston station in order to be sick in a park and for much of the journey he had been in the train's toilets (he had used several rather than just the one at the end of his carriage because he thought he would in this way be less likely to draw attention to his discomposure), arriving in Stoke drained, almost literally, and tired. He was introduced to the head in his office shortly after arriving at the school. He knew of Stanford Horsfield from his training, where he had spoken to Morant's year about the mission of the comprehensive school. He was a head teacher of a type that became extinct at some point in the late seventies, early eighties, a charismatic figure who believed absolutely in the capacity of education to raise up the lowly and create a more just society and who saw the comprehensive school as the perfected instrument of individual self-realisation and a necessarily equalising social change. Morant knew from students who had been placed in his school that he was always on the corridors, knew every child by name, refused to tolerate negative comments from staff about children, fought the local authority tooth and nail for the resources his teachers and pupils needed and ran the school with a benign, paternalistic authority. Morant had responded to Tim's offer because he admired Horsfield's moral seriousness, his, even then anachronistic, enlightenment zeal. Where modern heads are, almost exclusively, administrators working to a bureaucratic ethic of operational effectiveness, babbling what he had heard someone on the radio accurately describe as the sorry, failed lexicon of managerialism, Stanford Horsfield, with his (it could only, Morant was to think, be described in this way) mane of grey hair and intensity of gaze, looked like what he was, a prophet and preacher of culture. He spoke to the head for about ten minutes before being taken round the school— curiously, not introduced to any staff—and given some lunch. He then waited in a small room for about an hour before Tim appeared to say he would be ready to run him back to the station in a few minutes. In the car Tim said, after a while, you probably realise you didn't get the job. They had interviewed a woman with several years' experience earlier this morning—she had been very good, actually—and Stanford wanted to appoint her. He could be an awkward bugger at times. He hadn't really taken to Morant when they'd talked in the morning. Morant said what, that ten minutes. What had he done wrong. Tim said that there had been nothing, really— the head had just said that he felt that there might have been a problem if Ron James, the deputy, had had to talk to him about something. Morant had asked what that meant.

Something disciplinary, something minor, like covering for someone who was absent—that he'd be likely to argue about it, wouldn't take it well. After a recess of about fifteen minutes, Dr. Armstrong invited him back into the interview room where he was offered a place for English, but was informed that he had not been successful in gaining a place for P.E. Mr. Holding explained that there was tremendous competition to get on the course and that they rarely admitted anyone who had not, at least, achieved representation at junior county level in their main sport and he had not met that requirement. He would, however, be welcome to try for the college teams in anything that interested him and he could, of course, make use of the college's facilities, the gym, pool and so on. Irritated, but immediately recognising that this is what he had expected, Morant thought but did not bother to say that the reason he had not achieved county representation was because his trainer handled professional boxers and had no plans for him to spend long as an amateur, and in any case, as far as he knew, amateur boxing didn't have county level competitions. Neither did he mention that, as he had written in his application, he had won all of the fights he had so far had, all but one, on stoppages, and, as he hadn't said in his letter, that he had already attracted the interest of professional promoters. He should, he realised, have been more careful when talking about the Hardy poem. Dr. Armstrong said that if he accepted the offer they would have to find him a second subject place. He said he would accept the English place and she said that there was a course, new that year, called Arts, a combination of drama, dance and film, which he might well be interested in. Shortly after he was interviewed by a quietly-spoken head of the Arts course, Tim Dawson, who was to become one of the very few people in education whom he entirely admired and who, now, in this moment, asked him what, as an English student, he had been reading recently and he said, Norman Mailer and Vladimir Nabokov. They talked novels for a while and then Tim asked him if he was interested in drama, dance and film. Film, yes, drama to an extent, but he'd never thought of performance, and dance—whatever that meant—was not something he knew much about. What sort of films did he like? Cowboy films, 1930s gangster and horror films and he'd recently got interested in Ingmar Bergman and Luis Bunuel. Tim, who looked like the photograph of Albert Camus on the back of the Penguin edition of The Outsider, but with the effects of what had clearly been a bad case of teenage acne, said that Morant would have to have a chat with Roger Caldwell, the drama lecturer, and a few minutes later, whilst Caldwell watched from a balcony, he was moving cautiously around a large hall to In the Hall of the Mountain King and failing to overcome resentfulness at being set this unforeseeable task. Afterwards Caldwell observed that he hadn't really let himself go and Morant said that he might have done better if he'd known beforehand that he'd be interviewing for drama and dance. They must have talked for some time after this, but Morant, tiring of all this inquisition, had ceased to put anything more than minimal effort into the discussion. All his life he was to detest interviews—the ones he submitted himself to and the ones he was obliged to subject others to— as dispiriting, embarrassing collusions between, on the one side, participants whose usually polite and sometimes warm manner masks, most importantly from themselves, a pitiless inquisitorial, judgemental will, and another who offers for inspection a self, calculated, sometimes shrewdly, sometimes with pitiful ineptness, to conform to what the interviewee imagines to be the ideal figure fantasised by the interviewer. Here, in this banal scene, was the epitome, the bodying forth, of liberal hypocrisy. On a couple of occasions—one harrowing, during an interview at Reading university for a place on their English course when the interviewer thought he was lying about reading Conrad, and the other invigorating when, halfway through his doctoral viva Morant questioned the external examiner's understanding of a cultural policy theorist's arguments—Morant had had interviews where the pretence that this was anything other than a barbarous exercise of power had been put aside and the actual nature of the encounter had been revealed as a court no different in essence from that in which the tyrant, the capo dei capi, the ganger before the roiling, desperate crowds at the factory gates, dispenses an arbitrary and capricious justice to beseeching supplicants. These two interviews had at least excused him from the wretched self-violence of concocting a persona that might seduce or appease his interviewer. It wasn't that he thought there was another way of carrying on but that these people thought that they had, through their civilised courtesies, their feigned, or at best carefully worked up respect for the interviewee's ideas, removed their activity from the unpleasantness of power. Eventually Morant was returned to Tim Dawson who offered him a place on the course, which he accepted. Morant had been fearful that he would not be able to work at college. In the sixth form he had found study near impossible. He rarely read any prescribed text to a conclusion and could never, even when he had something he wanted to say, manage to fit his ideas into the writing structures that were offered to him. In examinations he always ran out of time, never answering all the questions. In part, he blamed this on the rigidities of the system, but he knew that there had to be constraints, conventions, legislated orderings and boundaries for anything intelligible to be written, read and assessed, and he worried that he would never find the strength to subject himself to such rule. He knew that for him it would be through writing that he would come to understand the world and himself, that he would remake and fit himself for what he saw would be struggle, but perhaps he just wasn't up to it. Colleges of education in those days catered for young people who had not got the grades to go to university and who would require, it was thought as well as teaching about teaching, the knowledge necessary to be plausible teachers of their subjects. In his first English session at college the lecturer, Dr Armstrong, who had interviewed him for the course, asked the group to write a personal reading history. This was the kind of call that Morant had been waiting for all his life, an official authorisation, a licensing, of self-investigation, and he wrote about the smell of a battered fairy tale book and its swirling drawings, going to the local library with his father, who took out books about Arctic expeditions, jungle travel and biographies of land speed record holders, his incessant reading of Alison Utley's Little Grey Rabbit stories until a woman librarian had suggested it was time he moved on, which he did, to Biggles and books about Jim Corbett and feline predators; he wrote about the Dandy and Beano, American cowboy and horror comics, Conan Doyle, Denis Wheatley, Rider Haggard, Henty and Ballantyne, Jack London, the Robin Goodfellow and Moomin cartoon strips and George Whiting's boxing reports in the London Evening Standard—Henry Cooper's mitt sinister—, P.G. Wodehouse, Conan Doyle, H.G. Wells, G.K. Chesterton's essays, and on to the more recent interrogations. He tried to trace his formation in these readings, to identify what it was that drew him to them, how he used them and how they shaped him. When, later, he tried similar approaches in his own teaching he was struck by how difficult it was to involve pupils in the ways that he found so liberating. Most of them were happy to write about important moments, experiences that had meant a lot to them, disappointments and even unhappinesses like family deaths or bullying, and some took to the task enthusiastically, adding to the record photographs, bits of text cut out of magazines, poems, song lyrics and lists of things loved and hated. Some could see no point in the exercise, a few clearly disliked it, but most engaged willingly in an often sentimental gathering together of significant moments in their lives. What he learnt from this was that self-reflection, purposeful consideration of how one had been shaped as an individual, was not an activity that came easily to most young people or one that was much valued. He realised that you had to be unhappy or dissatisfied with the way things were, but, at the same time, conscious that by taking thought you might understand and thereby begin to address the causes of your unease. This seemed to him something that was, in those early years of teaching, central to his role as a teacher of the humanities, that what literature, philosophy, history, social and cultural study promised was that in coming to an understanding of how one had been made as a person, as a social being, one could acquire some sort of control over one's life and that this endeavour was pleasurable and rewarding. But most people, not just children, had no desire to understand, were wary of insights that might be painful, disturbing, were of the view that you could think too much about things, didn't believe that much could be changed anyway, that they inhabited an inevitability, a time and locale in which history had no significance, in which things just unalterably, incontestably were. Decades later he read of a German poet—Gottfried Benn perhaps—who said, in 1913, that the only way of being happy in the appalling circumstances of his time was to be stupid and have a job. He could see how history had made his pupils like this and how they were the kinds of people required by the times. And who was he,

Morant, to demand that they think in ways that he valued. There, though, at that time in that college, he began, gratefully and exultantly, to think purposefully. He was uncertain how his assignment, which it was after all perfectly possible to view as a rambling exercise in self-indulgence, would be received, but the following week another lecturer approached him and told him that he'd read it, indicating that it had been interesting enough to pass on, and he felt what can only be described as a suffusion of contentment throughout his body, centred somewhere between his chest and his stomach, something close to joy, an unashamed gratification that would accompany him through his time at college. He knew he was exceptional and now he had been seen for what he was.

When he was older Morant saw that as a young man he had had a sense of his life as heroic. He felt that he was or was about to be engaged upon great things. In light of the life he'd led subsequently he knew that this was absurd, comical, but he didn't feel it had been unhealthy. A woman, a teacher he had been involved with, had once criticised a friend of his, characterising him as thinking he was wonderful. She had said that he was the kind of man who loved himself. He had thought this was unfair, but he knew what the woman meant. His friend occasionally displayed what the English call a blokishness, an unthinking and confident assumption of the naturalness of one's own outlook on things, an assured humour that is oblivious to what one would have to call its gendered narrowness of outlook, its roots in male privilege. This was the late seventies and some women were very alert to these things. He always thought that it was a pity that in the next couple of decades so many of them seemed more tolerant in these matters. It was also the case, Morant recognised, that in criticising his friend, the woman, Trish, was trying to hurt him because she was annoyed that she was becoming involved with him. On a later occasion they sat in a dismal Italian restaurant on the periphery of a market area in what they subsequently realised was the red light district of a rain-soaked northern town, the kind of northern town that is filled with, suffocated by, the memory of a lost industry and productiveness and that had its own gloom that was distinct from those sad southern, impotent towns that at night time sink under the weight of their own meaninglessness. (For a moment that evening it seemed to Morant as if the town were constructed out of the sodden newsprint that filled its gutters so that he could see not just the bricks and constructed fabric of the town but the rooms, the inhabitants of those rooms, every instantiation of atoms into some kind of thing in that town, even the relationships between these people, all those things as made into and out of the detritus, the poisonously shit-soiled, rotting waste filling those gutters). Trish said, guilelessly, purely descriptively, that for him, Morant, involvement in illicit relationships—she was engaged to an officer in the air force—was easy because he was Joe Cool. He had been surprised and irritated by this, not least because he recognised that it pleased him, that it produced, if he was honest, a certain sexual stirring. Trish, one of several history teachers he slept with over the stupid, stupefied middle years of his life, was one of the prettiest women he had ever seen, not sweetly pretty but serenely so, in fact he would almost say beautiful if that weren't such a slippery and untrustworthily inexact thing to say. He had been drawn to her on an occasion when he came through the school library to the landing which opened onto several classrooms, one of which was his, and he saw her pinning down a fifth year boy, fair-haired (like Trish), a pupil in one of Morant's classes, an arrogant young man who he had noticed expressed incredulity at any suggestion that he should give attention to his studies, and Morant heard her say, so don't do that again you sexist little bastard. But Trish had not said that he, Morant, was in love with himself, that he thought he was wonderful. Trish had an uncomplicatedly feminist analysis of almost everything that she encountered in life. Many women seemed reluctant to face the fact that most men were frightened of them, uninterested in them, didn't really like them or were just very unsettled by them. It was as if so many men seemed to believe that the possession of a Y chromosome was a marvellous stroke of luck, a 50-50 gamble that they'd won. He had never felt this. He neither feared nor hated women, although this had not prevented him treating them at times thoughtlessly, cruelly, disgracefully. It had always seemed to him that men could be easily thrown into bewilderment or panic whenever women asserted themselves. It was clear, as some feminists alleged, that society was largely constructed around men's need to defend themselves against women. But Trish would be wrong if she believed that he did not love himself, because he did, as the necessary foundation of his self-heroics, love himself. He loved being in the body he was in. He had minor dissatisfactions: his legs could have been more chunky and his back a little longer—all his weight and muscularity sometimes seemed packed into his upper body—but he didn't really worry about these things. In his teaching he'd sometimes bring newspapers and magazines into the classroom, examining perhaps how language and images were used to produce particular responses in readers, how stereotypical views and perceptions were deployed, how the language was working on the reader, what it assumed about readers, and he'd noticed, particularly in magazines aimed at teenage girls, a game, an amusement, where readers were invited to choose between the body parts of celebrities—

eyes, noses, mouths, hair, legs, breasts, hips, to build the ideal woman which, of course, was an ideal self. To Morant there was something gruesome about this appeal to a longing for a different body. Sometimes you came across it, heard it, people wishing for a different kind of body, like Brian who would have swapped his stubby build for something more willowy or women who say that they would like smaller hips, thinner legs or different breasts and, of course, men often wanted to be larger, more threatening in all sorts of areas, an impulse that had been distilled in a comment Morant had once heard at the men's pond on Hampstead Heath, when a body builder, admiringly and it seemed enviously, described another body builder as a human fucking penis. Sometimes this was actually a wish for someone else's body—a wish to look like some athlete, some actor, some model—and even when it was just about having someone else's more attractive life, he could never shake off the horrific thought that this would involve inhabiting a different body. Perhaps these people weren't thinking this through because they weren't really serious. They couldn't have considered the possibility of assuming someone else's flesh, their bones, the unthinkable strangeness of differently damp armpit and crotch hair, of different genitalia, mouths and the tastes inside those mouths, different excretory organs, and the smell and feel of alien skin as it tightened across their faces when they smiled or grimaced and the sense of unfamiliar internal organs sitting heavily and wetly inside those unfamiliar torsos. And what would your laughter sound like to you as it came out of that newly assumed body, what strange dislocating transformations would be felt as you sweated, ate, experienced orgasm, sneezed, became aware of your breathing, shat and cleaned yourself after you'd shat. What would thought itself be like. Sometimes he very much liked alien flesh, but on other people. In early adulthood

Morant had done many bad things, committed wrongs—lies, deceptions, betrayals, acts of violence. He was never quite sure where these transgressions were precisely located in that part of the moral continuum that crowded together mistakes, misjudgements, cruelty, selfishness and failures of self control. As he grew older he regretted many of the things he had done, even if he could not quite rid himself of the memory of the pleasure that some of these episodes offered. Even later he felt little guilt about most of his behaviour; he could see that he had sometimes been stupid and had acted in a way that was morally wrong, although the latter was a concept that for him always had a certain remoteness to it when sex was involved, something uninhabitable. It was only much later that he felt sorry for the people—his partners, his lovers' partners—to whom he had been false. In those troubled decades between Liz leaving him and her return the thing that did besiege him was shame and embarrassment, that he should have been seen to behave foolishly or disgracefully, that he should be judged by others as unserious or bad. He felt this as a weakness in himself; he wished he didn't care about the opinion of others. As a young man he had seduced or allowed himself to be seduced by friends' girlfriends and, although in later life he would never have thought of sleeping with a friend's wife, most of the affairs he had had were with married or committed women, a few of them the partners of people he knew professionally. This was, looked at from a conventional perspective, despicable behaviour. It wasn't that he preyed upon these women, just that if he found them attractive or interesting and detected a susurration of curiosity, of desire, he would always want to sleep with them. It had to be admitted, though, that the subterfuge involved often added to these encounters and relationships and there was sometimes a competitive pleasure in taking another man's woman, if he thought the man was worth competing with. He knew this was infantile, disclosing something grotesquely unevolved in his nature, an ungoverned impulse to power and gratification that was bound up with an ingrained refusal of authority. Why, he wondered later, could he not have behaved more like the older brother he was. On another view, though, part of the pleasure was derived from the subversion of accepted regulation, of respectability. It was pleasing that within the imaginary harmony of socially approved and legislated alliance there lurked an appetite for unlawful, ungoverned pleasure, and pleasing too that he was the bearer of that rogue satisfaction. He didn't feel uncomfortable recognising this, although it would be a difficult point to argue for in public and there was vanity here too, of course, but it wasn't all vanity. These were, however, rare occurrences and he would have been unhappy if his relations with women had been dependent on securing betrayal and the humiliation of another. It was easy to see that he became involved with married or already committed women because there was a barrier in place that preserved what was for him a reassuring distance. There was an explanation for this. He didn't want to start on a new life with a new woman; from his late twenties into early middle age he just wanted a particular woman back, to resume their life together. It had to be said, however, that he was in those days convinced that if he found a woman attractive he could always get her to sleep with him. This, he knew, was no testimony to his own erotic power, since he was only attracted to women whom he sensed found him interesting. But sexual attraction could be a brutal business. It was what would be to some a distasteful fact, but nevertheless a fact, that all heterosexual men judged women on their looks, their bodies. Some did this relentlessly and undiscriminatingly, in that they consciously judged all women, most of the time, as desirable or undesirable. The judgement of some was only called into play when they encountered a woman who presented one or several of the features that they found attractive. These triggers of sexual interest varied from man to man. There were the familiar prejudices in that, undeniably, some liked pert or full arses whilst others preferred what his friend Davey had once described, approvingly, as boyish hips; some were excited by large breasts, others only by small or beautifully proportionate breasts; others again were drawn in by a frail or waif-like vulnerability, hippy chicks; some perhaps by pretty faces which had to be framed by hair done in a certain way. He guessed that attraction was prompted in many by an unconscious calculation of ratios, hips to waists, length of legs to lengths of bodies, and of course some kind of estimation of body mass index was operating all the time. He had met men, mainly when he was younger and mainly West Indian men, who only liked plump women. All men, at some time, submitted women to the judgement of this kind of internal court and some, sometimes, felt a certain shame about this. Some did not and their judgement was often tied to their essential contempt for women and this was unpleasant, disgusting. Any man, any straight man, who denied that this was the way it went with him was either a liar or horribly repressed. When all was said and done, there would always come a time, on occasion immediately but more often not, when he would find something intriguing in some woman, a line to cheekbone and jaw that suggested sensuality, a wry expression, self-possession, the way her waist flowed into her hips, perhaps a principled scepticism, the way she used her hands, an aggressive intelligence, and then he would begin to notice and to imagine her body and how she might use it, how he might use it. There would come a moment when he and she would touch for the first time; sometimes this was a full embrace, at others the back of his hand against her thigh as they stood together in a crowded space, her hand placed over his in a café. These things and what they led to were irresistible. But they had effects. He never really felt bad about the possibility of breaking up someone else's relationship; in truth he didn't think about such consequences, but if he had he would probably have thought that there was perhaps something wrong with the relationship he was disrupting if the woman had wanted to move outside it and if it didn't withstand the impact of the affair it wasn't strong enough in the first place. In later life he could not, did not want to, rid himself of the memory of one involvement. The woman was younger than him, in her mid thirties, and she had joined his school as head of history. In meetings she was intelligent, with a clear political analysis of education and, when their departments liaised on a unit of work he ended up—he hadn't arranged this; it had just fallen out that way—team-teaching with her. She was the best teacher he had ever come across. She worked quietly, without showmanship or selling of herself as a personality, absolutely clear about her purposes, holding the class and the lesson together through the focused attention she gave to the work, to her pupils. In those four lessons he saw her talk to groups of boys who initially responded facetiously, rudely, to her questions, but who, because of the patient, serious concentration she offered them—an attention that made no attempt at ingratiation—through the carefulness of her regard, were always drawn into the work. She believed that through knowing things these awkward young people could become more free. Morant felt clumsy beside her. He became aware later of how much her classes loved her. What she did was absolutely removed from the caricature of the inspirational and charismatic teacher. If there was in her any small particle of that kind of self it was subdued. A few weeks later he sat next to her on a sixth form trip to Stratford–upon–Avon and she told him what he knew already, that she was married and had two children. Her husband was a civil servant working in Sheffield on employment and training and she had grown up in poverty in Liverpool. It was soon confirmed that they had shared views about education and about how it was organised in the school in which they worked. The following week he asked her if she fancied a coffee after school and they drove into town. Afterwards he drove her to the village in which she lived and on the way he took her hand and she instantly nuzzled into him. He stopped the car on a track that led into a field that was sheltered by trees. They scrambled into the back of the car and they fucked. This was the beginning of an obsession that lasted for two, perhaps three years. There was a kind of rapt heedlessness to their affair; they hardly cared to disguise their relationship. They felt heroic and envied, although their behaviour presumably appeared sordid, disgraceful or stupid to many other people. He had fallen in love with her teaching and thus with her. He was mesmerised by her northernness, her class anger, her feminism as much as her shameless white body. They were loving and kind before and afterwards, but sex was intense, a zone in which they explored the possibilities of degradation and pleasure. Sometimes they made love at his flat, but not often because it was too close to where other people they knew lived. Sometimes they went to a house belonging to a friend of his in another school, but he didn't like using another man's bed. Often it was in the car after a drink, perhaps in a back street away from street lights, hurried, transgressive sex, transgressive because it was so clearly wrong to do this outside people's houses and transgressive because they used to do it in the interstices of social events, between, say, the end of a parents' evening and meeting other staff for an after event drink. He met her husband several times at social events and liked him. On one occasion she and Morant had slept together at a conference and they had made love again just before they left. Afterwards he dropped her off at her house and went inside to meet her husband and her children, a girl of eight and a boy of four. He was uncomfortable because he felt they must have stunk of sex. But these couplings were not driven by a delight in their illicit nature; they were simply scarce opportunities that presented themselves and which they could not bear to pass up. He discovered that as a child she used to hide under the bed when her father came home drunk and roaring, she hugging her younger brother who grew up to be a fantasist, always stumbling from one transformative project to another, always needing money which, if she could, she supplied. Her house, he noticed without surprise, was what his mother would have called immaculate; tidy, fiercely clean and furnished with a precise and restrained stylishness, every object—flowers, clock, hi-fi, lighting, fruit bowl, the few, as if carefully rationed, items of ornamentation—arranged in judicious balance. It was impressive, but surprising considering that there were two children in the house. She could be astonishingly inflexible in her views, often bringing meetings of senior staff to a halt with her refusal to compromise on some proposed change to school policy that she felt disadvantaged some children. He remembered one meeting, held to discuss the possible adoption of a vocational curriculum for older "non-academic" children, when she hunted down every argument in favour of introducing such a curriculum for these children—every plausible justification for such a change—as a lie, a capitulation to a fraudulent agenda, a cynical government initiative intended as a solution to a problem that education was on its own incapable of remedying: the obstinate non-compliance with educational goals of working-class children. Like every other work-orientated scheme that Morant had encountered, this one claimed to equip young people with skills that would secure employment, a dishonest promise since it offered no qualifications that would be tradeable in the employment market, presented itself as a hands-on, practical course when it was not and was in fact a ludicrously crude and inept attempt to address the difficulty of how to keep a restless cohort occupied within a system that had no notion of what an education for such children should be now that the jobs that they might have looked forward to taking up no longer existed. The room was thick with embarrassment and anger, in part because this was a direct affront to the head's authority, but mainly because she was bringing into the open what almost everyone in the room knew but had been too cowardly to address—that the head had already made up his mind on the issue and the debate they were being invited to participate in was a pretence and that the initiative had no educational value nor any purpose other than to keep a particular group of children occupied and subdued. Almost always he stood with her on such issues, but often, an unusual experience for him, he felt as if, alongside her intransigence, he were being weak-kneed, too ready to trade concessions, lacking a necessary zealousness in support of the cause. Where others would concede defeat she would take arguments up to and beyond the point of embarrassment, leaving the head teacher or some other senior member of staff angry and feeling that their authority was undermined and others furious or desperate to get out of a meeting that had become too full of affect. After one such meeting an older member of staff who encouraged a view of himself as a fount of common sense wisdom muttered to Morant that he needed to be careful about getting too close to that woman. For a moment he was shocked into silence, uncertain of the breadth of reference in the remark, but soon deciding that both he and his colleague knew precisely what he meant, he said fuck off Joe. From early on she would take sudden stands against him, often on issues that seemed to him to be unimportant, as when he told her that as a child he had learnt that if you shook a Cox apple you could hear the pips rattle and she expressed what seemed to him an extraordinary level of scorn for the idea, as if he'd been trying to impress or deceive her. On one occasion in the staff room, seizing on a statement he had made about the ambivalent educational effects of teaching standard English to working class children, she said that of course they had to learn the dominant form if they weren't to be disadvantaged in life and English teachers needed to forget all that romantic, middle-class guilt-trip shit about working-class culture and just do their job properly. Immediately Morant knew that there would be no possibility of refining his remark, filling out what she well knew was a more nuanced view. This was an attack that had no interest in debate; it was a display to him, a signal that he could not always expect her concurrence. The disproportionate vehemence with which she spoke produced a nervous silence amongst those around them in their corner of the room; everyone knew that this was about something other than pedagogy and everyone knew roughly what that other was. Apart from such moments she was the gentlest and most patient of people whose judgement, for all her indiscretions, was respected by other women on the staff. From time to time, he wrote something to her, something meant to show how powerfully he felt about her, but she almost never wrote back. He could recall one card she sent to him, when she was back in Liverpool for the funeral of her father, in which she described the strangeness of her situation, immersed in grief but unable to ignore her longing to be with someone, him, Morant, although she did not name him.

Where he used it as an instrument for living his life more intensely, she distrusted writing. In every professional situation she would prefer to talk face to face rather than argue her ideas on paper. In his work, if he wanted to secure change he would write a paper in which he sought to cut off all possibility of escaping from the inevitabilities of his argument, of avoiding the conclusions he aimed at, and then he would talk, using that text as a site of struggle, the ground that he had carefully prepared to achieve maximum advantage for himself. Perhaps, he thought later, she was right to be wary of what was going on when he wrote to her. On a few occasions, always during sex, she said that she loved him and once, after one of their periods of estrangement that began after a year or so, she said that he could have no idea how good it was to feel him inside her. Usually, however, she seemed guarded, careful of what she was committing to him, of what she was ceding in the words she offered. Once, towards the end of the summer term, they had, unusually, gone to his flat after a school training day in which they had both spoken against a proposal to introduce setting according to ability for first year pupils, a step that was described by the head as an experiment. This was one of several such changes in a school which had always defined itself as a progressive, even radical, institution, changes which a new head appeared to hope would make it more competitive with other schools in the area. These schools had responded to the recent abolition of the regulation that they could only recruit pupils from within their own precisely defined catchment area, by marketing themselves according to a traditional model of pre-1960s education—as academically rigorous institutions peopled by happily obedient children in dazzling white shirts, neatly knotted ties and, what were considered to be smart, blazers. It seemed to be overlooked that no such school had existed in reality because the vast majority of children in the fondly remembered period had attended schools which had varied from training establishments for society's more menial occupations to grim, brutal penitentiaries, whilst a minority went to other schools where the intention was to groom the selected few for recruitment to the governing classes. This was the beginning of a change that was to take place over the next three decades. What teachers like Morant had thought of as education in schools would be replaced by a technical process of preparation for life in a society ordered to economic priorities. If it had once been possible to think of education as an art of freedom, concerned with shaping its subjects as intellectually disciplined and curious individuals who had some concern for the common good; if it had once been possible for teachers to believe that what they did increased civility and the possibility of a more just society; if this admittedly quixotic conception of role, this commitment to an austerely noble or irredeemably romantic notion of teaching and learning as a liberatory and civilising endeavour, had made it seem possible to teach honourably when it was plain that actual education, real schooling, was a brutal system of social differentiation and control; if all this had once been, it was to be no more. What governments wanted of schools were young people who were multi-skilled, which seemed to mean flexible, adaptable, enterprising individuals who would eagerly, unquestioningly, accommodate themselves to the ever-changing requirements of employment in a global economy, to the flux and delirium of markets that had some time ago spun beyond governability. In truth, governments had no idea what they should do to bring about the state of affairs they desired, so what they did was to govern schools more, often and oddly whilst claiming to be governing less, in a kind of frenzy which sought control of the curriculum and of teaching itself. Schools now did not concern themselves with educational matters but with demonstrating success in attaining targets set according to a range of statutorily imposed measures, and what and how teachers taught was tightly regulated by inspection and assessment regimes. Thinking about teaching and learning—the ends and meanings of education—had been replaced by statistical and pseudo-scientific conceptualisations of the tasks of schooling which indulged, not dreams of democracy and freedom, but fantasies of economic competitiveness and populations translated to entrepreneurial consciousness. To achieve their ends the most decisive move made by governments was to enter schools into the market place, through league tables of performance, by opening the running of various aspects of schooling to private companies, by severing the link between education and public mission by way of the destruction of local control of education and by the setting up of schools as competing institutions. It seemed to Morant that the education system had openly and shamelessly abandoned any pretence that it operated according to rational principles, that it was more chaotic, its purposes more purely regulatory, than at any time in its history. He sometimes reflected that what had perhaps happened was that an exhausted governmental project—the education of national populations—had tired of the pretence that it enshrined some elevated socio-moral principle and had let slip its humane and democratic guise to reveal what it was, essentially and ontologically: an apparatus powered by nothing more than an insatiable will to control and order. One warm Saturday afternoon in early July (he could not remember how it had come that they were together on a Saturday or why they had chosen to come to his house), they lay on his bed after making love. They had talked about work, sharing their pleasure in what would later seem to him small and inconsequential victories, a pleasure that somehow mingled with his love of her body, her small subtle hands, her arms so lovely, her back at once pliant and strong. They looked at each other with unguarded love. Then she had asked if he was sleeping with anyone else. He told her the truth, which was that he wasn't and she asked if he would sleep with anyone else while he was sleeping with her. He reminded her that except for one occasion early on they had never technically slept together. He immediately regretted being clever because she became angry and said all right would he have sex with someone else while they were having sex together, clever boy. He said no, which was the truth as far as he could imagine it at that moment. He said that he hadn't been attracted to another woman while he had been with her and that she was all he thought about all the time. She said he was a liar and he asked her why she thought that. As he said this he spoke as if he were surprised or puzzled and was aware that this was mainly a manufactured response, that he wasn't really surprised or puzzled by what she said. Afterwards he wondered why he had made up this surprise and it appeared that there were several reasons for it, all of them tactical or about disguise in one way or another. Firstly and obviously, he had hoped to indicate how remote such a possibility was in order to calm things down. Secondly, he had decided to appear shocked because it would not be wise to let her see that he liked the thought that she was jealous of him, that she doubted her hold over him, because it indicated that he had a hold over her. This could be put in a light that made him appear less brutish—that it reassured him that she loved him. Thirdly, he had wanted to obscure the fact that she had guessed right and that it would be possible for him to sleep with someone else, although he could not at that moment imagine it happening because he was obsessed with her. Fourthly, he wanted to obscure the fact that he was flattered that she knew he was a man who would have opportunities to betray her. She said that he was a liar because he was the kind of man who wouldn't pass up the opportunity to sleep with someone he found attractive. It was the kind of man he was. He was arrogant and would think that she wouldn't sleep with anyone else while she was sleeping—sorry, having sex—with him. He had become alarmed that things were slipping away into uncomfortable areas and depths. He said that he assumed she was still sleeping/having sex with her husband, although he didn't want any details, and she said that he knew fine well that she didn't mean that. Forget her and her husband, she said, he thought she wouldn't go with anyone else because he couldn't imagine any woman being interested in another man while she was going out with him. He said that he hadn't thought about it and she made the little yelp of mirthless laughter that she used to suggest disbelief at a ridiculous idea and said that if he hadn't thought about it—and she bet he had—it would only be because he was an arrogant bastard. He enjoyed the idea of power over women. He said that he didn't and she said mockingly yeah, right. There was a silence and perhaps then, although probably later, because then he was taken aback by her anger and could think only about getting out of this hole, he was left thinking about how much of her attack was accurate and true and what this meant for the kind of person he was. Then she said did he ever think about his daughter and he said yes. She asked why he didn't ever see her and he said that she knew why. He knew, however, that she wanted to make him go through it again. He had seen her, admittedly erratically, for the first three or four years but then his wife had remarried and had successfully petitioned for custody so that he was denied access. There was another silence before she said that she would still have seen her, it wouldn't have stopped her. It suited him not to see her. He knew she was right and years later he was to feel great guilt about this, the one thing in his life that more than anything made him doubt if he could ever consider himself a good man, but then, at that time, he did not feel shame. Why had he been denied access. He said that they had been through this before and she said, yes, but why. As he'd told her before, it was because he had missed some maintenance payments and his visiting record was erratic—in fact, not very good at all—and in court his solicitor had been exceptionally inept while his ex-wife's had been relaxed, fluent and persuasive in a linen suit (later he was to think he was a kind of craftier Atticus Finch). She said, you shouldn't have missed the visits. He knew that. Why had he missed them. Because he'd been too busy shagging women (if he had been truthful, he would have said, falling in and out of love, and then back in, pursuing his destiny as someone for whom life could only be fulfilled through this strange business of immersion in and absorption of another) and because he was wrapped up in writing and then teaching. Because he was enjoying himself running around getting pissed, fighting and generally being an irresponsible, rootless, lawless young man for far too long. It was unusual not to get access, for all rights for a father to see his child being withdrawn. Usually, as far as he understood it, this only happened if the ex-husband had been violent or psychologically abusive or if it was thought he would be likely to be a harmful presence in the child's life. None of these things were true of him which was about all that he could say in his defence. He said that perhaps the judge had concluded that his unreliability would damage his daughter. There was quiet for a while and then she asked what he had felt when he realised he would not be able to see his daughter again and he said that she would probably like him to say that he had felt downcast, wounded. In fact he had had just this—a sense of something slipping away, something that he didn't fully understand but which he perhaps then but certainly afterwards felt as an absence, a vacancy that would grow and pull on him more and more over time—guilt and loss, that sort of thing, a tear that he could never mend. He had chosen to cause pain to a child. Then she said that she wanted to go home. He said that he knew he had done wrong and they were quiet for a while and then she said, I know, and snuggled into him, that faint smell of a soap, astringent, that he had never identified, and skin that had been warmed and chafed by the sun, although she was always pale, and she reached down to his crotch and they made love again. She rarely spoke of her children but said enough for it to be clear that she was devoted to them. Several months into their relationship, when they were together there would be occasions when she hardly spoke and dismal evenings would be spent sitting in his car or some pub, with Morant trying to find out what was wrong, worried about asking too many questions and worried too that he wasn't asking enough. At these times she would talk obsessively about her father and her inability to deal with his loss, or her brother who had nowhere to live because he'd lost his job, and the burden it placed on her mother. Typically she would cry quietly, sniffling through the evening and Morant would rack his brains to find ways of penetrating this sealed-off gloom, aware that her emotions were on a hair trigger and likely to erupt if he said the wrong thing, whatever that might be. He was worried too that he might say the right thing, might touch on the true cause of her misery and that this would enrage her because he knew for certain that she was very angry with him and the last thing she wanted was the intrusion of his perceptiveness. When she was like this they did not usually make love and if they did she would be entirely mute afterwards. Years later he recognised and wondered at his obliviousness to what was at work. All he cared about was to keep things going, to hold on to this woman, and this made him blind and deaf. His memory of the next couple of years was of long troubled periods interspersed with briefer episodes of manic closeness, when once more they were together against the world and its enfeebled respectability, against its corruption, mediocrity and political timidity. Then one day, on their way to a presentation they were to give to other teachers in the local education authority on how English and Humanities teachers could co-operate in an integrated curriculum she took exception to something he said. It was about an item he'd heard on a news programme on his way to pick her up, which suggested that scientists had come to the conclusion that women could turn their forearms outwards at the elbow to a greater angle than men because this enabled them to avoid contact with their wider hips. She was furious and said that yes, of course, he'd like to think that, that it was just the sort of evolutionary bollocks that men came up with to explain why gender was destiny. He was so taken aback by the wildness of her attack that instead of saying what he thought, that the theory did indeed sound like the kind of crude and blithely over-confident assertion that scientists sometimes made, he said that surely you couldn't dismiss all evolutionary thought as driven by a conspiracy to oppress women and that the idea was a possibility, given that women did seem able to turn their arms outward at the elbow more than men. This last provoked a level of scorn that was new; he was sexist, arrogant, stupidly smug, and nothing he attempted by way of retraction or defence could calm her rage, so that as he went to stand up at the meeting to start the presentation she pulled at his sleeve and whispered in his ear that she was going to fuck this up for him. This was the only time he heard her swear. After that she cut him off for a longer period than at any time before, refusing to speak about anything but work. This exclusion was a darkness in which he incubated humiliating jealousies. He convinced himself that she no longer loved him, that she had met someone else. To his shame he rang her at home several times when he was drunk, hanging up once when her husband answered and having her hang up on him when she answered. In this period she seemed to join in staffroom conversation much more than usual, nearly always with women, and with a brightness, a vivacity, which seemed to Morant artificial. He wrote a note to her and they had a coffee together one lunchtime in a local pub. She gave no explanation for his excommunication and spoke in an emotionless way about her younger child, the boy, who had been ill, and her husband who was having too much piled on him at work. Then she said that when she was visiting her mother a few weekends ago she had gone for a drink with someone she had known at university and they had had sex together. He was a bit of a tosser really. Morant asked why and she said that he obviously went to a gym and was stupidly proud of his body. She told him that she was seeing a psychiatrist for depression and that she was on medication. Then she had a long period off sick. One day he rang her, knowing that she would be in on her own, and he said that he was thinking of coming round at lunchtime. She said that he shouldn't bother and that anyway she had flu. He said that he'd like to see her anyway. When he arrived at her house she did indeed look unwell. She put her arms around him and snuggled into him. She smiled at him and looked into his eyes, for the first time in months. They went upstairs and, conscious that she was fragile, he made love to her gently, tenderly. Afterwards he said that that was nice and she smiled and said, yes, but she wouldn't want to do it like that too often. When she came back to school she again kept him at a distance and he was aware that she was applying for jobs and at the end of one day she said could they talk and in her teaching room she told him that she had got a job in Birmingham as a deputy head and she'd be moving there. He asked was her husband moving to a new job as well and she said no. Morant said it would be a long commute for him and she said, if he comes. He asked what she meant and she said if he comes. She didn't know if he would be moving with her. After she left he got in touch and met her one Saturday in Chester and, as had often been the case, they didn't speak directly about how they stood with one another, how they felt or what they might do. He was numbed, unable to act and she kept up a surface brightness that told him she wanted no intimacy. When it was time to part he held her and she was stiff and unresponsive. She told him that she was divorcing and when he asked about the children she said that she would probably be having the kids during the week and he'd usually have them weekends, but it'd be flexible. She had exhausted and bewildered him and at that moment he could find nothing to say. Afterwards, some time later, he realised that he had felt a sense of release from a relationship that had been, for obvious reasons, punishing and draining, but he recognised too that in accepting that liberation, allowing it to claim him, there was a faltering in his strength, a self-protectiveness. He still loved her, still trailed a tatter of regrets and longing, but this ending allowed him to put all that away, to store it somewhere safe from his shaming fantasies. He didn't have to find out anything more about her, about himself, about them. If he asked no questions he would be beyond the reach of the pain they had traded. A few years later he learned that she had remarried. He didn't have to think what this meant. He never, ever, forgot her and her goodness, nor the irresistible division in her nature, between the need for tenderness and the need for violation. So, that was somewhere where he'd behaved badly. He'd participated without a thought of right or wrong in the break-up of a family. He'd pursued a woman and driven her into a relationship that had caused her breakdown and at the time his self-absorption, his unpitying need, had made him unable to see that her illnesses were triggered by the irreconcilable conflicts he had imposed upon her. He had been merciless in the demands he had made and in the end he had offered her nothing. On the other hand, she would have been incandescent at this characterisation of her as a victim. And he hadn't thought about the children. He never ceased to have dreams about her and once or twice he had awoken from them tearfully. At times he could hardly bear to think about what he had been like from his mid twenties to most of his forties.

One Friday evening in the seventies before he and Liz broke up he had gone for a drink with some colleagues and after perhaps six pints had gone back to the flat where one of them lived to listen to The Who, Steely Dan and Pink Floyd and possibly Ry Cooder and to drink gin and smoke dope. This last was a first for Morant as he had never smoked a cigarette in his life and to share a saliva-wetted joint was a major achievement. He then suggested that if they went to the airfield, a private club with a bar, that, as far as Morant could make out, let anyone in, they could get some more drink. Several people demurred but the rest he drove to the airfield, hitting kerbs and missing lights on the way. The bar was packed and after they'd got a drink, as they stood in a tight circle in that crowded bar, Morant, because he didn't know where the toilet was and was too tired to find it, and also because he knew that he could do this and no one would stop him, unzipped his fly and pissed on the carpet. Driving home in the early hours of the morning and noticing that it was a clear night with a full moon, he turned his car's lights off to see if it was possible to drive by moonlight. It was. A car came up behind him, flashing its lights. Annoyed, he braked hard. He did this several times. The car followed him back to his house and the driver exploded from his vehicle, but stopped on the far side of Morant's front lawn, his girlfriend pulling at his arm and pleading for him to get back in the car. Morant could think of nothing to say and just observed the man, who was younger than him and wearing a suit, thinking about what would be the best way of ending this if the man decided to attack. He didn't want a wrestling match in his front garden and he might, given that he had drunk so much, mistime a punch. Liz came out of the house in a towelling robe and said for christ's sake get inside. He was aware that all this was shameful but he didn't intend to retreat into the house, leaving the man yelling outside, nearly crying with rage, pretending to himself that he'd scared Morant away, but he didn't want to humiliate him in front of his partner and he didn't want an injured man with a ruined suit on the grass at the front of his house. The man took Morant's silence for an arrogant confidence and this increased his levels of rage and noise, but in the end the woman persuaded him back into his car. This happened near the end of things with Liz. On another occasion he got into a fight with a pimp outside the toilets in a market place pub in town. Morant had gone for a drink with some colleagues after a meeting of the local English teaching association, which he chaired, and a female colleague returned from the small courtyard out the back, saying that she'd been turned away by some prostitutes who were having a meeting. Morant went back with her, although she seemed somewhat reluctant, and asked if it would be possible for his friend to use the toilet as she was desperate. Hardly looking away from what seemed to be an intense conversation with her co-workers, one of them said go on it'd be OK. He was waiting for his colleague to finish when a man came through and started talking to the prostitutes in a way that combined wheedling and menace. Then he noticed Morant and asked what the fuck he was doing there. Morant explained and the man told him to fuck off. Morant indicated that he intended to stay where he was and the man pushed him in the chest and said just fuck off out of here. Morant declined to shift and when the man approached again, more slowly this time, and he knew from the way he held himself, the slight tilt backwards of his head, that he intended to head-butt him, he stepped back and slightly to one side and hit him on the jaw and when he was on the floor, on the wet, uneven concrete that seemed to Morant possibly to be stained not only by the urine and shit water that leaked from the lavatories but possibly also by every other excretion that human beings were capable of, kicked him in the stomach. One of the prostitutes said you'd better leave love, he won't be pleased about that, he won't let that go. His frightened colleague came out of the cubicle and Morant's party left. Later he became aware that his behaviour had shocked and unnerved people. There were other occasions of violence and rage, nearly but not all drink-related—fights during or after football and rugby games, a staff evening out when he had erupted at a pub landlord who refused to serve one of his colleagues on the grounds that his long hair was dirty (it wasn't) and on one occasion fury directed at some police who had caught him and friends pissing against a wall on some waste ground—and he knew that things were bad when he met a former pupil in town who said that he'd seen him having a fight the weekend before at a barn dance. Morant knew that he and Liz had gone to a barn dance, an excruciatingly dull entertainment, popular at the time, laid on in some farmer's giant shed, involving barbecued meat, huge cans of watery beer and, if he remembered right, attempts to get people interested in something like square-dancing—but he couldn't remember fighting. Apparently someone had accused him of pushing in at the bar and it had developed from there. Morant didn't ask if he'd won, but since he'd not been aware of any bruising and had no dulled feelings of defeat and humiliation he assumed he had. He would never become entirely clear about the causes of his unboundaried rage at that time, his loathing of propriety. Neither did he know what cured him of all this, why he eventually became calmer, although it had something to do with study, with his return to academic work that began with a masters and moved on quickly to the doctoral research that eventually led to work at the university. It never occurred to him that he was frightening people he knew and one day in his fifth decade he realised with horror that although these incidents were infrequent he must have been viewed with the same distaste as he felt for any man who traded on physical threat. In all this time he ran what he knew was the best department in the school and colleagues would sometimes tell him that they admired his teaching. He should have given his career, its progress, more thought, but he was too busy for that, dividing his energies, he was later to think, between a commitment to Dionysian excess or, the same thing put differently, behaving disgracefully, and, through his teaching, working towards the downfall of capitalism and an era of love and social justice.

One of the things that Morant liked about Alison was how much she enjoyed sex. She was always warm and affectionate but there was also something both mischievous and practical about her approach to it. As their relationship developed she revealed an appetite for sudden sex in risky places. One Saturday morning he had driven the pair of them into town for a lunchtime drink and sandwich and after they'd parked she said, let's do it here, in the back of the van, now. Morant put up some half-hearted objections to this proposal but soon gave in. Subsequently she had persuaded him to do it, to do it to her or, once, making him laugh, to give her one—on a number of occasions in the bathroom she shared with four other girls on her floor, in a cloakroom before an end of term dance and, one morning just as everyone was making their way to lectures, in the women's toilet just outside the student common room. Alison's everyday behaviour, her demeanour, was at all times controlled. This is not to say that she appeared at all repressed, but that she presented a calm, composed face to the world and, as far as he could make out, this was the outward expression of a well-ordered personality; she was someone who was at ease with herself, managing with some success the miseries and doubts, the fantasies and the yearnings that affect everyone. These mild sexual delinquencies were not the inevitable overflow of a cruel regime of self-denial, of self-violence, but an ordered, pleasurable experiment with desire and abandon. Such usually brief engagements, which, Morant guessed, were for Alison more enjoyable for their disgracefulness than the physical satisfaction they provided, were balanced at other times by a purposeful investigation of the possibilities for sexual pleasure. They quickly identified what they each enjoyed. She established early on that sometimes she would like penetration from behind and on one occasion suggested they try anal sex, but after a few seconds she stopped him and said it didn't feel right. On another occasion she said she wanted to, as she put it, fellate him. Morant hadn't quite understood what she meant at first and she said, give you head. These experiments with the sexual demotic amused and charmed him. He said, fine, although he had always found this a tedious activity, only once experiencing orgasm in this way and this had been a couple of years earlier whilst he was driving along the North Circular Road with his friend Maurice's girl, Vivian. He was driving to a pub in New Southgate where Maurice was playing guitar in a group and although he and Viv had been playing at surreptitious touching and feeling for some time it was the unexpectedness and inappropriateness of the event that made him come. Alison applied herself for half a minute and then said, is that nice. He said yes. I quite like it, she said, but she obviously found it a bit more like work than pleasure and the experiment wasn't repeated. What Alison was particularly interested in was that she should come when they were in bed; it was clear that she expected it to happen at some point, by some means or other. This, he thought, was a reasonable expectation. Her mother was French, and this seemed to explain certain things that had intrigued him. Alison was always neat and tidy in her dress, in a way that had appeared to him a little old-fashioned—she was the first girl he had been with, at least since he had stopped seeing working-class girls, who always wore a slip. Her skirts were just slightly below the knee. She wore matching sweaters and cardigans and always something else like a scarf, a necklace or a belt that—he understood these things imperfectly at the time—had a purely decorative function but which struck him as conventional, conservative, although somehow managed with a pleasing freshness. He liked this about her. A girl on the Arts course said to him one day how beautifully turned out Alison always was, but it wasn't until she was complimented on her perfect French by Jack and she said that hers had been a bilingual household, her mother from the Lot, that what he had previously seen as a slight staidness about dress became Frenchness, a conformist aesthetic valuing restraint and properness above the kind of individual expression that many English women were beginning to explore. Suddenly the fact of her mother's nationality seemed to explain all her behaviour; her poise and self-containment, her quiet practicality about sex, emotions and study became the rational pursuit of a good life in which pleasure and necessity, the life of the body and mind, were held in balance. He knew that this was a simplification borne partly out of his own francophilia, an enthusiasm based on limited experience of France or the French, in which Frenchness served as an idealised alternative to everything that he disliked about the self-satisfied pragmatism, the insistent, arrogant myopia of Anglo-Saxon thought and culture, but it was appealing nevertheless. Later that evening he was in bed with Alison, her back to him, his legs enfolding her endearingly short legs, his face pressed into the side of her neck, holding her by crossing his arms over her body and cupping her small breasts in his hands. He said, why didn't you tell me your mother was French, and she said, you didn't ask. There was no reason to. Then she said, do you love your mother. He asked where that came from and she said that he never spoke about her and she'd told him about her parents. He was silent for a while, not knowing how to begin, so he began without thinking. He had always tried to get away from her. She chose him as the one she would confide in, which is to say unload her unhappiness. She had always been a very discontented woman. Even before his father died, when he was twelve or thirteen, if he was alone with her, say when he'd gone with her shopping for some reason, she'd tell him how she hated the house they lived in. They'd just moved after twelve years in rented rooms off the Caledonian Road, but their first house wasn't what she'd imagined and the area was grey and featureless. She'd wanted somewhere nicer, a place in somewhere like Southgate, but this was a terrace house in a working-class suburb that didn't even have the liveliness and family of Islington. She wanted—she hadn't put it this way—a different kind of life. She never used to complain about his father on these occasions, although she moaned at him a lot in the house. All sorts of things like that, that he could barely remember. He had an image of them walking down a wide street in Tottenham, going to the bus-stop, her telling him things that worried him and made him sad. He said to Alison that he didn't know. He didn't know if he loved her. Probably not. He felt sorry for her and was grateful for how she'd helped him. I'd like my brother to look after her—not me. He just wanted to leave all that. He hated families. She asked if he looked like his mother and he said no, that she was tiny with a round face and a small nose. Would he like to look like her? He couldn't imagine anything more disturbing. And he said that before she asked, no, he didn't look like his father either and that he would hate to look like him. Alison asked why, had he been ugly. No, he had always been thought to be a very handsome man. She asked who did he look like then. No one. And then he told her about his father. The youngest child in a middle-class family and the only one to lose social position. A mechanic in the army during the war. Afterwards a chauffeur, electro-plater and finally an insurance agent. Visits to his father's brothers and sisters in places like Egham, Muswell Hill and Leigh-on-Sea, in photos both he and his brother as carefully turned out by their mother—in flannel shorts, grey socks, white shirts and sandals—as their uncles' and aunts' gardens, which seemed to the boys intentionally or negligently inhibiting of play. His father was the one uncle who played football or cricket with however many of the sixteen children—all but one boys, born to his mother and her brothers—as were present on occasional family outings to Dunstable Downs or the south coast. The uncle who gathered all the children into a darkened room at Christmas parties and told them ghost stories. The man who liked cars, especially foreign ones, who adored Stirling Moss and wanted one day to own an MG, who enjoyed trying to cook what he thought French food must be like and who, when he was working at the electro-plating business, gave him and his brother knives—letter openers—which he said they would have to carry with them on the day, one day, when he would take them for a meal at a Chinese restaurant, because these places were dangerous and they might be attacked. He was the man who bought books of practice tests for the 11+ examination and was, it seemed to Morant, a little taken aback when his older son coped well with the exercises. He was the man who had a screaming row with his mother over a woman called Milly, a woman who was retained in Morant's memory only as a blurred face. He had been with him when he died. They had been moving some gardening equipment into a house in Enfield which they were to move into the following day, when he said, you'll have to finish this, David. I don't feel too well. He had sat in the car while Morant finished unloading the boot and carrying, he couldn't really remember what, probably plant-pots and trowels, into the garage. They had reversed out of the drive and his father had tried to drive home but had had to stop just one street away. He lay down on a grass verge—many years later, visiting his brother, he had driven past the spot and there were no longer grass verges in that street—a householder called an ambulance and—he remembered thinking this was unusual when it shouldn't have been—he held his father's hand and said, are you feeling a bit better and his father had said, no, not really, a bit worse since they moved me. At the hospital he was wheeled away and he, Morant, was left alone amidst some rows of empty chairs and feeling as if he was in the wrong place—this wasn't a normal place for him to be. After a while a nurse came out and took him to a doctor who said something like, I'm terribly sorry, but I have to tell you that your father has died. He never really knew him but he had begun to think his father didn't like him, that he couldn't make sense of this son who was good at games, academically successful and what he would have called dreamy, introspective, reading too much, not down to earth. Perhaps he detected the lack of focus, the imaginative excess, that had afflicted his own life. He said to Alison that it was probably an early adolescent thing, the beginning of the struggle to make sense of your relationship with your father. She said it must have been terrible for him, Morant. He said that it had been. He had understood instantly that he would never see him, hear him, touch him, again and felt the void that had opened. All children fear this but here it was in reality, it could really happen, this violent removal of certainty, this destruction visited upon your life. He had used to dream that his father was still alive and had had this fantasy that one day a friend would say that he'd seen his dad driving a car and this meant that he hadn't died but had just left them, moved on to a different life with a different wife, a different job, a different family and kids. But it was much, much worse for his brother. He was eleven years old then and his father was the one important person in his life. When they were little children living in the two top floors of the house off the Cally, every evening their parents used to stand them in two round bowls on the kitchen table and wash them from head to foot before they went to bed. Raymond would never let his mother wash him. His uncle Tommy collected Morant from the hospital and took him home to his wildly grieving mother. He had had a lot of attention, particularly from his aunts who said how horrible it must have been for Davey. He was uncomfortable—he didn't want this and he was aware of his brother, not centre stage like him, past tears, stunned and, as Morant later saw it, knowing that now he was bereft, without the one person who would defend him in this world. When he was older he recalled his brother standing alone and uncomforted and he couldn't summon a picture of him being held and consoled by his mother. Later that evening he passed his brother on the stairs and said, are you OK Raymond said, piss off. What he meant, Morant saw, was this: he loved me the most, not you, I'm the one suffering. He had always loved his little brother and, it seemed now as if this was the last time he would feel this: his heart was pierced by pity for him. But you loved him, your father, Alison said. He must have, but he couldn't remember what that was like. But he had grieved. It was a bad time for him to die, for himself he meant. Alison turned and snuggled into him but—he was glad of this; it was part of her gracefulness—made no other attempt to comfort him in word or gesture. He had one big memory about his father. His brother and he and his uncle Tommy's two sons were playing in the street near his uncle's house and up at the corner, about fifty yards away, his Dad and Uncle Tommy were talking to two men. After a while there was shouting and he saw his father being held back by Tommy and one of the other men trying to restrain his companion. Suddenly the angry man had broken free and pushed his father to the ground. A sickening flood of terror and humiliation had swept over Morant. His father was quickly back on his feet and, although the shouting and threatening behaviour continued for a time, the group split up soon after and his father walked back down the hill with Tommy. He told Alison that that never left him. He was caught by surprise, overthrown, cast down, upended. At some point after that, Morant said, he had decided that that would never happen to him. You'd be the one to do the humiliating, Alison said. I don't want to humiliate anybody, he said. No, I don't think you do, but perhaps you think that that's what happens in the end between people. They humiliate you or you humiliate them. He said again that he didn't want to hurt anyone. No, but you would do if you had to—not because you like to be cruel, but because you need to protect yourself. He said doesn't everyone. Alison said that yes, need to protect themselves, but that didn't mean that they saw their lives as needing to be organised to avoid pain being inflicted by other people. Was he horrible then. Yes. He was a monster. Years later, when Alison had passed out of his life, he had a dream and when he woke from it, he thought instantly that he wished he could tell Alison about this. He had discovered his father, sick, frail but still alive and he had brought him home and cared for him, but knew that he would still die, probably soon, but they had had him back for a brief time. Home was a version of the rooms they had lived in as a young family. His father told him about his time on Gibraltar during the war and spoke about other things in a way that had never been managed when he had been alive earlier. His heart was heavy with love for his father and he thought how pleased his mother would be when she came home, but he couldn't recall her being there. Then his father had to go.

One afternoon Morant sat in a high, light-filled room listening to a lecturer proving that Troilus and Cressida revealed the conservative nature of Shakespeare's social and political thinking. The room overlooked a hillside meadow of long grass that rippled and waved in a wind that seemed to blow from no set direction, producing swirling tides and currents that swept down, across and up the field, combing the luscious grass into sinuous, sometimes cross-cutting flows that played with the sunlight and cloud shadows of a high Staffordshire sky. Morant tried to discern some repeated patterns in this voluptuous display, but could see none. It reminded him of a television film he had seen of young polecats playing in a clearing, tumbling over a fallen tree trunk and each other, hiding, pouncing, advancing and retreating, wrestling together in lithe, wriggling collisions of movement that— almost, but never quite, predictably—exploded into separate darts and scurries of flight and self-assertion. He could see clouds propelled across a vast, towering sky that reached out and beyond this English midlands landscape, connecting it to regions of mountain, forest, sea, desert and steppe, to twilights, star-strewn nights, dusks and dawns, snows, tempests, heat and drought, to cities, civilisations and to bewitching lives of which he knew nothing. All of it cried out to his heart, his imagination, filling him with a desire that he knew for now could be satisfied here, just where he was, now in this teeming moment, this prolific space. The lecturer, whom Morant had not come across before, was saying that take but degree away, untune that string, and hark what discord follows. He appeared to be saying not just that Ulysses represented Shakespeare's view of social order but that these were indeed wise words to which we might all give assent. None of his fellow students seemed to think it remarkable that their lecturer was arguing in favour of a rigid hierarchical organisation of power in society and, presumably, the necessarily ruthless domination of the bulk of the population by a fascistic leadership. Perhaps, he thought, he was being harsh and the lecturer was simply envisaging a demagogic leadership that contrived the masses' acceptance of its rule through the instilling of false consciousness—a genial, communally sensitive authoritarianism. (Ten to fifteen years later he would have been tempted to use the word installation rather than instilling, the former one of those exhilaratingly brutal locutions he would come across in theoretical writing, which he would be obliged to question for its mechanistic over-simplification even as he relished its wonderful offensiveness to humanist idiocies). He waited a few minutes to see if he had correctly understood what the lecturer was saying and to see if anyone else would have anything to say. Then he raised his hand and made a number of points. Wasn't Ulysses just a character in a play whose given lines represented one point of view, one argument that was current at the time, an expression of the anxieties of an age that was panicking about the evaporation of old certainties, the emergence of new classes and the individualism that was being fostered by early capitalism and a few scholars who were excited about the possibility of new intellectual freedoms. In any case this was a speech that had a narrowly practical purpose, to get the Greeks to stop falling out with each other and unite purposefully against the Trojans. Ulysses was just using the most persuasive argument available to achieve what he wanted, a calculated, you could even say cynical, deployment of an idea rather than something he, or the man who wrote the speech, was himself deeply committed to. You might just as well say that Thersites—all the argument is a cuckold and a whore—represented Shakespeare's view of things, that history was not driven by noble ideas but by human weakness. Anyway, why should we be bothered about Shakespeare's views. And shouldn't we be wary of the imagined ideas of an imagined man, Ulysses, who was clearly imagined as a cold-blooded realpolitiker whose only interest, whose only idea, was to seize and exercise power for his side on the grounds that it was better to wield power than to be subject to it. Or something like that. The lecturer paused briefly then said, yes, the speech could be read in that way, but the play's structure, its trajectory, tended towards the conclusion that violence, barbarity and moral breakdown flowed from the failure of social authority. Morant said, you mean a failure to respect social authority. Yes, I do think that that is what the play argues. And you agree with that. I'm not sure that it's to the point what I think, but, yes, I do think that. And Morant would have liked to say something of what he had been writing for a philosophy of education essay in which he attacked the idea, then dominant in educational theory, that education should be a process of initiation into a culture and its values; it had seemed to him that there was here an unexamined assumption that what the dominant culture had to confer was an unquestionable good, that its values had an unanswerable authority, and he wanted to say to this lecturer—who, he had noticed, tended to look around the room, down at his notes or out the window when talking to him—what if people have lost respect for social authority and the morality that they claim underpins it, a morality which is in fact very useful to one particular class, perhaps we should say ideology rather than morality, what if those who govern have come to be seen as liars and hypocrites who uphold injustice, exploitation and the maintenance of privilege that was originally won by a lawless violence, by originary acts of theft and slaughter. Might people not conclude that such a system of rule has forfeited its authority and might they not refuse to behave in accordance with its dictates and, indeed, seek its overthrow and replacement by a more just system. He managed to say something of this and the lecturer said that he thought one should be very wary of overturning a social order. Decades later Morant would agree with this, insofar as he would have to concede that revolutions were dangerous affairs—since, as someone he admired had written, we know from experience that the claim to escape from the system of contemporary reality so as to produce the overall programmes of another society, another vision of the world, may lead only to the return of the most dangerous traditions—and shortly after he was to wonder if he had done the lecturer an injustice and whether less belligerent questioning might have yielded a more nuanced and instructive statement of the man's position. However, Morant would never lose the conviction that it was necessary to imagine an entirely different way of being. He traced this recognition to a moment at morning break in his first year at school, just inside the gates of the recreational quadrangle. He was standing so that on one side to his left there was the swarming asphalt playground and to his right, through the gates, the Victorian school building that he had just left, a few boys straggling across from it. About fifteen yards in front of him was a large iron gate that consisted of two fixed structures on either side and the gate itself. The gate, hinged on the left, had been pulled back to the wall to allow access to a doorway that led, a further five yards ahead, to the school tuck shop and to the left the prefects' common room. There was a space between the wall and the gate inside which a boy had been imprisoned by a group of other boys. This happened to this boy almost every break time. The boy was fat, broad-hipped, an androgyne and Jewish. A few friends, of similarly low status, none of them Jewish, kept him company, talking to him and perhaps passing him a bottle of lemonade or a chocolate bar. Morant was not shocked by this although he felt sorry for the imprisoned boy, but he was perplexed by certain aspects of it—why the boy submitted to it so readily, why his tormentors pursued this ill-treatment with such an efficient regularity, why no one in authority had noticed that this was happening—and he had no wish to involve himself in the persecution. The day before his father had chided him for not looking alert and sharp when he had been walking down the road with his cousin Daniel, whose eyes, his father said had been darting everywhere, taking in the details of his surroundings, whilst Morant had looked as if he were in a dream; he'd never get on that way. He had had a conversation with his friend Tommy earlier in that school day in which Tommy had said that he was sick of the way that girls always got all the praise—this was something to do with a cousin who was always held up as a model of behaviour. He had just had a religious instruction lesson in which the teacher, a priest, had said that their school did not go in for things like striped blazers because it was long-established and had no need to advertise itself by such means. He remembered a kind of epiphany in which he saw that this school and what it did, its organisation and its purposes, this life, the city whose violent system whirled around him, the ways in which the schoolboys amused themselves at break, everything that people did and all the arrangements, the duties and commitments by which they made sense of their lives, did not have to be like this. There was no more detail to it than that and this was not a moral vision, not connected at all to an imperative for change. Neither was it alarming. It felt as if something had been lifted off him, or as if a filter had been removed from his gaze so that he saw things, not as they really were, but in their contingency. He just saw that everything was made up. This was where his puzzlement seemed to begin, his constant surprise at people's readiness to accept the existing organisation of the world, their keenness to embrace the certainty that this was how things had to be disposed. On

Shakespeare, Morant would later be attracted to the Borgesian view that at the centre of his plays there was an emptiness, a blankness onto which we project our fantasies, at their heart an originating nothingness, only a bit of coldness, a dream dreamt by no one. Borges, of course, tells us that Shakespeare recognized what other men refuse—the fundamental identity of existing, dreaming and acting, the vacuum around which our language revolves, agitatedly, desperately spinning its stories, its justifications, brewing its copious storms of meaning and action. Later in the week of the Troilus and Cressida lecture Tim Dawson was showing him how to fix an audiotape onto super 8 film and said, I see you've been upsetting Clive Howson. Morant asked who Clive Howson was. Tim said that it was the chap who took the session on Troilus and Cressida a few days ago. Morant asked if he'd really been upset. Tim said that no he hadn't but that he'd been a bit taken aback, that Morant had been extremely fierce. Oh, shit. I shouldn't worry. Howson had said it had been quite stimulating. Morant explained what the exchange had been about and said that Howson hadn't appeared to be stimulated, more embarrassed. He seemed a bit right-wing. Tim smiled and said that he was new and he didn't know a great deal about him, perhaps suggesting at the same time that he had already come to certain conclusions about Howson. There was no hint of collusion in Tim's response, no silent endorsement of Morant's impression, but neither did he make Morant uncomfortable by communicating that there were professional boundaries which, of course, he could not cross in talking about a colleague. There were, certainly, scruples of this sort at work, but Morant admired the way in which his tutor managed these small things. Few people, Morant thought, could be completely without side or malice, and he wasn't sure that he would have been much interested in anyone who was, but Tim came as close as anyone he was ever to meet to that kind of poise. At least in relation to his students he played the exchanges of power at work in all human encounters gracefully and with respect. Morant never consciously adopted Tim as a model of how to teach, but years later it occurred to him that he had learned almost everything about teaching, about education, from him. He had no idea if Tim ran his department in a way that pleased his colleagues. His approach mixed instruction and heuristics; he would tell you what you needed to know—that this film, for example, played around with the conventions of classical film-making—and then stage a discussion of what those conventions were, before watching a film or a sequence from a film during which you were asked to look out for what was happening in the narrative, the dialogue, sound, editing and camera work. Then there would be another discussion in which he used what the group had found out to build a more conceptualised understanding of what was going on. Then you would be asked to do some investigation of your own or to go off and shoot some film, experimenting with what you had learnt. What was important in this was, of course, the combination of an unequivocal assertion of his authority as a teacher—he knew more than his students—and his insistence on practice, that you could only learn by doing. But what was more important was the bearing that he brought to his teaching, his focus on what the student had to say, what she knew and what she needed to know, a seriousness about the work that communicated that here was something important and something whose study was pleasurable. And beyond that, he demonstrated that there was no final, settled knowledge to be aimed at, that teaching calls itself into question, seeks always to forge new concepts. Nothing in Morant's previous experience had been like this. He remembered the time in the sixth form, in an English lesson, when a boy had questioned the teacher's statement about a character in King Lear, or it might have been an interpretation of a particular passage, and the teacher had paused for a few seconds, allowing a certain dread to fill the room like a freezing mist, a grey menace spreading out from his entirely motionless, erect and gowned body, before informing the boy that, as someone who had just come to the play he had no authority to question the judgement of someone who had spent the last thirty years studying Shakespeare, watching his plays, keeping abreast of the thinking of scholars and critics and reviewing performances of the plays for a national newspaper, and that the boy would be better off listening carefully to what he had to say and trying to understand it, if he was to gain any benefit and real enjoyment from the work of this most important of all writers, rather than offering his unthought-through, disrespectful—to the writer, not to the teacher—half-baked concoctions for general consideration. Half-baked concoctions became a popular phrase amongst these A level students. What have you said about the incident in the Maribar caves? I've only been able to come up with a few half-baked concoctions as usual. I left a few half-baked concoctions here somewhere. They were in a blue folder. Has anyone seen them? Danny Engel said that he had been in the loo having a piss and had caught Davis looking across longingly at his half-baked concoctions.

One Easter holiday, when he was sixteen, Morant and his friend Tommy Davis hitch-hiked to Scotland. Morant had been fascinated by the north since primary school days. He remembered looking at a geography text book and seeing pictures of industrial towns, miners, moorland wildernesses and mountains, everything so different from what he knew. Terry Bryan, who sat next to him in lessons, told him that he had stopped with relatives in Sunderland in the summer holidays and that it was always sunny and hot there. When his family had gone on holiday to Cornwall Morant's heart had filled with excitement when he saw what he thought were white mountains. He knew that Cornwall did not have real peaks, but for a moment he thought that there were indeed a few small mountains which, through some extraordinary oversight, no one had thought to mention. He was told that these were china clay spoil tips, the heaped residue of mining, and neither the astonishing coast nor the satisfyingly bleak moorland they drove through on their way home quite compensated for this disillusion. He and Tommy were picked up north of Manchester by some friendly young builders from, it seemed, Wigan who, to shared amusement, could barely understand what Morant and Tommy said and whose accents were just as impenetrable to the two boys. Much later Morant seemed to recall, although he couldn't be certain, that they said thee and tha, a usage that he came across twelve years afterwards when he started to teach in South Yorkshire. The builders dropped them off just after they'd crossed the East Lancs Road, at a junction near Warrington. The slip road back onto the motorway was overpopulated by hitch-hikers and they walked to another exit on the roundabout, where the map indicated that a road led off, running parallel to the motorway, and rejoining it about twenty miles further on. After a while a car stopped and the driver, a middle-aged woman, wound down the window on her side, away from them, and said something that was lost in the noise of traffic. Tommy and Morant indicated that they couldn't hear her and she angled her head out of the window and spoke again. Tommy shouted,

I'm sorry we still can't hear you. The woman closed her window, leaned across, opened the window on their side a few inches and said, them that hiketh, let them hike. Then she drove away. In the back of a large saloon car, just after Lancaster, Morant looked to his right and saw in the distance a range, a lavish sprawl of hills and over them all a vast, snow-hung mass, his first mountain. His heart heaved. As would always be the case when he saw at distance, or entered the hills of the north he was filled with exhilaration and longing, with a certainty that here he would, in this immense desolation, find some sort of unnameable completion. He read later that English hills are always too small to achieve grandeur and that one could not therefore attain amongst them an experience of the sublime, that supposedly ineffable condition of terror and exhilaration felt before a beauty or immensity that exceeds the mind's comprehension. Yet that was more or less what he felt, apparently illicitly, in these places. That evening they stopped in a small town or large village and queued for fish and chips. Morant's expectation that everyone, customers and staff, would know one another and be friendly, was satisfied, and many years later he wondered if his memory that these working class people were dressed plainly, without any obvious desire to distinguish themselves from their fellow citizens—not really like, but in overall impression not completely dissimilar to the images he was familiar with from photographs of football crowds before the 1960s—that their good humour, their amiable sociability and their calm and dignity was just a nostalgic imagining, a wish for a working class like, but more like, the one he had grown up in and unlike the one or ones which, after their existing composition and deployment had been deemed useless for further exploitation, had been shredded and the remains distempered by a cunning and idiot capitalism, so that where it once, as a class, cherished respectability, fellowship, modesty and honesty, the virtues it had learnt as now necessary to flourishing, to survival, were the competitive assertion, pursuit and display of one's uniqueness, a gluttonous appetite for food, drink and possessions and the cultivation of an ethic of aggressive masculinity. And let no one say that they authored this, that they chose their destiny. (A walk through the centre of any working-class northern town, on, say, a Saturday, when people were out to spend and to be seen—and he had no reason to believe that matters would be different in similar places in the midlands or south—was a lesson in historical abuse, a case study of the strange cultural flowerings of systematically applied social neglect. What one saw were the marks of weakness and woe, the blighted faces and bodies of a populace bereft of social purpose or meaning. His friend Matt had told him about his unease at the revulsion he felt walking through town. Eating in the street distressed him, the gluttonous, impatient heaping of bad food into, it seemed to him, desperately ravening mouths. Why did they feel such irresistible hunger? The vastness of the bodies fed by these despotic appetites so that you wondered how the bones and sinews could support such heaviness and what selves were inside, hidden and protected by this fat-swollen flesh. The nakedness of young—but not always young—people baring arms, legs, bodies no matter how inclement the weather, and skin covered in tattoos, as if some interiority that could not be expressed, would not be heard, were now inscribed on those skins, truths that could not now be ignored, truths that had to be seen, that no one could now avoid; and the young men bulked up on steroids and exercise; the loudness, the unruly public display, everything from bitter rows of the most personal nature to gossip, flirtation and banal exchanges of information, shouted for all to hear, and then the shameless brutalisation of children by way of command, threat and sometimes blows. This was not all, Matt said, for most people on those streets, or more accurately, concourses, were not like this and moved through these dismaying, monstrous scenes as if they were not taking place, keeping their heads down, minding their own business, shrouding themselves in a protective privacy. And this, Matt said, was what our public spaces, our public lives had become. They are sites where battered, confused, unarticulated selfhoods are aggressively asserted, advertised to a contemptuous world, the respectable world, that has placed its faith in the safety of private life—or, Morant said, that has locked away its fears, which are surely only dangers we refuse to face, in a secure box placed inside a safe inside a home which is itself a safe. Matt felt guilt for these feelings because these were the people whence he came and because he had to struggle against what he recognised was an inclination to despise them). Morant knew that he, Morant, fantasised what had once been, that his was an idealisation of a heroic working class he would, as he was presently constituted, have hated to be part of, but Morant always wanted to say these things because hardly anyone else was and they were true. When it was their turn to be served, Tommy and Morant were careful to order fish and chips because they had noticed that this was all anyone asked for. In London they might have asked for cod, haddock, skate, plaice or rock, or they might have had the options of saveloys and faggots; a London fish and chip shop could have had large gherkins—wallies—pickled eggs or sometimes, pickled walnuts, on the counter or at the back on a shelf. These northern people had lacks they were not aware of, uninformed appetites. What struck Morant above all was that once the fish and chips had been placed on their wrappings the woman serving them had herself applied the salt and vinegar, in the quantities Tommy and he specified. This would not have happened in London.

When he read about them in his forties Morant found that he agreed with the Daoists who opposed the world of consciousness and order to an unseen spirit world, accessed by shamans and unresponsive to rational command, an anarchic world beyond logic and governmental design, a world that mocked and undermined the empire of reason. This, the hidden world, was the sphere that, for better or worse, determined human existence. In the winter of his first year at college Morant sat in a friend's room, listening to The Mothers of Invention's Freak Out! and not smoking the joint that was being passed around. Later, the thing he would remember most of all from this afternoon was the song It Can't Happen Here. He was with a group of friends who sometimes referred to themselves by a name taken from a conversation overheard by Morant in a queue for coffee one morning break when Jack De Rossi and Simon Greaves had been about a dozen places ahead of him. Jack was wearing, as far as he could remember, a sleeveless Afghan coat, flared trousers and some sort of oriental hat, like one Morant had seen Gary Brooker wearing on Ready, Steady, Go; Simon was dressed in black in tight-fitting trousers that were a little short, chelsea boots (which Morant knew should more correctly be called dealer boots) and a buttoned-up jacket, again just slightly too small for him, with a white shirt, an assembly which was quite successful in what Morant guessed was meant to suggest fin-de-siècle decadence; it was possible, it was sometimes the case, that Simon was carrying Huysmans' most famous novel. Both young men had long hair, in Jack's case down onto his shoulders. A student in front of Morant had asked her companion who those boys were and her friend replied that they were part of that way-out, psychedelic in-crowd. So way-out, psychedelic in-crowd, it was then. Simon's room, tidy enough, Morant remembered, was as dingy as all the others in what were little more than long huts housing students. A wall on the side away from the door sloped inwards towards the ceiling, something that Morant found oppressive. Somehow a bed, a table, a wardrobe and several chairs were crammed into this uningratiating space. The college was dominated by the PE wing which saw itself as the sole cause and origin of the institution and behaved with all the arrogances and assumptions of superiority associated with sports fraternities. But this was the late sixties and the counter-culture had reached this damp corner of the English countryside. There were freaks, there were heads in this room. Morant could remember little of how it was decorated, but he knew such rooms and their suffocating joss sticks. They might have been lit by an orange or green bulb whose subdued lustre might have been further diminished by a paper lantern lightshade; there could have been a poster or posters advertising Pentangle, Incredible String Band or Cream performances, a Klimt or Beardsley print, or, he remembered, a poster of Che Guevara dead, the smudgy graphics adding to the desolation of his stricken body, his face; in one room there would be the clutter required to make Turkish coffee, in others a tin of Old Holborn tobacco and Rizla licorice papers, a Philips tape recorder, a Bush mono record player, an old white acoustic guitar, a few bottles of Newcastle Brown Ale, a clarinet, a jew's harp, harmonicas; there were photographs, of a field of poppies, of the woods, in snow, above the main campus of the college, some of these featuring an indescribably beautiful girl; one a close-up of a bearded young man, apparently lying down, his right eye covered and swollen by a magnifying lens—this was Jack; on one wall he recalled a picture, taken from Oz magazine, of what appeared to be, beneath the swirling design, a woman having sex with a pig. These rooms had copies of International Times and on the door of one room an IT front page headed Free Hoppy; there were vinyl LPs of Sonny Terry and Brownie McGhee, Jacques Loussier, the John Mayall Blues Band, Graham Bond, Vivaldi, Country Joe and the Fish, Jimi Hendrix, The Brian Auger Trinity with Julie Driscoll, Love, The Soft Machine, Davey Graham; there would have been books—Bomb Culture, The Politics of Experience, Catch 22, A Season in Hell, The Third Eye, The Function of the Orgasm, and others by Franz Fanon, Hermann Hesse, William Burroughs, Jack Kerouac, Angela Davis; on one table some scribbled song lyrics, some copies of a scurrilous magazine produced by some of the residents of these rooms, the main targets of whose mockery were the college's Home Economics and PE students, the apparently alcoholic manager of the college bar and any poems contributed to an official college magazine; in another room a letter from a famous film director which said that a student was welcome to visit the set of the film he was about to start directing and a large original painting of what might have been a protesting student, by an Italian artist who appeared to have been influenced by Francis Bacon; a time unlike afterwards, deeply imprinted by consciousness, by an irruption of generational desire, a time of excess and overflow. Morant and some friends decided towards the end of the first year to participate in the college concert put on annually by first-year students. They told the organising committee that it would be a presentation mixing dance, music and theatre. They did not tell the committee that this would be a happening. Their slot came after a female student who played an accordion and sang what Morant remembered as sea shanties and music hall songs with astonishing verve. They began by switching off all the lighting in the hall as an Ornette Coleman track played at full volume; then Morant on one side of the hall and Jack on the other, both dressed in what they hoped looked like African robes, were picked out by spotlights as they moved towards the stage shouting instant salvation and throwing sugar lumps into the audience, some of whom threw them back. As they reached the stage the lights went out again and Jack and Morant rushed to the steps at the side just as Kenneth McGuire, centre stage, threw a match into a tall waste bin that he had filled with an incendiary mixture. As the explosion flared, Jack and Morant ran onto the stage to join a group of girls, Alice, Cheryl and Liz, who it had been planned would be dancing around the bin, but as he ran up the steps and onto the stage Morant tripped over Cheryl, who was crouched in terror, and smashed his mouth into the back of Jack's head, severing his, Morant's, labial artery and knocking Jack unconscious. Liz, in her radiance, accompanied him to the hospital, holding a basin to his mouth, in a car driven by the deputy head of the PE department and, as Morant remembered it, periodically emptying the blood out of the window. He spent two nights in hospital and one in the college sick bay. He remembered a patient in the hospital bed next to him complaining how hot the ward was and asking another patient who was able to move about if he could open a nearby window and the second patient inspecting the window and saying appen it's oppen. Liz visited him in the sick bay and he was aware that they would now start a relationship. The happening, as an attempt to disrupt the flow of bourgeois consciousness, to fracture the unifying mask of the spectacle, had its limited success, in that several people, including rugby players, approached Morant to say how much they had enjoyed the performance and that it had been different. Morant did not have a room, at least not a room of the sort most first year students had, since, as a mature student of twenty-two he was required to live off campus, in digs, firstly on a pig farm and then near the beginning of his second year, in a suburban Newcastle-under-Lyme house which a fellow student, whom he did not know well, and who was living there, had suggested to him when Morant, newly divorced, love-stricken, forlorn, attempting to subdue his tumultuous feelings by drinking vast quantities of ale, and, never attending lectures and seminars, was on the verge of being excluded from college because he had nowhere to live and had been caught, reported by cleaners, for sleeping on the floors of friends' rooms. The college principal had told him that he had to find somewhere and get back on track or he would be asked to leave the course. Morant had asked what was wrong with sleeping on friends' floors and the principal, because clearly he could think of no good answer to Morant's question, had said that apart from anything else the college had to guard against the possibility of homosexuality, not that he was saying that this was involved in Morant's case. He could never remember the name of the student who came to his aid—he had red hair, ginger in fact, and glasses, tall with a receding chin. He had been insufficiently thankful towards this young man, not friendly enough. In those days he was reflexly dismissive of anyone who was not subversive or an athlete. This was one of many sins and omissions about which, later, he was to feel wretched, guilty and ashamed. If he had had a proper room, one that was more than a bedroom in someone else's house, it would not have looked like his friends' rooms since he had qualms about advertising himself, his selfness, through the artefacts he might decide to put on display in that room. He was, however, interested in these student rooms and didn't attribute base motives to other people's desire to surround themselves with the texts and objects that had significance or usefulness for them. Some rooms he admired; in most he felt comfortable, in spite of the lighting, at once lurid and dismal, and the joss-sticks. Where occupants had chosen to give prominence to a particular wrought thing in order, as it would be put later, to make a statement about themselves, to associate themselves with what they thought were the values or glamour of the image or object, he could be irritated or he could be charmed; only later would he think that all this was getting out of hand. As far as he understood it, his uneasiness about involving himself in such display had three components. He was reluctant to disclose himself, to offer whatever choices he made to judgement and inquiry. This had nothing to do with concerns about adverse commentary on his taste; it was about not having his subjectivity on show. He never knew for sure why he felt like this, but at its most humiliating, it appeared to be a simple fear of being found out for what he was, for all the acts of nastiness, cowardice, idiocy, dereliction, dishonesty, self-serving, envy, whose stored weight he carried with him, the task being to come to terms with it all, accepting the damage caused that couldn't be repaired. More honourably perhaps, if the self was to be subdued and life lived well, this was an endeavour best undertaken quietly. Then, he had misgivings about territorialising spaces, of laying down the scent of one's ownership, one's residence, about marking these boundaries off and proclaiming this ground as yours and not someone else's. At the university at which he later came to work he had colleagues whose rooms were made comfortable and fit to purpose or, in some cases, barely adorned, decorated only by a jumble of books and papers read and yet to be read, assignments to be marked, post-its and notes scrawled on paper, stacks of journals and policy documents, a newspaper open at the comment pages or the sports section and perhaps some family photos; these rooms he approved of. Other colleagues turned their offices into shrines to their own personhood, carefully elaborated compositions designed to proclaim themselves as they wanted to be known; and these were nests. Where in an earlier Enlightenment imagining such a room might have been an austere chamber dedicated to the increase of knowledge, now it had been converted into a welcoming home for receiving visitors, for calming nervous students, for not making learning too perturbing—he had heard world music of a wholesome kind being played quietly as he passed one of these rooms and he had been told of water features. On another view these were cells for suffocating difference, airless, smothering enclosures that had something of the spider's web about them, spun out of the body itself and meant to entrap. Not that he begrudged others their comforts, but what was endearing in students was distasteful in grown-ups. He knew that this was a form of puritanism and an unfashionable view, but he felt that the endeavour of projecting one's identity was unpleasant and embarrassing. And then he felt uneasy about identity itself. But there were other reasons why the student Morant's room would not have been like his friends'. He had no taste for decadence in literature or art, particularly the shrivelled erotics of late Victorian aestheticism and he hated the Pre-Raphaelite paintings that were another feature of student rooms. In later years he saw more clearly the pervasiveness of this ruralist nostalgia for a more beautiful, a more simple and gracious past, a retreat to an age of social harmony, of courtesy and calm that was occasionally rent by transfiguring states of feeling. This was a condition about which there was, as had been said, one certainty, that it was and always had been, always would be, in the past. He learned that this horror of modernity, its turning away from machine society to an imagined at oneness with nature was a recurrent impulse of western thought and was always a kind of despair about the inhumanity of the present time, a despair that always incurred political pessimism. But the hippie variant of this was a strange hybrid, a melding of this yearning with fantasies of sexual liberty, forgotten knowledges, magical thinking, utopian futures and, occasionally, a faith in the insurrectionist power of trash (henceforth, popular) culture. Morant had listened to conversations, about orgone energy, ley-lines, geodesic domes, the activities of Aleister Crowley, the iconography of comic books, which were often lightly brushed with what seemed to him a defensive humour and scepticism that was meant as cover for genuine engagement with the transformative potential of these things. In these exchanges he had learnt not to be too direct about his incredulity. He was ill at ease with sixties subfusc, the distaste for illumination in favour of half-light, magazines in which texts were heavily overlaid with graphic designs, a love of obscurity and a tantalisingly veiled past, a twilight out of which something exquisite, astonishing, prodigious might appear, strange and wonderful things that had retreated, hidden, from the violent light of an oppressively rationalist age. He had no love of that scouring, obliterating light but also little faith in gloom, preferring chiaroscuro, stolen light by which men and women show the truth of their conditions. He read books by writers whom his friends did not bother with—Marcuse, Sontag, Norman O. Brown, Mailer, Roszak, Germaine Greer, Leslie Fiedler—opinionated, quite bossy books, heavy with argument, which he was aware a few of his acquaintances felt were too declamatory. They detected and disliked a coerciveness in such writing and, in any case, preferred their nonconformability dressed more aesthetically. He did not realise it at the time but these encounters—with books and his friends' distastes—were his first engagements with what was to become for him more than an idea. It was a disposition to think and feel in a certain way, which was this, that language was infected by a narrow and corrosive rationality that faithfully served an inhuman power. And this implied the need for more than the critical unveiling of the ideologies that peopled words; it required a profound and vigilant scepticism about the capacity of language to knit together stories and accounts, by means of which we understand ourselves, which are not also closures around cruel hierarchies of power. Later, in a different age, he was to come across other ideas about the unconscious, more rational, more scientific ideas.

Science, Morant had concluded, presents itself in two contrary ways. On the one hand, it can horrify by laying before us the vastness of our universe which, moreover and even more disturbingly, may be only one of multiple universes, and thereby confront us with our unimaginable inconsequentiality; it can lay before us the prolific, unrelenting diversity of life in its ferocious, blind drive for survival; and it may offer the bleak truth that we exist within a cosmos that is slowly, irreversibly ebbing towards inertia and the oblivion of all things. It had always seemed to Morant that when scientists spoke of the wonder of this universe, the inspiring beauty of the real that science set before us and the stupid redundancy of the desire to people this vastness with meaning, with gods and banal normativities, they displayed a certain lack of imagination, a characteristic insensibility—or perhaps they were just whistling in the dark. For Morant felt the same way as Pascal and the religious on this. Science tells us of the meaninglessness, the blank impersonality of the universe, on one inexpressibly tiny speck of which we strut or cower, and it is horrifying. Science thus does us great service because it tells us that we have to look to ourselves to make sense of the life we have quite haphazardly been given, but this is a long way from saying that contemplation of the technicolour majesty of spiral galaxies and the abundant complexity of the ecosystems of tropical rain forests is on a level with the meanings and consolations enjoyed through the self-surrender of the pious. What was more, the majesty and beauty that some scientists point to is not the majesty of the life we live, the life that Camus refused to trade for the hope of another, the magnificence of sunlight on skin, the coupling of bodies, of a natural plenitude to be felt and unthinkingly sensed. This scientific majesty was just a cold, blank sublime, terror reduced to the level of glossy photographs in weekend colour supplements, like postcards you send or receive that are intended to signify, to retrieve and retain something someone experienced and enjoyed, or perhaps never experienced, so this picture will have to do instead. Science here offers its own facsimiles of feeling, of meaning. Better to just say here is nothing, a nothingness we have arranged into some sort of provisional order, which we can describe but whose existence in its nothingness we cannot account for. There is much to admire in what we scientists have achieved and it may amaze you, but the main service we have performed is to show, through the implacable operations of the scientific method and great ingenuity, that we have discovered nothing which indicates how you should live, so look elsewhere for that. But, my goodness, look how big it all is. On the other hand, science has a, no doubt necessary for its purposes, bias to orderliness and rationality. It may recognise and be intrigued by randomness and chaos but its impulse is to restore things to order. It made this offer: here is something sure that we can hold on to as the tectonic plates slide about beneath our feet. Morant watched a television programme about how scientists now believed that the unconscious, rather than the conscious mind, controlled human behaviour. As he had expected, this was not the Freudian unconscious but a Darwinian one, the unconscious having apparently evolved as a behavioural guidance system which provided impulses to appropriate action in the situations encountered in everyday life, which is to say, the everyday life of the Stone Age. Afterwards he looked up some articles on research into the unconscious mind and in one read that there are a multitude of behavioural impulses generated at any given time which derive from, not only evolved motives and preferences, but cultural norms and values, past experiences in similar situations, and from what other people are currently doing in that same situation. It had emerged that the unconscious, highly intelligent and adaptive, was in fact rational. The writer remarked that it was nice to know that the unconscious was minding the store when the owner was absent. Morant could see that for some it might indeed be comforting, in a numbing sort of way, to know that the unconscious, far from being a pit of unbearable horrors or a troubling source of creativity, was a sort of benign, paternal presence, a very active guardian angel, seeking always to put us out of harm's way and get us through life's challenges and travails as comfortably as possible. The television programme said that this sophisticated mechanism sometimes went wrong and this was because of faulty wiring in the brain. Scientists, we were assured, were working on how misfiring circuits such as these could be mended. During his reading, he noted that some scientists allowed the play of a certain irrationality, a recalcitrance, in these subconscious systems, so that moods that coloured the day or decisions to take certain courses of action were determined by chance encounters with trivial phenomena. Other psychologists suggested that cognitive biases or ingrained predispositions to understand the world in particular ways caused us to think we were acting or judging rationally when we were not. These misconceptions or confusions were often illustrated by the illogical outcomes of logical conundrums which reminded Morant of the sort of IQ questions he laboured at successfully in order to pass the 11+ as a child and which he had avoided as tedious exercises in cleverness ever since. Testimonies to the silent wisdom of subconscious thought were thus mingled with quite pleasing rebukes to the vanities of rationalism, including the judgement that bankers and fund managers are consistently outperformed by index tracker funds that unthinkingly, passively, follow market trends, although we continue to ascribe wisdom and unimaginably sophisticated skills to such individuals even after their complete incompetence is exposed at moments of market failure. Not all psychologists were optimistic that humanity's habit of misreading the world could be cured, but they all hoped it might be, and it turned out that rational self-reflection and practice of positive behaviours might be the way forward. Everything, then, might be OK and the rule of reason restored or, perhaps, finally achieved. Morant was far from unsympathetic to the notion that subconscious perceptions and know-how played a large part in steering us through life. Any brief reflection on the amount of time spent in apparently idle musing whilst engaged in purposeful activity like, say, driving a car, shopping in a supermarket or writing a paper for submission to a scholarly journal, would confirm that focused intentional thought was a fitful phenomenon. Something was guiding us through the journey, around the store or through the byzantine protocols of academic composition and it wasn't the unflinching gaze of the cogito. On balance, however, Morant loathed all this sort of stuff—the unseemly folksiness of the researcher's prose—minding the store while the owner was out!—the reduction of the fictive, convulsive resources of human thought and feeling to a set of looping self-help instructions or programming errors, or the horrific optimism, the panglossian faith in the positivity of scientific endeavour. The shift from cognitive mistakes to emotional disturbance seemed unwarranted. He could see how cognitive bias, as they called it, could lead to mistaken calculations, illogical conclusions, irrational judgements in encounters such as—one of the examples offered—interviewing, and to an overvaluing of expert opinion, but not that the misery that saturates a soul and consigns it to despair or the impulses to rebel or conform that can rule a life, might be reduced to cognitive miscues, faulty assessments of actuality, to errors in reasoning. Perhaps these irrational judgements were more than mistakes to be effaced and replaced with correct, rational understandings. Perhaps they had their own rationality; perhaps they were based on originally accurate perceptions of the sufferers' histories and situations; perhaps these people, like the rest of us, had not been loved enough; and perhaps, if they were to achieve ordinary unhappiness, a measure of control over their fears and pain, it would take more than an adjustment to someone else's idea of correct perception. Above all, he despised the obedient, domesticated, small-minded love of tidiness, the urge to reassure and bring the strange back to familiarity, the commitment to banality. He cherished what he had read in a novel where an admittedly unpleasant professor of literature, required to teach Communications, rejects as preposterous—utterly implausible—the discipline's foundational premise that society has created language so that human beings might exchange their thoughts, feelings and intentions, convinced instead that speech originated in song whose own origins lie in "the need to fill out with sound the overlarge and rather empty human soul". Oddly, he also objected to the domestication of reason, the overlooking of its madness. And where was desire, anxiety, despair, hope, hatred , mischief and love in all this? These scientists dismissed Freud on several grounds, one being that his conclusions were based on observations of extreme cases of human experience—people suffering from delusions, neuroses and great unhappiness—rather than on the run of average or normally functioning people. So that was that, as it almost always is with the activity of western reason—there was one thing and there was another; there were mad and dysfunctional people and there were sane people who got on with things. As Morant understood matters, the problem with this was that everyone was mad to one degree or another. It was just that some people were unable to contour their madness to forms that were socially acceptable. The whole cognitivist enterprise seemed like a sanitised, rationed version of stuff that had been covered more honestly by philosophers who had doubted or scorned the claims of reason. It was an attempt to make the infinite disquiet, the multiple drives of the soul safe for these blind times, skipping life completely and stuffing it in a cup. In the mid-seventies, Morant became head of English in the school in which he spent most of his teaching career, at the same time as William, a social studies teacher, newly trained at the London Institute. He was an unbending radical of a kind that died out at some time in the 1980s. They had both joined a humanities department that had been the core of the school's educational programme, staffed by intellectually fearsome young men and women who were fully signed up to a 1968 political agenda, inflexibly oppositionalist, feminist and ultra-democratic. A few years earlier, Morant was told, at the head of department's suggestion, salaries had for a time been pooled and shared equally and all departmental decisions were voted on, with no greater weight being given to the views of what the official school hierarchy would have recognised as more senior members of the department than to a teacher in the first year of her career. It had successfully put a stop to what had been annual visits and displays from the army who were keen to recruit, as it always had done, from what one retired general later referred to as its traditional reserve of semi-feral young men who grew out of the bleak pit villages and vast city council estates in that part of the country. It had forced staff votes on whether the police should be allowed into the school to explain their role to pupils, managing to impose strict conditions on the content and form of these intrusions and to have every proposed visit examined by a committee drawn from all curriculum areas and from ancillary staff like caretakers, dinner ladies and secretaries, and then to be voted on in staff meetings. It was taken aback but not downcast by the fact that ancillary staff, if they turned up to vote, often did so in quite reactionary directions. It had not been successful in a proposal to integrate staff and student social areas so that there would be no staff common room, access to which was denied pupils, but for a period the department had chosen to take breaks and lunch-times in the sixth form common room. The humanities curriculum was unequivocally political, organised under themes such as poverty, war, race, law and order, class and the family, its ethos ceaselessly unaccepting of the existing ordering of society. Morant, appointed to take English out of integration within humanities, was uncomfortable with a lot of this and later came to see the problem in this way: he thought that the department's political analysis and consequent local strategy was naïve and likely to lead to entrenched and unthinking resistances in those it sought to change, that its pedagogy veered between being disturbingly didactic and anarchically irresponsible, in that it was marked by what he thought of as the emancipatory left's typical and fatal ambivalence concerning authority, and he didn't really want to be eating his sandwiches and slandering other members of staff surrounded by pupils. On the other hand he recognised later that many of the students who went through this regime had a confidence, a sense of where they were located in the world and a social awareness that was rare amongst the graduates of the standardised, centrally regulated curricula of subsequent decades. In truth, however, by the time Morant and William joined the school the humanities department had passed its heyday. Impressive, politically committed young people had grown a little older and moved on to posts in other schools, to be replaced by younger people who, although progressive and well-intentioned, were less certain in their politics, not so convinced of the likelihood of wholesale social change, and perhaps less eager for it, and they were as well less convinced that education was the vital site for bringing about that change. William was an exception, already an anachronism. In his first term in the school he took on the role of school representative for the largest teachers' union and in a staff meeting urged all staff to lobby their unions to petition government to condemn the Somoza regime in Nicaragua and to declare its support for the Sandinista rebels. He attempted to sell copies of the Socialist Worker in the staffroom, without much success, and was reprimanded by the head when he began distributing the newspapers to pupils. He worked the staffroom industriously, spending lunch hours sitting and arguing with the most unpromising groups in an effort to recruit them to his views and causes. The teachers he targeted seemed quite tolerant of these interruptions, although some treated them as opportunities for amusement. On one occasion Morant heard William arguing the iniquity of the death sentence for murder with some technical studies and science teachers who were convinced of its effectiveness as a deterrent to homicide and its desirability in the case of a man who had recently been found guilty of the murder of a policeman. William made an eloquent case for the barbarity of the punishment, its vitiating effect upon the nation's moral health and the inevitability of innocent people being executed, concluding by drawing parallels in the recent case with several instances where subsequent revelations had established the innocence of individuals who had been sent to the hangman. There had been a pause and then one of the teachers had said well, that bloke who killed the copper, just hang him a bit then. William made regular interventions in staff meetings, calling, amongst other things, for staff to encourage children to address them by their first names, for student governors who would sit in on interview panels, for teachers to refuse to correct misspellings because in modern communication such observances were becoming redundant and for all staff to undergo racial awareness training. He also expressed the view that the school should subvert the examination system, which he said was set up to discriminate against working class children and to sustain an unjust class hierarchy. This subversion should take the form of manipulating pupils' results in their favour. These contributions caused fury amongst most of the staff, who were already resentful of the high status accorded the humanities department and suspicious of its political motivations. Most of the time Morant just squirmed with embarrassment when William made these kinds of proposal, although, along with some others, he occasionally found himself trying to explain on William's behalf what might be a sensible core to his suggestions. It was as if he were trying to defend him against the outrage that he provoked, although, beyond the wish to rescue good ideas from mangling, it was never clear to him, Morant, why he did this. He didn't like William, whom he found humourless and who, on the evidence of what he said, seemed devoid of an inner, or indeed outer, life that might engage interest. William didn't know what to make of Morant and on one occasion accused him of tearing up some copies of the Socialist Worker that he had left on a staffroom table. Morant explained that they had already been mutilated when he had sat down at the table and that yes he and some others had been laughing at this, but only at the idea that anyone would be so angry and prejudiced as to want to damage them. This was only partly true as he and a couple of friends had also been laughing in anticipation of William's reaction. William refused to believe him and seemed for a moment at a loss as to what to say before muttering that he had thought that Morant would be an ally. On another occasion Morant and a maths teacher conducted a conversation in which they assumed the views of an English football manager who had resorted to racist stereotyping of black footballers, doubting their capacity to cope with harsh winters. William overheard this and was horrified, accusing Morant of being racist. When it was explained to him that the football manager was being ridiculed, that racism was being derided and that Morant and his colleague had been adopting the persona of this stupid man in order to expose the idiocy of his ideas, he seemed unable to understand and just said that he wouldn't have expected it of Morant who then said fuck off you po-faced knob, very angry but pleased to be in a position for the first time in his life to apply the adjective po-faced to someone. At some point towards the end of that first year it became apparent that William was a drinker. His breath smelt of alcohol in the mornings and he had begun to disappear at lunchtimes; someone told Morant the he was going to a pub in the village. Never a well turned-out individual, he became conspicuously dishevelled. He began to phone in sick quite frequently and his evangelical activity became more sporadic. As far as Morant could make out he had no friends on the staff, apart from a young technician in the science department who was a heavy metal fan. Morant suspected that he had no friends outside of school. After a parents' evening Morant had gone with some other teachers to a nearby pub and when they arrived William was already there sitting on his own. It would clearly be impossible not to sit with him. During the thirty minutes they spent in the pub William spoke twice, on both occasions in response to direct questions. As the group were leaving Morant offered him a lift into town. Afterwards he tried to work out why he had done this as he found William unpleasant on several levels, including the physical; his body seemed wretched, his movements awkward, as if he were struggling frustratedly with some interior foe. He concluded that he had felt a mixture of pity, for an individual who was not simply socially inept but who seemed to have subsided into an acceptance of his ineptness, and curiosity, thinking he might discover something of what made this person what he was, and guilt, since he had spoken roughly to William on more than one occasion. There was also the discomfiting possibility that he had wanted to feel generous. When Morant pulled up at a large, run-down Victorian house and William asked him if he wanted to come in for a coffee, his curiosity and compassion had ebbed but he said OK. The house, its hallway and stairs, the landing which William's flat gave onto, were minimally furnished—worn carpeting, a table piled with mail, faded and chipped paintwork and oppressive anaglypta wallpaper. The place smelt of the dust of years. Morant thought of emptiness. He had been in such places before and had lived in a similar house for a few weeks as a student. It reeked of neglect, of isolation, of absence. William had two ill-lit rooms, one that contained a sofa, an armchair, a dining table, chairs and a bed and a bathroom that was reached through a narrow corridor that contained a sink and a cooker. Everything seemed filthy and the apartment smelt of damp. Morant had dreamt of such rooms. In one there were steps leading up to a door in the back wall of the living room. Behind the door was an unimaginable horror, an unappeasable malice whose breath seeped under it and through the walls, filling the room and the house beyond with chilling menace so that he felt as if he would be annihilated by this something that wanted to burst the door and release its terrifying, extinguishing contagion, suffocating and absorbing him into its rotting being, but he had to withstand it because it wanted to destroy everyone he loved, everyone he felt responsible for and he was the only one awake. In this dream he had children, daughters. He knew that it would overwhelm him but only he could deal with it. William's room was strewn with the familiar detritus of a certain kind of young male living without a woman—empty beer cans, unwashed crockery, a few cartons and trays that contained the dried remains of takeaway meals, discarded clothing and packaging, a couple of soft porn magazines, all this mixed, across the table, the sofa and floor, with the litter of teaching: children's assignments, some of them marked, most not, worksheets, reading material, mark sheets and schemes of work. Piles of Socialist Workers were distributed around the room and other SWP publications could be seen on an open desk and at the foot of a large cupboard. Also on the table was some sheet music for the violin. Morant said to William that the flat was a shit-heap and if he was making coffee he wanted to see the mug before he'd drink from it. William said the mug would be clean and actually he was having a brandy, did Morant want one. Morant said he'd stick to the coffee. When it arrived the coffee was good and he asked William how he'd made it and he said filter. He said that he supposed Morant's house was very tidy and Morant asked why he thought that and William said you seem an orderly sort of person. Morant said that no one had ever thought to call him that before. William drank half a tumbler of brandy quickly, returned to the kitchen and came back with a larger brandy. He said that Morant despised him, didn't he. Morant said no, he sympathised with many of his views, it was just that his attempts to persuade others to his positions seemed disorganised. William said that he'd given up pussyfooting about some time ago, people needed to be told the truth. Morant asked William if he had come across the idea that the revolutionary needed to adopt the tactics and persona of the guerilla fighter, to take on the appearance of ordinariness, to seem like the rest of the population, to disappear into the sea of the people like a fish, emerging at carefully calculated moments to strike and then dissolve once more into the water. He hadn't. Morant suggested that it might be a more effective strategy than hitting people over the head with evidence of their stupidity and moral dereliction. He asked William why he'd become a teacher but he didn't answer. Then William said that Morant didn't have to despise him because no one could despise him more than he despised himself. Morant knew he was going to hear something that he didn't want to, more engagement with William's life than he would be comfortable with, and he could feel an unanswerable anger mounting against him, an insatiable fury, and yet he found himself asking what William meant and he got a story, a terrible story, a middle class version of parental fucking up, the father a vicar who interspersed his habitual lack of interest in his son with regular expressions of dissatisfaction at his timidity, his lack of intelligence, his idleness, his emotionality. William said nothing about his mother. He had been sent to what he described as a shit little public school where he had, it seemed, been carefully bullied. Morant asked why he was telling him this and he said because he wanted to tell someone and he had decided that Morant was that person. He despised himself because he was a failure. He hadn't coped with school, hadn't gone to Oxford, hadn't become a professional musician, had failed in his one relationship with a woman. Morant, knowing that what he was about to say would be useless, nevertheless said that he, William, was in his early twenties, why was he talking as if his life was over and done with. Because it was. He would never do anything with his life. Morant suggested that he was being too accepting of his father's assessment of him. William said that he didn't need Morant's analysis, to just listen. Did Morant know what he did with his time, how he occupied himself. No, and he didn't want to know. Then followed a story of masturbation, fantasised cuckoldry, masochism, self-hatred and abjection. Morant was repelled, not by the content of what William said but by the loathing, the hatred of self and the world, the miserable, impenetrable banality. He said, I don't mean this to annoy you but unless you want your life to be shit for ever you need therapy. William said yeah, then I'd be normal and cured and fuck lots of women. Morant said that the sex thing wasn't the problem, there was something deeper, prior to that, but this enraged William. Fuck off, you cunt. He didn't want advice, just listen. What was exquisitely—he said exquisitely—pathetic was the imaginariness of the imaginary woman who was imaginarily betraying him. She had to be imaginary because the only woman he'd lured into a relationship had certainly not, he could assure Morant, been the kind of woman he or any other man would have fantasies about and that had been a disaster because he found her disgusting—someone had said to him that she looked as if she didn't have a cunt so much as a cloaca—but she was the only woman he'd met who didn't find him disgusting. What was most appalling, most humiliating about these little masturbatory scenarios he staged, and Morant needed to hear this, was that the men who fucked his imaginary girlfriend were all young working class men, the sort of men living the sort of lives—working within an exploitative, dehumanising system and accepting the narrow crampedness of those lives—from which through his political activism he'd been trying to free them, to rescue them, the sort of young men who if he was in town on a Friday night he hoped would not notice him, the sort who had a few times mocked his appearance as he passed them. Morant said that someone's sexual inclinations didn't invalidate their political dedications. William laughed and said inclinations, such delicacy. The truth was he was shit at politics just like everything else. Morant asked why him, why he had decided that he was the person he would tell all this to. William said how do you know that I haven't told others about this. Morant said you haven't, have you. William said no and that he had wanted many times to smash Morant's face and that he hoped Morant didn't think that he was getting some masochistic pleasure from telling him these things and Morant said, partly to annoy him, that the transference he was getting was more sadistic than masochistic feeling. William said fuck off now unless he wanted to have a look at some of the pornography he had collected. Morant said that no that would be OK and left. William made it through to the beginning of the following year, although he had been put on a formal warning about his negligent and wayward behaviour, presumably given targets to achieve, and placed under the supervision of a kindly deputy head. There was a complaint from a parent about him discussing with his A level students whether sexual relations between teacher and pupil could be justified and shortly after this he was suspended for a time. One miserable late October morning after he returned the school carried out a fire drill which involved all classes taking up designated positions on the school field. Morant's fourth year tutor group was lined up next to William's who was becoming increasingly angry because several boys in his group were refusing to stand with the rest of the class and were chasing one another around on a raised grassy bank immediately behind the assembly area. Morant was about to intervene when William appeared behind the boys and launched himself into a rugby tackle on the most annoying of them, taking him and the boy down the bank and into a wrestling match in which he attempted to punch the boy, shouting you little bastard, you cunt. When Morant and another member of staff disentangled them William walked off and the following day, it was later revealed, informed the school of his resignation. At some point after this the science technician told a member of staff that William was working as a guide, conducting parties of tourists around historic sites in London. And Morant thought later of his mother, an ordinary person, valued by friends and admired by many who knew of her for her independence of spirit, who had been consumed by envy and by the fear that she was not really loved, perhaps not deserving of love, and that others were more loved. She doubted her own husband's love. Morant remembered returning home from a Sunday afternoon drive and his father stopping the car at a zebra crossing to allow a woman to cross the road and his mother saying that he had only stopped because she was a pretty girl and his father saying not to be ridiculous and his mother mocking his protestations, insisting that he had wanted to get a better look at the woman, that he was lying, that he looked at women all the time, and his father eventually exploding with rage, a terrifying row ensuing and Morant and his brother cringing and fearful in the back of the car. When she was very old and dependent on Morant to organise her life, to ensure that she got the care and support she needed to go on with her miserably impoverished and diminished existence, and when he used to visit her at least once a day for four or five years and a great deal more frequently for the two years before she went into a nursing home, she would sometimes say that she knew that he didn't really want to do all this, that really he wanted her dead, out of the way, once even suggesting that he couldn't wait to get his hands on her money, and when he said that he did this, the care, the sitting with her, because he loved her, she said that no, he didn't, not really. Then she would say, perhaps the next time he visited her, that she was indeed very grateful for what he did and that she really did love him, he knew that, didn't he, and she knew that he loved her and would look after her and wouldn't leave her. He wondered if she really thought he might leave her. It occurred to him that everyone had left her—first her sister, then, cruelly, her two husbands, both of whom died young, and eventually her brothers and her sisters-in-law—and in some earlier period—who knew when, but at some point in that comfortable childhood, in that large family—something had occurred that had made her doubt that anyone would love her. Sometimes it seemed to him that her life had been infected by terror, by some dreadful deprivation that had stunted and warped her ability to deal with the world. She never held on for very long to pleasure or joy. She loved flowers but complained that they weren't worth buying because they didn't last very long. All her life she was discontent and resentful, feeling that things were stacked against her, that life was unfair, that there was nothing she might do to improve her lot, that nothing would do any good. She was suspicious and harshly judgemental, often ascribing the basest of motivations to people she felt threatened by, whether it was the superior manner and manipulativeness of the woman next door who wanted her to go halves on mending a fence that had rotted behind a beech hedge, or Liz's beauty, which she detested from the start and which she associated with vanity, deceitfulness and a proclivity to sexual waywardness. In Liz's absence she would complain to Morant that Liz was always titivating herself, that she wore too much make-up—Liz wore none apart from lipstick—and she would warn him that when the three of them had been out together she had noticed Liz looking at other men. In her presence, she found occasion—perhaps in relation to an actress on the television or a photograph in a newspaper—to comment on the shallowness of beauty and once, to general embarrassment, when one of her brothers was visiting and his wife, with an artlessness that was typical of her, had said to Liz that she liked her dress and, dear, you are a lovely-looking girl, and his mother said that beauty was only skin-deep. And yet she was admired for her spirit, her good housekeeping and she could be kind, loved her grandchildren and had friends who liked and admired her. And the result of all this was that she was unhappy all her life and as she reached old age became increasingly bitter, isolated, spiteful and afraid, refusing, or complaining about—as intrusive—every form of assistance that Morant tried to organise for her. Perhaps the first and most terrible of these renunciations was when she severed all contact with her younger son over something he had said to her during an argument about a divorce that he was going through. Even when she was nearing the end of her life she refused to have contact with him, even after she had admitted to Morant, with a shrug and the briefest of laughs, that it hadn't really been about very much at all. He never found out from her or his brother, who seemed content that his relationship with his mother had come to an end, what had been said. Later this moment seemed to Morant like his mother's first and decisive step in a process of narrowing her life down towards nothingness. A consultant gerontologist who visited her twice told Morant that she had been the most uncooperative patient he had had in a long time. She refused physiotherapy and so lost mobility, refused to have carers in her home and thus had to be taken into a nursing home where she refused to mix with anyone else, refused to have a television in her room and thought two of the nurses had it in for her, refused to take medication regularly and showed neither gratitude nor interest if old friends visited her so that eventually no one did apart from Morant whom she blamed for removing her from her home and for not making the doctors put an end to her life. She never succumbed to dementia but willed herself towards death, which came early one spring, an hour before Morant arrived for his daily visit, after she had for a few weeks refused food and eventually water. In a room that had remained, at her insistence, almost entirely unadorned, except for a potted plant, a yellow chrysanthemum that he had brought in a few days earlier, she lay on her back, her mouth open, her skin stretched tight and shiny over her skull, looking as she always did when asleep, but now there was not the slightest sigh of breath. Death was as he had expected it would be, uninformative, without revelation. He kissed her on her forehead, wishing desperately that he had been with her when she died. He wept at the wasted, shrunken life, a life whose stored-up longing had reduced to an assiduously managed self-destruction. The girl who looked out from old black and white photographs, sometimes seeming a little puzzled, sometimes boldly inquisitive, the smiling young woman who had not yet met his father, on the front with her friend Cissy at Brighton—he would never know what she had wanted, how she had pictured the life ahead of her, nor whether it had necessarily to end in something like this, in this miserably impersonal room, wishing only to be free of life. Throughout that time and after he considered whether he did love her. When he grew older he had come to feel pity for her and, of course, to accept a reluctantly assumed responsibility, and sometimes, sitting in her garden drinking tea or orange juice on a summer's day, listening to the bird-song and traffic noise from a nearby motorway that she could no longer hear, he felt almost love. At such times he perhaps approached what he had felt when she had taken him to Chapel Street market as a child, always it seemed in November on a foggy day, and they had visited a café with steamed up plate glass windows, a photograph of which he was one day astonished to find in a Penguin collection of writing and illustrations aimed at adolescent school children, where he always had a hot blackcurrant drink; or on those grey afternoons when he and his brother played with toy cars or toy soldiers under the kitchen table in that high room that looked out over the low slate roofs of the street behind and, beyond, the railway lines, and it seemed as if they were held, drowsy, in the warmth of their mother's care. He had loved her so much then. If this later feeling was love, it was of an attenuated kind, carefully sculpted around his mother's abrasive presence, her easily aroused antipathies and prejudices, and he wondered how well love mixed with pity. As time passed he did not forget her harshness of judgement and her selfishness, but there was no bitterness in that remembrance and, although her death had been a release he welcomed, he remembered her with something more than fondness and great sadness.

At college Morant had a car, a light blue Austin A35 van, unlicensed, untaxed and uninsured, which he drove, from London to Staffordshire and back and around the villages and countryside near the college. It drove well, except that it had a tendency to throw off its windscreen wipers, although this had only once caused real inconvenience when they had dislodged themselves on the M1 during heavy and incessant rain, requiring him to lean out of the driver's window during periods of particularly intense downpour. He had been giving a lift to two young women students he knew, having picked them up at a tube station on the outskirts of London, probably Edgeware, possibly Queensbury, some place beyond the outer boundaries of where, as an authentic North Londoner, he was normally prepared to go. They had been remarkably unfazed by what could have been a frightening experience, offering sensible advice and the one in the passenger seat doing her best to see what lay ahead from her side, and Morant was intrigued years later that what remained in his memory was the admirable composure of these two; he remembered nothing about them—who they were or what they looked like—except their gameness. The van went well until one weekend when he was away on a rugby trip he lent it to Kenneth McGuire, Simon Greaves and Peter Morgan. When he drove the van on his return it seemed to sit lower, closer to the ground, and made a grating noise when he changed gear. The door on the passenger side wouldn't close properly, either. The following year, after sleeping in it for several weeks, he left it, unresponsive, inert, at the farm near Stafford on which he and Simon had been working during the summer of love. When he returned a month or two later with John Guzman, who drove a Ford Anglia which he had equipped with a Cortina engine and extraordinarily fat wheels, the vehicle was still in a corner of the farmyard, undisturbed by the alcoholic farmer. John removed what he said was the cylinder head to, as he explained it, inspect the head gasket. Inside, were two or three tiny, pale beige spiders moving delicately on top of the engine block. John laughed and said he had never seen anything like this and soon established that the van was not going to start and that it was not worth attempting its repair. Morant asked what they should do and John said leave the fucker. Before that, Morant used it to go to discos and concerts at the nearby university or to drive to The Place, a club— although later he doubted that it would have been called that at the time; a decade or so later it became famous as a centre of Northern Soul—in Hanley, sometimes to dance to a live act, more often to recorded music. At about three o'clock one cold Sunday morning in late winter, early spring, he left The Place with Alison and walked across the road to where his car was parked by some abandoned land—how he missed the dereliction, the unchartered waste spaces of those times—and as he was adjusting the rear mirror he saw a police car pull up on the other side of the road. He said, Christ, the cops, making Alison laugh. He said it wasn't funny, he was well over the limit and he was driving the car illegally. She said it was funny, he'd sounded like Z-Cars and very cockney. He said Z-Cars was Liverpool, not London. It was still funny. After a couple of minutes the police car moved on and he drove back to the campus, neither of them talking. When he parked outside her hall of residence she said that she didn't want him to come up and he asked why, although he knew why, and she said that she just didn't want him to. He said, overcoming the tumultuous impulse he always had at moments like these to persist and try to persuade the woman to sleep with him, I'll see you tomorrow then, meaning later that day. On the way back to his digs he thought about how Alison had been since he went to her room at about eight o'clock the previous evening and she had met him with the words why didn't you tell me your wife was pregnant. After a while he had said that he had meant to and she said liar. He thought that perhaps he was a liar. Certainly he had been wondering how he could tell her. He asked who had told her and she said that it was none of his business. At the pub he told her what had happened, that he and his wife had agreed to split up, but a few weeks later she had told him she was pregnant. Afterwards he admitted to himself that this was a lie. Although he had for some time meant to leave her he had not told her he was leaving until a few months after they found out she was pregnant. He said to Alison that the previous weekend he had gone down to see her and he had said he would support her and the child but there would be no reconciliation. This turned out to be a lie because he did little to support her after the baby was born. Alison said and how did she feel about that, how does she feel about it all. He said that she was grief-stricken and had been throughout. Morant knew that Alison, sensibly, had little faith in him. Early on in their relationship she had said to him that he would leave her, probably sooner rather than later. When he asked her why she thought that, she had said that he was beautiful and she wasn't. He had been puzzled by this, partly because he certainly wasn't beautiful. He knew he was attractive to women, some women, but he knew he wasn't beautiful—although some part of him, as they say, felt that he was—and he didn't see any disparity between them in terms of looks. Also, why would being beautiful make you less likely to stay with someone. He said all this to her and she said that it was just him; he was restless and it made him more so that he knew he could attract women. Alison was one of the least didactic or opinionated people he knew but there were times with her when he felt like a child listening to a sensible, kindly adult. He didn't mind this; dreamily immersed in their early relationship it was pleasant to be told such things, particularly when they included flattering, if ridiculous, judgements about his appearance or his sexual performance. Everything, the pleasing things and the more unsettling insights into his personality, came from her honesty and clear-sightedness. Decades later he was watching an Ingmar Bergman film in which a young and entrancingly beautiful Liv Ullmann was playing the role that the director often assigned for her, the good, emotionally healthy woman who is bewildered by the irrationality, the madness of some man, and the Max von Sydow character, on one of the few occasions in the film when he shows warmth towards her, says to her character that she has a wholeness that he lacks and that seems lacking in the world around him, and this made Morant think of Alison, except that Alison was never bewildered by any man, never surprised. Morant did not see Alison later on the day after the trip to The Place or hear from her for weeks. He knew that she had gone home because her mother was ill. He got Jack to find out her phone number from Michael Tanner and he tried several times to ring her but on the one occasion that the phone was answered a male voice, perhaps her brother's, said that she wasn't there. He said to say that David had rung. One Friday a girl on Alison's floor came to him in the student common room and told him that Alison was coming in tomorrow afternoon to collect her things. She was leaving college. The following day he saw her in the foyer of the main building and she told him she'd got everything from her room and was waiting to see the vice-principal before she left. Her mother had had a stroke and she wanted to be near at hand to help out. Her father was trying to be supportive but, if anything, this had made him even more hopeless. He had, she said, taken to drink, and he was once more charmed by the slight oddness of her language. She had always, occasionally, used expressions, words and phrases, as if she had recently come across them and they would have to do. She'd try to pick up her course again later, at a college nearer home. She said don't talk about us, we both know that it was winding down. This was summary judgement and even though he knew it was true he felt that pang to hold onto things, to bring them back. He knew that he would never again see her sitting on the edge of the bed in her singlet and knickers, never hear her talk about the films she loved, never again dance with her, never on walks have her tell him which bird's song they were hearing, never have access to that body, that mind. He said nothing except that he'd drive her to the station if she wanted. She said that a family friend would be picking her up at two. He said, I'm sorry and she said there's no need. Some friends of hers appeared nearby, looking away but hovering. He said goodbye and she said yes. He heard about Alison on and off for years afterwards but did not meet her again for nearly thirty years when his university got the contract for a research project examining school governance in the north west of England and she was the head of one of the schools involved. In later life memories came to him and one was of sitting up in Alison's bed at college, his back cushioned by a pillow. Earlier they had had sex and she was lying beside him on her stomach reading, a bracelet that it amused her at these times to wear around her right ankle, and her bottom, its perfect skin, rising in a lovely arc from the hollow of her back, and he knew that in a few moments they would make love again. He remembered too, another college room in which Liz's cello leaned against the wall next to a dressing table whose surface held in addition to the familiar, entrancing paraphernalia—the bracelets, the scatter of bottles and jars, some lidless, containing unguents and fragrances, the brush, the beads draped over a side mirror—three stones that she had found in the woods above the college that afternoon, the shuddering joy that ran through him as Liz, kneeling on the bed where he lay, took off her dressing gown and he saw for the first time her breasts and he remembered the brief, obliterating perfection of making love to someone with whom you were newly in love.

Every Thursday evening for nearly two decades in the middle of his life, Morant met his friend, Matthew, for a drink at one of the pubs in the village where they both lived. Morant admired Matthew—Matt—more than any other man he knew. He was married to Theresa, a civil servant working in town planning, a woman who, like Matt, seemed grounded—confident in a settled understanding of what she was doing with her life—in a way that Morant had never achieved. They had two children, boys, and it was a pleasure for Morant to spend time with this family which was happy, tightly knit and yet open to the world and its possibilities. Matt was the only one of his friends who shared anything of his intellectual interests and the only one who would not have been embarrassed in the unlikely event that Morant had disclosed a hitherto unrevealed fact about his inner life. He had been Head of History and the Humanities at the school where Morant had been Head of English. Subsequently, Matt had become a deputy head at a school in a nearby authority, a school that drew its pupils from working class estates on the edge of a city. Under the leadership of a head who insisted on respect for all pupils, however repellent their behaviour, and who believed that all children were educable, that all children could be brought to a clearer understanding of their place in the world and the possibilities available for making their lives fulfilling, the school had persisted throughout the nineties and beyond in by then unfashionable practices which attracted the suspicion of the local education authority. Its unanticipated reward for refusing the technicist delusions that were being foisted on schools was that annual national league tables which took into account the social and economic situation of a school's intake, judged the school, in the shameless language of modern education, to have added a great deal of (contextually adjusted) value to its pupils, presumably as learning units, perhaps as economic units. As a result the school for several years featured annually amongst the highest adders of value in the country. Inevitably, the local authority had made repeated attempts to get rid of the head teacher or close the school, since it represented a scandalous aporia, an intolerable contradiction of the set of delusions it had hugged to its bosom. In this it eventually succeeded when, after the head had retired and the school continued in its recalcitrant ways, to the extent that its performance was judged as outstanding by inspectors from the office constituted by government to monitor standards in education, it was amalgamated with a nearby failing school and placed in the trusteeship of an evangelical Christian organisation which appointed a Christian head and governed the school from London. Although he had a few years earlier left the school to work on community education for a university which Morant regularly pointed out had an inferior academic reputation to the one at which he worked, these developments had vexed Matt. It was not just that the school was now driven by the sole goal, against which any educational initiative was measured, of league table success, but that it had become, as Matt put it, a horrendous exams factory which had given up on any educational purpose—this was to be expected and was the fate, to one degree or other, of most schools in this period (in his final years of visiting schools Morant had been dismayed by the increase in classrooms of posters proclaiming what the school alleged were its values or exhorting desired behaviours, often expressed in acronymic format, and formulae or algorithms, again often set out as hopefully catchy acronyms, imploring submission to step-by-step procedures that it was promised would lead to successful learning). It was also the fact that the new management had chosen to ignore its published values and was, in fact, less Christian than the old, happily secular school which had been concerned to know and respond to individual children in order to identify how each might best be helped to learn, a school which had some responsibility to the idea that education had a social purpose beyond equipping its pupils with more or less tradeable qualifications, a school built around the injunction to look after one another. On these Thursdays they talked, amongst other things, about education, sport, friends, people they didn't like, politics, beer, films, music, books, mountain areas they had walked in or might walk in and radio and television comedy programmes, often from the 1950s and 60s. Matt came from the elite working classes of South Wales—his father had been a miner—a background which Morant envied. For some time after Matt had been appointed as a head of department Morant's contacts with him had, apart from brief exchanges at lunchtimes and breaks, been in meetings where he had been impressed by the clear analytical focus that he brought to discussions and, what became more marked as he got to know him better, a quality of moral precision applied to the professional and pedagogical issues that schools encountered in those days. Matt knew his way around meetings that Morant had found impenetrably procedural, the province of senior teachers who were expert at reducing debate about schooling to points of order and information, to quibbling about precedent and the detection of obscure technical reasons for not engaging in discussion about the composition of the curriculum or what kinds of teaching might and might not lead to children learning. Matt taught Morant how, at these meetings, to insist upon the connections between, on the one hand, hitherto stupefying problems about timetabling, rooming and stationery and, on the other, the right practice of teaching. Like many historians educated at the universities of the seventies Matt was a Marxist who entered the profession, as he put it, fresh from an unequal struggle with French structural Marxism. Opting not to engage his pupils in discussion of Althusserean theory he developed a curriculum based on the notion that a culture could be analysed by looking at how its use of technology interacted with its environment, thus determining the nature of its social and power relations, belief system, its values, and its mode of communications. This model was applied to hunter gatherer, agricultural and early industrial societies, and to contemporary Britain. It was, said Matt, a productive model. Children could use it to identify how, for example, in early societies their technologies were so simple that no one group could control their use, with the consequence that societies remained fairly equal in terms of social and power relations. In early industrial society on the other hand, control of the forces of production passed to wealthy men who became very rich while impoverishing those who worked for them and also those who tried to compete with their factories using older technology, people like handloom weavers. This always seemed to Morant a helpful analytical schema, one that could be contested and whose moral implications allowed for debate, much like Darwinist thought, although for reasons that may be readily understood it was a mode of analysis that had not attained the sanctified status of evolutionary theory. One evening, early on in their friendship, Morant told Matt that on his appointment he had very soon seen that he was on the left but thought that he would probably not like him. Matt asked why did he think he wouldn't like him. Morant said that he thought that Matt would find him lacking in seriousness. Also, in the early seventies he, Morant, had worked in a school whose humanities department had been driven by an absolute faith in the authority of certain kinds of Marxist analysis, whose premises he couldn't accept. Try as he might—and he did try, as his initial assumption was that, since he shared his colleagues' hostility to the ways in which society was ordered, he must have misunderstood their ideas—he couldn't convince himself that history was going to unfold in the ways they regarded as inevitable; he had less faith than they in the susceptibilities of the working classes, whose children he taught, to arguments about class struggle, their state of preparedness for the revolutionary transformation of society; it all looked a bit more complicated than was allowed. He was troubled by a naivety, or perhaps a contempt, for the detail of how a new dispensation might be brought into being, how it might be managed, what government might look like in such circumstances. In one of the underground magazines of the sixties he had read that the Hell's Angels might well be the police force of the new order, an idea, Morant thought that was an expression of millenarian faith in the purifying, transfiguring effect of unleashed liberty, an idea that was soon to be put into question by the murder and violence of the Altamont free concert. These teachers he worked with seemed to have a social and educational theory, a theory of government, barely more developed than this: once the bourgeois order had been swept aside everything would fall into place and an epoch of love, peace and justice would materialise, releasing the creativity of the proletariat and disclosing hitherto suppressed modes of relation and social organisation. What was more, Morant said, there seemed to be quite a bit of keenness to administer punishment for economic and social crimes and an appetite for forcing people to behave properly. Matt had said that Marx's economic analysis was more impressive than his theory of history and that the sixties had come up with some perverse ideas; obviously you needed to organise and to plan if you wanted to be involved in changing society, although it was a disaster that communist states had adopted a command structure of government. Morant said, yes, but who was going to be the police in the new order. What would happen to authority, what would it look like. Clearly a new power-free set of social relations wasn't going to appear overnight. But it was more than this—it was about how you changed what was in people's heads and how you gave yourself the right to try and do that. And people's heads did need changing. He told Matt about his cousin Bill, a P.E. teacher in an East London school, who had once been supervising a detention class, attended by three boys engaged in fitful labour, one of whom sat in front of him and who, unlike the other two had written briefly and with purpose. After a while he asked the boy, whom he knew but did not teach, if he could read what he had written—he had an idea that if he showed interest he might be able to help him—and the pupil had said yes and passed him the paper which said that last week he and some others had got some machetes and gone down where the Pakis lived and chopped some of them and there had been blood everywhere and that this was great. He asked the boy why he had written about this and he had said that Mr Wilson, the organiser of the detention, a head of year, an English teacher and one of an influential group of left activist teachers in the school, had told him to write about an interesting experience he had recently had. After half an hour Mr Wilson had appeared to end the confinement and collect the pupils' work. His cousin asked what he intended to do with the writing he had collected and Wilson had said, probably throw it. Bill asked him to read the piece he had read and then asked him what should be done about it. Wilson had replied, nothing—what did he want him to do. Surely, this should be investigated—even if it was fantasy it represented an attitude that the school should be addressing. Wilson had said, no, it was OK, it was self-expression. Bill had asked Morant if this was an accepted belief amongst English teachers, that allowing children free expression would lead to whatever English teachers thought education was for. Morant said such accounts should never go unquestioned, but that it wasn't unusual, in English teaching during the seventies and eighties to encounter this idea, amongst unpoliticised teachers as well as those with ideological dedications. Having taught briefly in a school where it held a strong foothold, Morant was aware of this melding of Trotskyism and a romantic belief in children's natural capacity for learning when it was untrammelled by authority. At this time there was a faith, common amongst liberal as well as radical teachers, in the sanctity of the experience of oppressed groups, its redemptive social power once it had been unloosed from its shackles through the grace of self-expression, and he had, briefly but without conviction, tried to teach as if this were true, but had soon come to the conclusion that it would be preferable to think about and explore this experience rather than view it as the hitherto confined source of liberatory energies. Amongst the working class people he had grown up with, worked with and taught, one was always likely to encounter the full range of prejudice and craziness that society makes available to all its cohorts—xenophobia, racism, fear and hatred of women and homosexuals, fascination with violence and a horrified obsession with sex, as well as an uncomplicated, comprehensive ignorance, a stew of prejudice that did not seem to produce social progressivism. In an early career as a pipe-layer he had worked with a man in, he guessed, his thirties who was a riot of terrified misunderstanding and error. He hated blacks and credited them with a prodigious sexual power; he admired aggressive potency, eulogising men who were skilful, pitiless streetfighters and almost every day he would, often repeating himself, relay experiences of fights he claimed to have seen or been involved in, relishing the injuries and humiliations inflicted; he thought everyone in a position of influence, power or celebrity was a Jew, although he didn't approve of Hitler; he was, as far as Morant could tell, without any secure knowledge of geography, history, sport or the country's day-to-day affairs; he loved his dog but said, bewilderingly, that he wouldn't insult him by talking about him. He was obsessed with homosexuality and wanted to get rid of queers, often visiting an East End pub that Morant knew, the Deuragon Arms, where he was greatly entertained by the drag queens who performed for an apparently straight audience. He had seen ghosts and once an orange ball, glowing with heat, had fallen towards him out of the sky and he had thought it would kill him, so that he had had to run away. One day, during the nine o'clock break, as they were drinking tea and probably eating bacon or sausage sandwiches that someone had brought from a local café, he started to tell Morant about a woman he knew whom he had recently had, who was apparently sexually rapacious, as usual possessing huge breasts, and who had asked him to do something disgusting. He had, it seemed, prior to this request, performed with great success and he spoke with some pride about the various acts he had induced the woman to undertake, but then she had asked him to do something that wasn't natural, that was just disgusting, that no man should be asked to do.

After some tactful questioning it emerged that the woman had asked him if he would lick her underneath. This had troubled him deeply. Like Lenny in The Homecoming he had concluded that she was a slag. It seemed to Morant that his fellow worker's understanding of what he had experienced of life, although offering an extreme and lurid instance because he was obviously more than a little mad, was not very different from what the mass of working class people had come to know. There were less mad, more respectable, even genteel, versions, and not all of them included fantasies of violence and sexual horror, but they all drew upon the same reserve of folk knowledge. In many it was tempered by a fair-mindedness and decency that he guessed was the residue of a communal morality that was throughout the seventies and eighties being broken by the calculated destruction of a way of life. Occasionally in the early years he came across individuals whose understanding had been shaped by a political consciousness forged in the workplace. But in any classroom it was clear that the educational task was to investigate what had been learnt from experience, and less often to celebrate it. He said to Matt that if you can't even see the truth that people are fucked up and education needs to unfuck them up and if you have no way of going about that task, how can you imagine that the new Jerusalem was on the way. Matt said, so Morant had thought that he would be that kind of humanities teacher and that would be a problem for him. Morant said, or worse; most Trots didn't bother with detailed thoughts about the practice of education or social administration because they were deeply authoritarian and probably ready to kill a few people in order to bring about the just society. Matt asked how he knew that they were like that. Morant said he'd read the Socialist Worker. He'd worked with Trots. Matt asked what sort of a Marxist he, Matt, had turned out to be. Morant said a thoughtful one, someone who wanted to teach, not someone who thought that children, if left alone, could build a righteous, free and shining city for themselves. Matt laughed and said that he wasn't a Trot, he was a Stalinist.

What was it, this heavy emptiness that sat at the heart of things, that, for example, sometimes weighed so heavily in the gaps that opened in conversations, so that you felt that you were talking about other things because you could not or dare not talk about this vacancy, this void that for a moment you shared with your companion, until one of you spoke, talking about something in order to cover over the perplexing, if you thought about it, terrifying, if you looked into it, nothingness that stretched out between you, that for a moment had wrapped around you? The only time Morant felt entirely free of this awareness was when he had been in love, so that the question offered itself whether love, the absolute immersion of two people in each other, was the one truly authentic mode of being or whether it was simply the most effective way of not considering the meaningless of things. And love, romantic love, this infantile emotional disorder, this reduction to a shared psychotic interlude of the possibilities of what love might mean, how could that make sense as a solution to the universe's senselessness, the fact that care is nowhere to be found beyond human hearts and minds. Other ways of ordering and conducting one's life—religious faith, sporting obsession, all-consuming hobbies, political commitment, enthusiasm for the arts, career ambition, absorption into family life, reading uplifting stories—although, for Morant, offering no plausible answer to the problem at least offered more long-term distraction.

When he was younger Morant had thought he would be a novelist, but as he got older the idea seemed preposterous. During his thirties and forties he read few novels, except for those he was required to teach, and he developed a distaste for what he thought of as art talk, in particular literary culture, the eager, busy work of propagandisation that he saw in the literary sections of broadsheet newspapers and heard on radio arts programmes. He also despised the unseemly wholesomeness of radio and television programmes where quite well-known people talked about books they valued or others where the same sorts of people had actors read their favourite poems and bits of prose. Sometimes these programmes took place in front of audiences who clapped the readings and laughed in appropriate places, reminding him of people at Shakespeare plays who appeared to find Elizabethan humour amusing. You always felt that the disturbing phrase "a love of literature" hung in the air, an expression whose deployment would, its user could confidently predict, elicit a warm and knowing approval. There was an unsettling cosiness and smugness here, a cultural performance, an enactment of taste that marked out these people as special, distinguished from those others who would not enjoy such occasions, such celebrations. He thought about this to see if he was being unkind, unfair, puritanical. These people, he recognised, were as entitled to their entertainment as the audiences who hooted and screamed at television talent shows or those who enjoyed comedy programmes that mocked current affairs. He didn't begrudge them their satisfactions. What was different, however, what particularly irritated him, was the ritual performance of communal value, the exclusionary reverence at work in these literary occasions. As well as simple pleasure at the play of words, membership of a faded faith was being practised here. These people were conscious of their goodness. He was surprised to find that he was also affronted by what seemed to him the reduction of literature to the function of a comfort blanket. But worse than this were the mountains of print, the oceans of verbiage, produced by the writers and the critics who kept this mode of production churning. Morant found it remarkable that these workers in literature rarely articulated the claims to value of the domain they inhabited; as they discussed a new novel or a biography of some poet or wrote about their profound respect for a neglected writer, they seemed to assume that their enthusiasms had a universal, transcendent cultural importance. He could never see why they were so confident about this. He noticed over the years that increasing numbers of these enthusiasts for literature revealed their enjoyment of popular fictional forms in a range of media and were careful to give them their due, whilst at the same time managing to preserve a notion of literary merit that was sometimes applied to differentiate pleasing or successful (within the terms of the genre) popular fiction from less felicitous examples, but which inevitably served a hierarchising purpose across fictional production in its entirety. There was some fiction that was special, that accessed discursive realms and did things there that were denied not just to popular fiction but to all other forms of language use. He noticed that when they considered whether the survival of serious fiction should be wished for in an age where so many other sources of apparently satisfying and fulfilling narrative were available to the population, through television dramas, films, computer games, celebrity magazines, the novels people actually bought and read in huge quantities or through social networking sites, they fell back on arguments that were more or less ingenious variations on the notions of literature as vicarious experience and as a privileged site of discursive freedom. Real literature, it was said, allowed the writer and reader to engage with the possibility of other ways of being through a discursive openness and generosity that was not to hand in the closed narrative forms—so often in hock to the market and its publicity—of the popular media. Proper fiction afforded a vital space of open inquiry, an indispensable alternative to the closed, rule-governed regions of religious and political discourse; it could be the stage on which the great debates of society were conducted. It was the least formally conventionalised and policed kind of language, the one that, trading in heteroglossia, let a host of conflicting voices speak. These advocates of literature sometimes claimed that the novel, in particular, had a way, a sensuous, telepathic way, of transferring thoughts and feelings from one person's mind to another's, that—a more sophisticated rendering of the same thought—reader and writer, through the medium of the text, become a collective being that both writes as it reads and reads as it writes, jointly producing the unique work, the novel. He had sympathy with some of these ideas but found them crudely expressed and theoretically undernourished. They were lazy formulations and some of them ridiculous. The idea that literature afforded unmediated communication between minds, the instantaneous transfer of ideas and experience, was obviously illusory—these were just words, treacherous words, that were inefficient at delivering a world from one head to another, words that were the best ones one person could come up with to approximate to what he thought he wanted to say and which were received by another person who used these unreliable words in ways that he imagined their writer used them in order to see what he imagined that writer intended. Surely, everyone knew that words were an unstable foundation for communicating intentions, that words were just tentative signs, stand-ins for the real thing, not some medium that conjured things themselves, and that the words writers chose often worked in ways that the writer did not intend, that sometimes they served impulses that were beyond the author's control. Some sort of communication took place but it didn't involve worlds being projected from one mind to another. As a teenager he had read several of William Faulkner's novels and had felt as if he was looking out of a window at a place, a society he had never visited, hot, dusty, breathing guilt and secrets, clenched fast by a mesmerising and immemorial folk knowledge. Lulled by the coiled, sprung rhythms of Faulkner's sentences, he had used the words Faulkner provided and what he knew, or thought he knew, of the American south, but he had also used what he didn't know about the south but did know about other places and other lives, attaching to his impressions bits of his own experience and knowledge that might or might not have some rough homology with the bits and pieces of belief, custom and social relations rendered in these exotic pages, to produce something that was pleasurable, intoxicating and, in a way that he did not then or now fully understand, somehow moral, but which, in representational terms, must have been only a blurred version of whatever Faulkner had in mind. But this was enough; it was just that it was less and more than a sharing of worlds. He had seen the task of translation from one language to another likened to an attempt to build a tree in a country that had no trees, using whatever materials lay to hand. This, it seemed to him, was the image of all communication in language. Literary discourse, its talk about itself, often seemed to imagine that it was exempt from these limiting conditions. It shared this delusion with scientific discourse. He saw that fiction could allow the collision and mingling of discrepant and contradictory voices in transgression of the boundaries that normally divided them and that this might lead to language that might undermine rigidified and conventional understandings; he could see that literature might stage the play of great ideas and events, that it might produce startlingly new and disturbing ways of seeing the world; it could, as its advocates sometimes claimed, serve the unfinished work of freedom, to act upon the limits imposed upon the possibilities of life. There were two things about this. One was that fiction was hardly unique in these affordances. The other was a question: if fiction could do all this, why did it do it so rarely. Why was so much literary fiction so obedient, so drenched in the way things are. He found himself agreeing with the statement that literature was the prescribed space for the amusement of the castrated, the formal freedom conceded to those who cannot accommodate themselves to the nothingness of real freedom. Why did so many novelists seem unconcerned by the fact that their genre was as rule-bound, as constrained by its (bourgeois) origins, as divisive in its modes of address (literature being what most people will not or cannot read) as any other. Why did so many well regarded novels offer comfort, the promise that guilt can be atoned for, human misery transcended by the novelist's art, that what is lost can be returned and broken lives made whole. Some displayed psychological acuity or beseeched understanding; they were said to move with their searing depictions of human suffering or to bring alive with a brutal honesty the reality of the human condition; by way of variation they sometimes sought, courageously, to lay bare the underlying depravity of humanity, the fact that psychopathy was its fundamental character, or they turned an unflinching gaze on the sadness and pain of life, the way that all lives are doomed to failure and regret. They showed the futility and sordidness of human existence or gestured towards hope and goodness, in both cases illuminating the nature of humanity. Why, in short, did novels attempt to reproduce reality. He sought none of these things in fiction. Although he expected to encounter expressions of suffering, despair, happiness, sadness, elation, the goodness and cruelty that is woven into human life, and, perhaps, the turbulence of history, he wanted neither consolation nor revelation, neither reassurance nor warning and he had no expectation of fiction making the world whole. He thought that psychoanalysis offered more subtle and informed accounts of the workings of human thought and emotion and that the nature of the human condition, if such a thing existed, was best explored through philosophy. What he wanted was verbal delight, beauty, rigour, strangeness, surprise and rebuke to the prevailing certainties of everyday thought. He had seen and enjoyed an American film, set in the early sixties in a small town in Montana, a settlement whose faint cultural footprint hardly marks the immense, inhuman landscape. A young teenage boy is caught, baffled, between his two parents who—it seems to him suddenly— decide to break off from the comfortable relationship within which he had been nourished. The father loses his job and instead of taking up employment that would pay the bills joins, for a pitiful wage, a group fighting vast forest fires in the mountains (the backdrop to the film). After a time mother and boy drive to the mountains, not because the mother hopes to find the father but, it seems, because she wishes to understand her husband's motivations, perhaps to fathom the incomprehensible, uncontainable destruction that has visited her family. On arrival at the chaotic scene of the firefighting they park the car and get out. The camera focuses on the boy's face, staring, and we see awe, incomprehension, horror, wonder. We hear the grumbling thunder of the wildfire. The camera cuts to the scene the boy is looking at, slowly panning up from the roadside to the nearby undisturbed trees and above to the full roaring violence of a mountainside on fire, an immense power beyond human reckoning. The boy is confronted by and the film presents its audience with an experience which is usually only glimpsed at the peripheries of human thought, at the boundaries and between the cracks in our rational order, something profoundly troubling, an ontological dislocation, a destabilisation of workaday human conceptual and emotional capacity, an event that introduces the thought of the soul's extinction, the dreadful puniness of human thought and feeling. And yet it excited. Not all art need approach the sublime, but this relatively unregarded film had and Morant could not forget it. There were other reasons why he decided not to write fiction. He deplored the way that novelists, the ones who were considered important, so often strained after significance, alighting hungrily on some recent or historical event or some cultural phenomenon so that the book was hailed by reviewers and critics as revelatory of a truth about our time or to be a moment in which all is changed. Here was a novel that would define our age, would display its essence for all to see in its pages, a novel that people would point to and say that here in these remarkable pages we were shown what we really are, what we were then. Morant guessed that novelists could write out of a number of impulses—anger, fear, anxiety, bewilderment, dismay at life, fascination with an idea, because it was pleasurable to invent things or because they wanted to amuse, perhaps to be admired, for the world to see them in their specialness, or because if they did not write they could not be themselves— but it seemed to him that a desire for acclaim, which was always a desire to outdo rivals, was not the surest basis for producing something worthwhile. He didn't want to be involved in such nonsense. How did you make yourself feel important enough to write a novel; how did you gear up to something that was such an obvious invitation to narcissism without indulging one's narcissism. The whole endeavour seemed an effusion of grandiosity, a fantasy of omnipotence. He had a friend, an academic philosopher who, as a young teacher of English, had returned to his old college at Oxford to deliver a talk in which he argued that the girls' magazine Bunty, if read with the necessary rigour, could yield meanings that were equal to those of King Lear. Rick combined an unyielding sardonic humour and unrelenting refusal of the current ordering of the world and had once, laughing, said to Morant that surely only a scoundrel writes a novel. Morant didn't agree entirely, but he could see that the novel offered temptations. He had in fact written a novel when he was young, in his mid-twenties, and although he could see that it was excusable as a young man's attempt to understand what was happening to him and to let off some surplus energy, that was no reason to inflict upon anyone else what was, in its essence, a crude attempt to show what a wonderful fellow he was. He'd enjoyed playing with different styles, a bit of brutal realism here, some nouveau roman disciplinarity there, occasional lyrical passages celebrating animal vitality, the whole subjected to jarring montage learnt from French new wave cinema, but, all things considered, it took quite a bit of cheek to expect anyone else to be interested in this sort of thing, and even more to imagine that the world was in need of it, that it might do people good to read it. And writers, all of them he suspected, all of those composers of literary fiction, were pricked into activity by a niggling itch to have their say, to stake a claim on the way things are seen, to make themselves heard and visible in their uniqueness—that old adamic itch. And then there was all that clanking machinery of scene setting, moving characters around, psychological insights, internal monologues, she said, he responded—breathing heavily or with a note of disappointment in her voice, as he smelt her skin with its familiar scent of drying cotton—

descriptive tours de force, subtly placed leitmotifs and endless plotting. In all this—this being the blather of English literary discourse—it was, of course, very much looked down upon to write in a way that drew attention to the unnaturalness of the novel, in a way that put on display or, worse, called into doubt, the conventions and mechanisms of producing fiction. To write in this way was to indulge a fashionable postmodernism, to reveal a lack of faith in the novel's—in language's, in story's—redemptive power or in its beneficence, a betrayal of literature's dedication to the common understanding and even more treacherously, a knowing, self-congratulatory nod to literary theory. The novel should be readable and that meant that the writer was to be judged on her hallucinatory powers, her mesmerist ability to draw the reader into her world, to bring into play all the admittedly various resources of the genre to provide a warm, morally improving, aesthetically delightful, immersive experience, or possibly a cooler, bracing, but no less morally and aesthetically etc. experience. As a reader he welcomed the experience of aesthetic delight and he knew he always stood in need of some moral improvement but these pleasures were too often cloyed by the novel's insistence on enfolding you in its immersive embrace, its intention of drawing you into its unique inwardness, into its infatuated selfness. He was struck by the number of times novelists expressed their admiration for writers like Sterne, Melville, Bernhard, Kafka or Calvino, even Robbe-Grillet, and who then went on to write novels which in style and form would not have upset Henry James. And yet there was fiction that was not like this, writing that knew that its essential destiny was to disrupt the smooth narratives of reason, to return to our accounts of life the primacy of the unconscious, the desiring and dreaming that drives us. Such writing set itself against the plausible storying of sciences, capital, religions, common sense and the great teleologies that have claimed to explain us, asserting that it is our fictions that constitute us, our imagined worlds that we need to attend to. One of the books he returned to from time to time was Calvino's engagement with the narrative allure of tarot cards. Calvino says in his concluding note to his experiment that he had become consumed by the idea of tarots as a machine for constructing stories and then by the diabolical idea that he might, like a conjuror, summon forth all the stories contained in the tarot deck. The novel begins by deriving stories from random groupings of cards, just as a fortune teller might, but Calvino becomes frustrated with this method because he wants himself to extract and explore all the narrative possibilities suggested by the cards, to bend them to his own fictive desire. For Morant what emerged from this endeavour was the recalcitrance of the narrative units, the elemental figures and tales that the cards incite, their waywardness and disobedience before the writer's will, and more, their imperiousness, their coercion of the writer's intentions to their own anciently sedimented and insistent meanings. Calvino concludes that the writer is like the juggler or conjurer figure in the tarot who assembles a number of objects and moves them around to create effects. He says that he publishes this book to be free of his diabolical obsession. There is the suggestion that it is not just the tarot that he wants to be free of but all the vast, unasked for, irresistible inheritance of mythemes, archetypes and narratives that are bequeathed to the story-teller. At one point he writes that the virgin page waits to be penned by the writer, noting the interlocking senses here, that that notion that is obscurely related to the production of fiction, "life", is also penned in—confined—as it is written and meaning itself cramped and constrained, compelled to speak within a pre-existing ordering of language. Here is a prison or a maze of a castle around which the writer is condemned to wander, confronting and being intrigued and then oppressed by time-worn but indestructible scenes and dramas which flow endlessly in and out of each other, a machine unstoppably producing and reshuffling the stock of meanings which is the inheritance, perhaps of the race, certainly of a civilisation, perhaps, he adds, particular income groups. What, the writer wonders, does he contribute, what survives of what the writer adds to this archive, what of himself, of the exquisitely personal, finds lodging and survives in this process.

One Friday evening in late October, or perhaps it was November, Morant was waiting in the foyer of the main college building, perhaps to meet Alison, and staring out at the car park outside. He had just eaten in the refectory which was just along the corridor to his left, past the cloakrooms, and students were coming from their meals and heading towards the common room and bar at the end of a corridor to his right, some perhaps to go straight through those rooms to a door that gave onto the campus and the halls of residence which were placed on the far side of neatly kept fields, some of which were for sports and some for less organised recreation. A few students were going up the stairs behind him, probably, perhaps improbably given that it was a Friday, to the library. Hardly anyone was leaving the building through the foyer doors, but from time to time a lecturer or college official and on one occasion a small group of students, late arriving from the first year campus, entered from what was clearly a wild and windy outside. As they did so a few leaves would blow in, joining others that had been admitted earlier and whilst the doors were briefly open the wind drove them in a looping, circular motion around the central part of the foyer. After a while three girls drifted along from the refectory, one skinny, pleasant-looking with a gamin, Leslie Caron haircut and slightly gap-toothed, one tall, large-boned with long, straight red hair and one dark-haired and beautiful. As they approached a woman in a rain-coat came through the foyer doors and the tall girl, as soon as she saw the swirl of leaves, went into ecstasies. She got the skinny girl to hold one of the doors slightly ajar which had the effect she desired of keeping the leaves in motion. She said oh my god, incredible, how beautiful and skipped around, light-footed and graceful, within the ellipse formed by the leaves, clasping her hands together, laughing and squealing in delight, occasionally leaning down to put her hand into the eddying flow. She kept this up for some time, getting her friend to open the door more and less widely to see what produced the best effect upon the leaves. Two P.E. students, who clearly knew her because they called her by her name, passed and said something in friendly ridicule, but she ignored them, keeping the dancing and cries of pleasure going for what seemed like several minutes. Looking back Morant was struck by how of the moment this was. A generation, or part of it, had somehow decided it was free to do this sort of thing, this slightly self-conscious, slightly defiant thing, to take pleasure in something that would, to the prevailing gaze, seem unworthy of attention. The sixties—the psychedelia, the attempts to expand consciousness through drugs, music and art, the implacable rejection of convention—was about this; an attempt to break a confining discourse, a definition of reality, of what counted as real and, therefore, of what mattered. Later he would think how brief this moment had been, how quickly calculative reason was to close around such impulses, this naive, blundering ambition towards a lightness of being. The girl wore jeans and a loose sweater—he could never remember what sort of footwear she had on—and everything about her suggested a dedication, perhaps a predisposition, to brazen display of pleasure at inconsequential things. Her behaviour testified that this small thing, fallen leaves blown by the wind, was proclaimed as truthful in a way that, say, bank statements, timetables, the life that is ordered for us, the life of getting and doing, the world given to us by newspapers and television, rules about how late you could have visitors of the opposite sex in your room, were not. And once, perhaps, on a beach on a Greek island, this girl had placed a large oval stone where from time to time the sea would wash over it, turning it from light grey to a glistening slate blue and then it had been another pleasure to see it quite rapidly dry to grey, one side fringed with sand, which made her think of the cocoa-stained top lip of her nephew. Perhaps, like Morant, she had walked in some streets one bright March day after showers and seen in a puddle how vivid was the blue of the sky, how much more intensely true was that reflected blue and the champagne and white of the clouds than what she saw above her. She might, looking at this, have felt the dizzying emptiness of the unvaulted spaces above and below her, nothing in between, just a thin film of appearance. Perhaps, like him—perhaps they would speak of this, or not speak of it, but think it at the same time—she had heard on a busy city street one hot afternoon when the day seemed to be struggling to keep going, a susurration, a breath of mischief and pleasure, of desire, that eluded and played about the ordered and rationed world that surrounded her. Of course this was a hippy chick and she wanted you to know she was. Morant was a little embarrassed by the component of self-conscious display, but intrigued. He had never spoken to this girl, but he knew that she was called Brid, that she was in the year above his and that she and her friends were an extrovert group; the skinny one was a gifted dancer, the beautiful one sang beautifully and the tall, red-haired one was Irish, flirtatious and, reputedly, sexually promiscuous. All these things he had been told by others. For now he was aware of how lovely one of these girls was and how beguiling another. In a year's time Brid Foley would be a passenger in a car accident which would ruin her nose and after surgery it would be shorter, no longer pre-Raphaelite, more snub, and at a lunchtime table in the refectory Peter Morgan would say to her, Oi, skull face, pass the salt, but before that in the January of his first year at college, he slept with Brid Foley and although Alison knew nothing of it, his deceit sapped their relationship. He had been in one of the two pubs in the village, in the first week of the new term and he saw her with a group of P.E. students he knew. The previous term he had turned out for the college's football trials and had, as he invariably did if he attempted to play football, triggered an injury, a groin strain that had been recurrent since he had had a hernia operation when he was ten years old. Running was impossible for a couple of months and the only way he could keep fit was to swim and to use the college gym to work out with weights, just lazy man, upper body lifts like the bench press. He had attracted some attention from PE students because he was regularly benching three hundred pounds—a lot in those days before serious weight training for sports—and some of them had suggested he try rugby, which he did in February of that year. Brid was with her thin friend, who, Morant could see, was not fully at ease amongst this group of boys, although one could not reasonably have described Brid as ever at ease, so much as engaged in what appeared to be a vigorous performance. She stared with exaggerated concentration into boys' eyes as they spoke, she laughed too long, too often and too loudly at things that they said, she draped her arms around them as they talked, she behaved as if she was drunk, but Morant could see that she wasn't. This was repellent but fascinating behaviour. He had never found her attractive but now he saw her in her black tights and short skirt and saw the swell of her large hips, her full, strong thighs, her disturbing craziness and he found her irresistible. All this movement seemed to promise abandonment but when she lapsed into stillness her face was serene, chaste. Her friend left after a while and he moved over and joined the group. She was talking about poetry, chiding the P.E. students for knowing nothing about it and caring less. It was one of those teasing games that young men and women play; she said that it was wonderful and beautiful and that it was about all that was important in our lives, everything that really mattered but that was ignored by the soulless system in which we lived and they said it was bollocks, OK for girls and poufs. It was a ritual engagement, neither side at all interested in convincing the other, a playful presexual skirmish, a flirting. He could see that none of these boys were going to end up in bed with her, something that she and most of them were fully aware of. One of them, Kenny, a pleasant young man from Barnsley who was in Morant's education group, said careful lads and that Dave liked that sort of stuff. Brid looked at him and said you're not a P.E. philistine like this lot then. He said no, that he did English. And dance, Kenny said. And dance said Morant. She said my god she adored dance, it was the most expressive of all the arts, more than music, she loved to do it all the time but she was too fat and lumbering to be any good. He said that he could see the appeal of dance as an art form but that he had no interest in it, it was the film bit of the arts course that he liked and she certainly wasn't fat, which was the truth. When he said that he was interested in film her eyes widened and she leaned forward and grabbed his hands and said film, Christ, listen, he must, he really must, make a film with her friend Liz who was beautiful, the camera would adore her, he must meet her, he must make a film with her, the world would be amazed. He said that if he made a film he'd audition her friend. He hardly spoke another word to her, content to observe her in this group, her white flesh, the way her neck craned forward when she wanted to make a particularly aggressive point, her eyelashes thickened with mascara, and no other make-up. She had graceful hands. A few days later she came over to where he was sitting in the common room and asked him what he was reading and he said it was a book called Life Against Death and she asked him what it was about and he said that as far as he could see it said that our lives, the whole of history, is driven by fears and a sense of loss that we are unconscious of and don't want to face and that civilisation and culture were just attempts to compensate for the loss, but he might not have it right because he hadn't finished the book. It also said that the genital organisation of sexuality was a problem. She asked what that meant and he said that it seemed to mean that the cause of human unhappiness was the way that erotic pleasure had been concentrated on the sexual organs rather than being spread across the surface and the interior of the body as it was with young children. She said you're different. He asked what she meant and she said intelligent. He said that he was maybe, but so were other people and she said no, you're different. Then she said something that told him they would sleep together. She said that she bet he could be a bit dangerous. Again there was that flaring temptation to accept this judgement, to accept definition as the predatory, amoral male who held the promise of physical and sexual power and again he was resentful of being seen in this way. He said that he wasn't dangerous, except perhaps that he wasn't very good at keeping to rules but that was probably a weakness. In her room she played some Bach and showered in the bathroom down the hall. When she returned they kissed, he undressed quickly and on the bed he removed her towelling robe but not the vest which, surprisingly, she wore beneath it and they had sex. She swore at him, accused him of wanting to inflict various obscenities and humiliations upon her, bit and scratched him and at one point hit him in the face with the flat of her palm, twisted and wrestled to get away from him even as she pulled him into her, and after a while started calling him—an odd but characteristic locution—lover, and told him in detail the ways in which she wanted him to humiliate her. In this he obliged as far as he could. It was a pleasure to subdue this woman, to have her turn, move, open herself as he required and he was gratified at the delight his grip on her body gave. At the same time he relished the smells of a new body, its living strength, these new arms, thighs, breasts, arse, the ways in which it arranged itself in its desire. Finally, on top of her, he pulled her vest, which he'd already lifted to her neck so that he could get at her breasts, up over her head. She came almost immediately, as he did soon after. A minute later Brid smiled at him and went again to the shower. When she returned she said, fondly, you're a bastard. She had work to do, an essay on counterpoint in some composer or other, so he left. They didn't kiss because she clearly didn't want to. It would be like this every time, no drowsy post-coital intimacy, no acknowledgement of what had been shared, no concession that they were now closer than before. For weeks afterwards they were, because of Alison, careful in their meetings, Brid more at pains to exercise caution than he. Then Alison left and Brid still imposed a furtiveness on their relationship. They never presented themselves around the college as a couple. After a while it would have been known to more than a few people that they were together, but Brid never allowed that to be publicly visible. At meal times she would usually sit with other people or, if at his table, never next to him and always paying more attention to others than to him. They never went to the college bar together, nor to either of the village pubs and they never went as a pair to college or university discos. Twice they went to a pub in town and once to a performance of chamber music in Stoke and once to a poetry reading at an arts centre in Hanley—tedious. They spent some time together in her room, whilst Brid played music or declaimed poetry and Morant tried to explain his reservations about art talk and sometimes Cheryl and Liz would come into the room to argue with him. Occasionally he and Brid would go for a walk in the woods above the college. He didn't ask her why their relationship had to be conducted within such limits. He knew that it was because he was married. She devoted great care to her studies, but having read some of her work, he concluded that this devotion was driven more by duty than a love of music or literature. She never missed a lecture, took pages of notes, always handed work in on time. She was a good, well-behaved student. Morant saw all this dutifulness as the price she paid for misdemeanour in other areas of her life. Later, however, Morant would think that something else was at work. Throughout his time of knowing her, before and after their relationship, she never offered herself to public attention as one of a couple, except for one period, some time after they had split up, when she appeared at college functions with an arty young man who, it turned out, was training to be a dentist. Morant was sure they weren't having sex and some time afterwards Liz told him that Brid had said that she'd finished this boy because he had made her feel sick. Morant knew a little about Brid's background from her friends—a hard-working but angry father, some sort of gamekeeper, who occasionally hit his wife and loved but terrified his young daughter. Their relationship lasted just a couple of months and towards the end his enthusiasm for an involvement that consisted of episodes of sexual abandon, interspersed with brief periods of awed reverie before Purcell or Shelley or Pentangle, began to wane, although in truth he was still a little mesmerised by her waywardness, the strangely constructed aesthetic of her life. In bed he was tiring of their tightly scripted sex in which he was cast as the cruel violator compelling her submission. Then she started not being there if they arranged to meet and when they were together she didn't want sex and she said that he was bad for her, but wouldn't explain what she meant. Then he found out that she'd been seeing someone else. Then he saw her with someone else in one of the village's two pubs. It was a third year P.E. student whom he had always disliked, Will _____ , a gifted athlete who was to go on to play as a back row forward for two first-class rugby clubs but who never did what he should have done, which was to play for his country. He was a caricature sports jock, loud, keen on women but uninterested in them, without any close friend but greatly admired by other P.E. students. Morant had thought about this before; what it was that the sports students whom he spent time with, at least the ones who were, or aspired to be with, high-ranking males, respected in another man, which was a way of saying how they liked to think of themselves. They liked someone who screwed a lot of women but who never settled with any of them; they liked emotional shallowness, a lack of sensitivity which could be realised as contempt for feeling itself, a contempt that was often directed at women; they liked intellectual shallowness, simple, easily graspable framings of thought that could guide them through life's complications, a preference for ready to hand ideas and opinions that made many of them firmly conservative in their cultural and social views. (Morant remembered an occasion when some activists were rumoured to be coming down from the university to urge college students to political protest, to join the demonstrations and occupations of premises that they were already undertaking, and on his way in through the main entrance he met three or four P.E. men in track suits looking a bit vigilant and when he asked them what they were doing they said that Stan Holding had asked them to keep an eye out for some university people who were coming down to cause trouble; when he explained about freedom of speech and political protest and the Vietnam war they were momentarily confused but decided to hold their station). They liked authority and responded well to leadership; some of them believed that physical force was a better way of sorting out difficulties than moral reflection. Later Morant had to concede that this was uncharitable and sweeping judgement and that many P.E. students were thoughtful, morally nuanced, maturely responsible and kind individuals, just not many of those he tended to associate with in rugby teams. And yet he found things to like in them, which was another matter. Will, however, was different altogether, the very model and image of what Morant's way-out psychedelic in-crowd friends referred to as a P.E. cunt, a sprawling, arrogant, cynical, over-mothered, six foot three and ripped, chunk of self-love. And Morant felt all this with intensified certainty when he saw him with Brid. Although he never saw them together again he knew that this was why, perhaps how, she had frozen him out. He dealt with the situation by excising it from his life. He spoke to no one about what had happened and, although he was polite when they met, he never tried to approach Brid as her lover, never asked her to explain her behaviour and this partly because he knew she would not give a truthful account of her decision and because he would never concede to her that he had been wounded and shaken, never allow her or anyone else to glimpse the pangs of rejection, the humiliating, raging, fantasising jealousy that gripped him and that made it impossible to think seriously about anything else in his life. This should not have happened to him; his life so far—and this would continue—had been organised around the avoidance, the exclusion from that life, of this kind of indignity, this surprise over-throw, this casting down. During the summer he visited his wife to confirm that despite the baby she would soon give birth to he still intended to leave her. He was moved by her grief but unyielding. His mother, who had never liked his wife, told him that she was ashamed of him and she had always thought he was a kind person. He returned north and left behind not just his wife but every friend he had had in that finished life, except Brian. He had thought that he would never doubt his masculinity but now, however he tried to reason himself away from the madness, he submitted himself to Brid's judgement, to what he imagined were the criteria of a masculinity according to which she had dismissed him from her life. He was insufficiently brutal, too thoughtful, trailing the reek of an ineliminable tenderness, an invasive, unmanly curiosity, a desire for permanence that offended the nomad spirit and in the end he could not satisfy her sexually. He had slept before with a couple of women whose enjoyment of sex had been lit by a fantasy of male power but neither had invited real cruelty and with both he had shared moments of warmth and affection. He knew that Brid had wanted him to hit her, to offer insult, to really bruise, to wound, and once as they approached the conclusion of their love-making, her legs wrapped around him, pulling him into her, she clutched at a pillow with her right hand and drew it in towards her side and he knew—it seemed to be so—that what she wanted was for him to smother her, to press a pillow against her face as if to smother her. Although he found the forms of her desire fascinating, exciting, he could do none of these things and was therefore inadequate to her needs. That warm summer was spent trying to avoid work on a farm just outside a small provincial town, work of which his only recollection was the chafing on his hands of baler twine and compacted hay, racing a tractor when the alcoholic farmer (every farm vehicle, every farm building, was littered with whisky bottles, some empty, most unfinished) was away, long breaks spent with Simon leaning back on, hiding behind, bales of hay, discussing the nature of love and making up songs about the farmer they called Farmer Pig because he looked like one, the near-dereliction and filth of the farmer's house whose uncurtained vacancy appeared to Morant like a memento mori that had been carefully set down in those gleaming, bristling fields, the small town that in the evenings swarmed with young people touched in their different ways by the fantastic possibility that the world was about to be governed by love and where he and Simon dropped acid for the first and Morant's last time. There was a bridge there where, one warm evening whose drowsy amiability he forever associated with the Scott Mackenzie song that like his friends, he affected to despise, Simon met a girl he had known at school and Jack visited once and got high, although he was always on an unassisted high, on a half-pint bottle of Allsopp's pale ale—he never had more—so that they were asked to leave the pub because he kept intervening in the conversations of older people, to their amusement on the whole, offering advice on, as far as Morant could remember, diet, their relationships and where in Italy they should go on holiday (not where they were planning to go), ending up on a table tapping the beams that ran across the ceiling to see if they were real wood. And in the town, as was very possibly the case in other similar towns, there was a droopy-moustachioed young man called Gypsy Dave who wore a Chinese skull cap and a kind of shorty kaftan. These things and a great deal of drink deadened any pain he felt and later he would look back to that time with fondness. Afterwards, much later, he recognised that enacted a simplifying violence on Brid, that he had done injustice to what he came to see was the complex and delicate organisation of her being, a construction assembled over terror and loss, with the cunning and deviousness necessary if she was to navigate life and pass as something like normal. On return to college, at the beginning of his second year, after he had found somewhere to live he found that he needed to drink less, could work again, and he started training for rugby. One November evening he was changing into his gear and bandaging his right knee because it had ulcerated after a second XV game at Wilmslow several weeks earlier when he had probably got some chemical that the pitch had been sprayed with into a cut—the doctor who treated him in what seemed to be a shed with a corrugated iron roof prescribed antibiotics which had no effect, so, taking it down from a high shelf, he gave him a bottle of thick yellow liquid which he said he had used to give miners when they got a knock down the pit. After a few days of applying this stuff the suppuration stopped and after a week the swelling had disappeared and he could run comfortably; the doctor was extremely pleased with this triumph of an old remedy over new-fangledness. As he finished the careful wrapping of his knee and started to put his socks on he heard Will talking about a girl he had been with recently, whom he called custard tits, and the things she had let him do to her which had concluded with him pleasuring her with a lemonade bottle.

The group he was with found this amusing and the joke seemed to be that she must have been—he could never remember the word that had been used, but it was something like loose or slack. Morant knew that he wasn't talking about Brid; it was customary to talk about women like this only if they were regarded as unattractive or contemptible in some other way. After circuit training and some tactical work outside they divided up for two games of sevens. Will was on the team opposing Morant's. It was usual to take these games light-heartedly, more as touch rugby, with no heavy tackling, but early on Morant took Will's legs away and tipped him over onto his face. It couldn't have hurt him but he could see that he was annoyed and the club captain, Martin, told him to steady on. Late in the game he got another chance, catching Will fractionally late as he released the ball, with a waist-high tackle that put him on his back with Morant on top of him. As Morant got up he was less than careful where he put his knees and feet and Will jumped up, grabbed him by the shirt and said you fucking idiot and drew his right fist back. Morant said go on then. After a few moments staring at each other Morant detached Will's grip on his shirt. Martin said come on lads this is stupid and eventually Will lowered his fist and said fucking mental-case and training finished for the evening. Many years later when he told Liz about this she suggested that his actions had perhaps not been motivated by purely honourable disgust at the other man's treatment of women, that perhaps in a way he had been expelling bad parts of himself by projecting them into someone else. He said did she mean that he would have liked to fuck a woman with a bottle and she said no, not that, but the things that he hated in himself and felt bad about and wanted to get rid of, to disown. He said you mean things I felt guilty about, ashamed of, you mean shitty treatment of women. She said sort of, but it wasn't really just about women. He knew that he had always felt as if he'd done something wrong, something more than all the actual bad things he'd done, something he didn't know about, something that might be discovered and his essential wretchedness made public. He knew, although he happily accepted that valid authority was a social necessity, that he had a fear of authority. He could dress this in some respectability as a visceral suspicion of anyone who was comfortable making judgements, decisions about how others should think or behave, or as a loathing of what went with high standing, the assumptions and habits that the well-positioned so much enjoyed and cultivated, the relish that you controlled the game, were on the winning side, knew the answers, that you and people like you had a realistic take on things, that you should be listened to, that there really wasn't any other way of viewing matters. But it was more than this. Authority would see through him, perceive his lack of authenticity and identify the lies and concealments covering the fact that he was not as he should be. He could, whatever the case, remember how good it had felt to dump Will like that and to stare him down, to know and have others know that Will had backed off. A couple of days later Brid stopped him on a corridor and spoke to him for the first time since they had finished. She'd heard that he'd attacked Will. He should leave him alone. Will had problems. He wasn't like him. He was sensitive. Later Morant heard stories about both Brid and Will. A few years after leaving college someone said that they had heard that Brid was living on a barge in Amsterdam and the story developed that she was on heroin, but Morant thought it unlikely that Brid would allow herself to take drugs. A while later someone said she was dead but Morant thought that it was just that she was the kind of person who attracted stories like this. What, much later, he heard about Will was that, like Bobby Brown in the Zappa song, he had come out as gay and was living not in New York but in Sydney. He thought this was probably true.

When he was an older man he was struck by a remark in a justly famous book on the photograph. Roland Barthes said that he had seen a photograph of Napoleon's son and had been transfixed by Louis Bonaparte's eyes, seized by the astonishing idea that he was looking into eyes that had looked into the emperor's eyes, but that when he had told others of these sensations they had seemed uninterested in—perhaps bemused by—his excitement. Morant had always been gripped by the thought of the recently become past. He remembered his grandfather waiting on the corner of his street where it met the Caledonian Road, holding a large paper bag of cakes—he remembered these as cheesecakes, although, in a short, or it might have been puff pastry case, filled with almondy macaroon and topped with coconut strands, they were entirely unlike what today is called cheesecake. He stood ready to give them out to his grandchildren when they passed with their mothers as they went about their shopping or continued down the street to visit the old man's wife. Something in the cake caused a mild burning sensation to the back and left of Morant's skull, a reaction that was also triggered throughout his childhood by plum jam, although his parents dismissed his attempts to explain this experience as being all in his imagination. He had been told by one of his cousins that he, Morant, had been his grandfather's favourite because he was the first-born son of his only surviving daughter. He had never been aware that this might be the case, only remembering the tall old man's long coat, his white stubble and blue eyes that glittered, staring out of the depths of an unknowable interiority, an archive of purposes, ambitions, achievements and frustrations, of passions, career and family struggles that had never, as is the way, been fathomed by his many sons and one daughter, so that grandchildren, some of them, are left to feel that they might know this person, might come to understand how he saw the world and how it saw him, if only they had a little more information. Morant remembered that he greeted his grandchildren with what was more a grin, an eager grimace, than a smile, an impression caused perhaps because his cheeks had hollowed as cancer wrung the life out of him, a grin that was hungry and desperate—he thought of a dog starved of water. It seemed as if he sought, this stern Edwardian patriarch, this formidable businessman who had been a chief buyer at Covent Garden in his twenties and by his thirties the owner of one of the first motorised haulage businesses in London, a landlord owning houses across London, Bedfordshire and Kent, this parent who had bribed police to take no action against his violent and miscreant oldest son, the neighbour who was petitioned regularly by poorer members of his community, the husband who was married to an illiterate Irish woman who refused to move out of the working class area in which they lived, thus retarding the family's progression to the middle classes by a generation, a woman who, it was said, after his death had everything he owned sold, the lorries, the houses, everything except the jewellery, and, surely implausibly, the money kept under her bed on suspicion of banks, it seemed as if this dying old man sought something, some sustenance, perhaps—this might be too sentimental a thought—something that he had overlooked, in his grandchildren, their smooth, unblemished faces, their wary, inquisitive gazes. It was in photographs that Morant felt most keenly the pull of that past. Going through two shoe-boxes of letters and photographs that he had brought home from his mother's house after her death he came across pictures of his family, his mother on the beach at Clacton with his brother's son and daughter, older ones of family outings to what might have been Dunstable Downs, showing his uncles and aunts as young parents and his cousins as children and teenagers, a picture of his brother and him, aged perhaps five and seven, sitting on the bumper of an Austin Seven with, in frame on the left of the picture, the front end of a large army tent, one of two that his uncles Ted and Sam had brought back from demob, to be pitched every summer on a campsite at Shoeburyness, and, to Morant's left kneeling and wearing a woollen swimsuit, a girl who had told his mother that she loved Morant and who pestered him throughout the two weeks he was there; there were shots of a children's coronation party, boys and girls seated at long tables, some wearing paper hats, most not looking at the camera—he, Morant, was, sitting next to his brother who looked bemused, uncomfortable—whilst mothers, all wearing coats and many with hats, stood behind them and they seemed to Morant to be ill at ease, wary, unsmiling, as if not sure of their role, and photographs, taken decades later, of his mother and step-father at Stourhead and Sherborne with his uncles Sam and Dan and their wives Nelly and Doffy, posing against the backdrop of the swooping, lush contours of the Dorset landscapes, looking happy, pleased to be visiting such places, an emptily democratised, twentieth century version of those eighteenth century paintings of landowners and wives in front of their manicured estates, all retired, except Al, his stepfather, all, except his mother, to be dead within ten years. There were pictures of his mother and his father and their brothers and sisters as children, in one his youngest uncle Terry, aged about nine, looking out cheekily from behind a deck chair in which

Morant's grandfather was sitting, in a garden, probably at their bungalow near Tenterden, smiling, almost laughing, in contradiction of his reputation for being a stern parent to his sons. Looking at these photographs, Morant was stirred occasionally by curiosity. In the photograph of his father with some of his army friends on Gibraltar, what had just been said, what had occurred, that they should, all five of them, have had slight, amused smiles as the picture was taken. There was a tantalising sense of being close to, at the edge of, an intimacy, a fold in his father's life that he could almost open up, suggesting a dimension, a way of being in the world that his father had lived and of which he, necessarily, had not known, but which seemed almost within reach. There was a series of very small photographs taken in the garden in Kent. Morant guessed that these were taken shortly after the house and its grounds had been bought, in the thirties perhaps, the family invited down to inspect the property. The garden was overgrown and the building in the background of a couple of the photographs was little more than a prefabricated shed. In later pictures it had been replaced by a much larger structure which still, however, had the look of a temporary summer home. In some of the images Morant's uncles, powerful besuited young men, looking, several of them, like prizefighters on a night out, stood, apparently well pleased, next to their father, their mother or with one of their wives. In one, Morant's uncle Alfred, the second oldest son, is leaning his right hand on a trellis arch, his wife, unsmiling, the beautiful Queenie, dressed in a trouser suit and as elegant as Katherine Hepburn. Alfred, a huge, guileless man, drove a potato lorry out of St Pancras and had been made to box in the army, but refused to continue in his only fight after he had knocked his opponent down, dismayed that he had caused hurt and humiliation to another person. After his death from misdiagnosed hepatitis, Queenie seemed slowly to go mad. In another photograph Morant's mother's older sister, Millie—who died of tuberculosis when she was thirty; in the picture she appears to be in her early twenties—is playing at wheelbarrows, in what must be the garden in Kent, laughing, her feet held by a young woman whose face cannot be made out, but who one guesses is in her teens, whilst Morant's mother, on the verge of adolescence, kneeling in the grass, dressed in a puffed and layered frock, her hair cut in a strikingly chic bob, looks on. Her hands are behind her back and somehow this suggests fearfulness, concern for her sister, as if she has to hold her hands back in order to stop herself from going to her support, although Millie is in no danger. The thought occurred, perhaps a ridiculous one, that this, as it seemed, solicitousness, might indicate an apprehension of a frailty in this robust young woman, whom he knew his mother loved. He wondered what left his mother's life with Millie's death. Morant also felt a simple pathos, a sadness at the passing of those moments, those lives that had borne such an intolerable burden of hope and desire, some of them blighted by mental illness, all of them firmly bound by the shackles of their time's morality, by class, by the merciless grip of their family's law, by an understanding, which no longer exists, of the way the world is and must be ordered. Although he knew that some of them had had lives that might be judged as fulfilling, he could not help feeling that they could have had more, that in the end all of them, nearly all of them, had been defeated, their passions frustrated. There were one or two of his aunts who he could be fairly certain had had a happy life, Nelly and Doffy, for example, kind and gentle women who had been tested in different ways during their marriages but had always seemed pleased with their lives, their children. Shortly after sorting through the shoe box

Morant dreamt that he met Doffy, smiling and full of life, as she was when Morant was a child, on a corridor and about to enter a room; she had said that she was sorry to hear about his mother and that she was just starting a new job. It was the happiness in these photographs that touched him most, the mischievous play between father and his youngest son in a 1930s Kentish garden, the beaming pleasure at the good day out, the smiles of his mother and her friend Cissie, young women, on the front at, it seemed, Brighton, apparently caught at an unguarded, unposed moment, his mother more uncomplicatedly enjoying herself than he could remember in life. As a boy Morant occasionally accompanied Terry on his trips to houses to remove old furniture and other items that he would take back to his shop, a lock-up at the Caledonian Road end of the street in which his mother, Morant's grandmother, still lived. Morant twice went to Barnet fair with Terry, spending his time at the livestock auction whilst, as far as he could remember, his uncle bartered for second-hand furniture. Terry became friends with Morant's father— two youngest sons—and later in life underwent electroconvulsive treatment for depression; he died in Australia shortly after emigrating there with his wife, Dolly, and three children, whether from cancer or heart failure Morant did not know. He had found amongst the photographs an airmail letter which Terry had sent to Morant's mother, which contained a poem Terry, clearly aware he was dying, addressed to his sister. In it he wrote that throughout his life he had always known that she had been the one person who had really loved and cared for him, the one person who had never deserted him. Morant knew that the dying generations made their bequeathments; as well as the wounds and impairments, the confusions, anger and inconsolable griefs, the unanswerable needs that families produce, they might pass on, along with some wealth, the benefits of a safe and loving upbringing, but what happened to their joy, to the all too quenchable vitality that he thought he glimpsed here and there in these images? He wanted to believe that a relish for life, a convulsive energy of desire, and love itself, were passed thrumming down the years, that that glimpsed uncompromising, insistent and undisguised seizure of life was not lost, that it too seeded itself in the future, but, looking at these photographs it seemed to him that very little of human energy and production survived from one generation to another except the pain and confusion, which assuredly did survive. Perhaps he had been looking at these images for too long; perhaps in the end they always told us, as Barthes seemed to believe, about death, about finality. There were several photographs of a street party, in one a thronged sunlit street, adults and children at what, if one could have seen past the chairs, the table cloths, the seated and standing people, must have been trestle tables, all down the road people standing on the steps of their formidable terraced Victorian houses and some leaning out of windows, bunting and flags—none of them the union flag, it seemed—on lines stretching between houses on the street, bunches of balloons hanging outside windows. This, he knew, because his mother had told him, was in celebration of a significant anniversary in the reign of the old king, as she always referred to George V. Perhaps it took place in May 1930, on the twentieth anniversary of his reign. In one photograph a man sits at a piano outside a house, his back to the photographer. To his right a group of people have arranged themselves by the piano and on the steps of the house to have their picture taken. They stare at the camera, the only person properly smiling, indeed laughing, his grandmother, next to the piano player, and beside her, a young, faintly smiling woman in a hat who may have been

Morant's aunt, Grace, who, for the first twelve years of Morant's life, with her husband, Stan and her two boys, shared a house with Morant and his family. Close to the camera on the left, partially in the frame—Morant had not noticed this at first as it was slightly out of focus—a man and a woman are hugging each other. Morant hoped they were lovers. Just behind them stands his uncle Alfred, young, with the large nose and high cheekbones of the males of his family and his hair centre-parted, looking down the street to his left. Morant remembered a story of Alfred taking the full weight of a piano that was being moved from upstairs in his parents' house to the ground floor. At times he felt that he had seen this happening and that it had taken place at one of the family Christmas parties that used to be held each year. A huge megaphone protrudes from behind Alfred's head, a hand holding its rim. To the left of the picture a young man wearing a flat cap stands staring across the street, holding a cigarette in his right hand, the trousers of his suit pulled up close to his chest. He and Alfred look, no doubt in an accident of the photographic moment, as if they are guarding the group at the piano. Another image is a posed group photograph outside two houses, the women sitting on the kerb, one or two of them in the road itself, Morant's grandmother, at this stage quite a vast figure, sits in the centre, and the men stand behind them. The shot is taken too far away to make out all the faces, but his grandfather, wearing a broad flat cap, stands on the left of the picture, hand on hip, and on the right, a man and woman who may be Stan and Grace. There are no children in this picture or even young adults, apart from the young couple. Morant assumed that the children and their parents would have been feasting at the tables further down the road, whilst Stan and Grace had not yet had a child. To the left three middle-aged women stand, one presenting her broad back to the photographer, talking intently, oblivious of the commemorative moment taking place to one side of them. Morant had doubts about the placing in time of these scenes— Stan and Grace looked too old and, oddly, Alfred too young— but the dress and grooming of the people in these photographs was closer in style to the first decade after the great war rather than the second. Morant was affected by these scenes in several ways. This was a street he had known well; he had slept frequently in his grandparents' narrow house at one end of it; he had played in it as a child and he was conscious of many of its inhabitants as part of the world that his family had admitted him to. It was a world that was physically more intact than the one he had known, since this street and the streets around were to have houses destroyed by German bombs just a few years later and then visited with more comprehensive devastation by the urgent, blind drive of post-war development. Now, he looked at these pictures and saw a world that had been utterly erased. It was not just that he knew that the houses on the street had been demolished. This vibrant communality, these men in their suits, caps and trilbies, some relaxing into the informality of waistcoat and white shirt, always a white shirt, the women in vast overalls, pinafores and smocks as they served at the tables, a few younger women dressed fashionably in small hats and, it seemed, always wearing coats, a young boy in long shorts darting from his chair because he appeared to have seen something irresistible happening further down the street, the woman wearing a red indian head-dress, the intensely inhabited frivolity played out against the backdrop of the handsome, two-story Victorian houses, so solid, so anchored, all this confident festivity, this vivacious energy, all this gone, effaced, devoured, as it has been put, by the future. He had partly known this world or its remains, had known people whose younger selves had daily walked cacophonous thoroughfares populated by street singers and beggars, German bands, street-criers, and the music of barrel-organs, who remembered hansom cabs and tottering, open-decked omnibuses drawn by horses, negotiating the swirling traffic of roads strewn with horse shit, quagmires in winter and dust bowls in summer, who had seen motor vehicles replace horses, for whom a black person was a curiosity and Chinese people a worrying presence, for whom suffragette activism had been fascinating, scandalous, perhaps exciting, people who worked in now vanished professions, as staymakers, draymen, saddlers, cabinet-makers, a world of knife-grinders, rag and bone men, pawn shops, people who knew that British was best and that they lived in—it was still just about possible to believe—the mightiest nation on earth, people for whom a farthing was useful currency, who had been used, in their families and along their streets, to deaths from typhoid fever and tuberculosis, to children dying from measles, whooping cough, diphtheria and scarlet fever, for whom it was not unusual that people should die in their forties and fifties, who had never been further north than Barnet, who saw and pitied images of the Jarrow march and feared that they too might fall into the destitution that lived close, who went every week to picture palaces, some of them enthusiastic followers of by now half-forgotten film and music hall stars, people who swarmed across the Epsom Downs for the Derby, had charabanc outings to the seaside, paid money into Christmas savings clubs, who had fish on Fridays, shopped at markets, the Co-op, Home and Colonial stores and the fruit and vegetable stalls at the ends of their streets, who bartered food, dubiously acquired goods and favours in pubs, ate scallops, eels and crab, and drank ales from long disappeared breweries, who were shamed by adultery and divorce, people who celebrated hugely and judged harshly, people who were, it seemed to him, at ease in crowds, confident, settled, unwary people. And then this convulsive, teeming multitude and the moralities, institutions, pleasures and knowledges by means of which they had seized the world and, as it were, built it to last, had faded and disappeared with a horrible suddenness. When he looked at these photographs, whenever he looked at photographs from that period, it seemed that for all that these people, in their faces and bodies, bore the signs of anxiety and disappointment that humanity inherits, it was as if they had inhabited, had claimed their places with conviction in a world that must have presented itself as ordered for their intentions, a world in which the chaos of history had been stilled. No modern photography could find and record what Morant saw here, the massive presence, the plantedness, ownership, fiefdom, a now unimaginable hold on being. And there was something disturbing about the family images. He was unsettled by an almost obscene wildness in his grandmother's laughing face, by moments when he thought he saw—in the features of a face, in a way of standing or holding a glass—something of himself, something unwilled but irresistibly given. These pictures told him nothing about himself except that he stood in a lineage of people, now dead, and that he would be dead. He could see evidence of a brute genetic inheritance and nothing else.

As a boy his family had lived on the top two floors of a Victorian house on a wide street that joined the Caledonian Road and Liverpool Road. Later in life he would be pleased that his childhood should have been linked to, had linked, two northern regions and that where he had been set down gave witness to London's immemorially mongrel character.

Where he lived no one owned their own house; no one was prosperous but he could not remember many extremely poor people, although you occasionally heard adults talking about children who couldn't go to school because they had no shoes or about men who drank a family's money away. When he went to school there were also children who wore clothes that looked old and sometimes dirty. As working class people would always say when later they looked back to their early lives, everyone knew everyone else. He had sixteen cousins living within a few streets of his house and another one a mile further up the Caledonian Road in the direction of Holloway. Without knowing it in any self-conscious sense he felt safe as a child. For a while he had everything he needed in these streets. His mother would not allow him or his brother go to the large primary school that his cousins attended because it was too far away, about half a mile, and too big. He and his brother attended a Church of England school just two blocks away on a road that no longer exists. This school had been damaged by a bomb during the war—he had a memory that it had lost an upper floor—and had gas lighting. Here he queued for malt each day, a school nurse taking children's spoons and filling them from a huge tin; Morant used to give his place away to a pretty little Scottish girl whose class always arrived after his. Here he longed to play the drums or castanets during music lessons but was always given the triangle and here he sped through the Beacon readers by means of which the school's children did or did not learn to read. Here he developed a slightly sore swelling on the top joint of his middle finger on his right hand where the nibs of the pens they used to write with dug in. He learnt about Joseph and his coat of many colours, the prodigal son, Daniel in the lion's den and felt sorry for Saul and was always ill at ease with David who seemed spoilt and treacherous. He was fascinated by Elijah who did astonishing things and he developed a filial love for this angry, severe figure, but also welcomed Elisha's greater calm and kindness, seeing in him something of himself. He didn't find out about the baldness though, the taunts, the bears and the children until he was older. Mr Nevis used to call children to his desk to mark their work or to hear them read and often it was a chubby, smiling girl called Barbara, whose bottom he would pat and stroke as he spoke to her. Mr Nevis showed them a book with pictures of Africans in bright clothes and he explained that these people had no sense of which colours would go with which. They wore yellow with red. They had no idea. Once a year in May they would go to the front of the school and watch as the union flag was raised for Empire Day. Morant had no recollection of particular activities or celebrations connected with this event. The school's head, perhaps her name was Miss Day, a severe-looking woman who wore tweed suits, the caricature image of an early twentieth century lesbian, had suggested to his parents that he sit a scholarship examination for Westminster school. For once he could look back with gratitude to his mother's excessive protectiveness. His father was interested but his mother said it was too far for him to go. He had found this headmistress forbidding until he realised that she had a particular fondness for him. He became aware that he had been shaped by her recognition. The qualities she had seen in him had been stirred into a becoming by her regard and he was grateful to this woman whose understanding of learning, of education, put to shame the technocratic heads he dealt with in later life. He had recently forgotten her name, something that pained him. This separation from his cousins by school was one of several things that made him feel apart, a little uncomfortably different, during his upbringing, others being the fact that his surname was different from his cousins since their fathers were his mother's brothers, and the realisation that his parents were the only ones in his street who voted conservative. There was also the difficulty about being clever at school, a problem that he overcame by excelling at sport and by making it apparent that he was one of the best fighters amongst the boys that he knew. In fact he had few fights as a boy, although he remembered with shame an occasion when he had been playing football in the street and another boy had called him a name and wouldn't back down when Morant confronted him. The other boys said that they should have a fight to settle matters and he agreed. The boy was thin, had bright red hair, slightly bulging eyes and a receding chin. Morant was divided between a distaste at going through with a fight that he knew he would win and a desire to impress the other boys. His memory, which he hoped was not false, was that he felt no urge to inflict violence, to satisfy a blood lust. The group moved into a nearby playground surrounded by high wire-mesh fencing. He knew that this boy's bravado was an emptiness, that he would not be able to protect himself, that he would not be able to defend himself against his, Morant's, blows. The fight ended almost immediately when he hit the boy once and blood poured from his nose. He remembered a flood of self-disgust. Except for one period in his life he always tried to avoid fighting and it was here that he learnt that it should be most carefully avoided when you were certain you'd be victorious. Where he lived every other street had at least one bomb-site, a debris as they were called, which provided playgrounds for children on which they could look for repellent but fascinating aquatic life in cratered and flooded basements, could whizz shards of asbestos at each other or peer into bomb shelters which stank of urine and always seemed to have old mattresses in them. Country childhoods are sometimes described as idyllic and in later years he realised that that was precisely what his city upbringing had been. There were what they called seasons, periods of obsession with particular pursuits—racing on carts made from bits of plank, wooden crates and pram wheels, marbles, various games involving the flicking of picture cards, now forgotten games like five stones or cobs, and playing with bows and arrows made from cane and string, an activity he somehow contrived to participate in despite his parents forbidding it as it could put your eye out, one of many things that could put your eye out. In memory he could tick off every cliché of a working-class childhood, from conkers to street games like Queeny-Eye-Eye, He, Kingey, Jimmy Knacker, hopscotch and a game where you balanced a stick on the edge of a kerb, hit it with a larger stick so that it flew up in the air and then hit it in flight as far away as possible, but as to what ensued he could not recall. All winter they played football and in the summer it was cricket with a wicket chalked on a wall and one day a young black man watched them, charmed it seemed by an activity that took him back to his far away life and perhaps childhood, and who showed them the difference in grip and finger and wrist movement between an off-break and a leg-break. He hoped that young man had had a good and fulfilling life in the cold and suspicious country he had come to. One grey day, as their mother prepared the evening meal in the back room that served as kitchen and dining room, he and his brother were playing under and around the kitchen table with toy cowboy and indian figures, or perhaps it was farmyard animals and farm workers, moving them according to shared intentions and significances that absorbed them completely, except that they—or perhaps it was just he, Morant—were all the time aware of their mother, her movements, the chinking and clattering sounds she made as she worked at the sink and stove; and then his father came in and Morant resented his intrusion, his breaking of that spell, that humming, spinning world. At night he and his brother used to look out of their bedroom at the back of the house and over the single storey houses behind to watch the trains go past, hoping that they would witness the thickly billowing smoke lit up, effulgent, from the fires of the train's engine. On other nights they would use tin can telephones to talk to John Rawson next door, the tightly drawn string magically abolishing the boundaries of bricks and mortar and parental sanction. On these nights the world seemed to beckon, to offer itself, the darkness an ocean promising to bear him to realms that were as yet formless, but which would be strange and thrilling, to places that—not now in this moment, from this safe room, but later—he would explore. He had only to smell summer rain on pavements to be transported back to those times: the newly tarmacked and pebbled roads; Wally West's corner shop with the iridescent dead bluebottles in the windows; he and other boys shaping to piss into the gutter in competition to see who could get their urine furthest across the road; the square, a small park, really a large garden at the centre of a square of Victorian houses, where children played on swings and slides and, in wet weather, clawed and dug clay from The Hill, a grassed mound, to make guns; the general store at the top of the road where he bought his first plants—some small marigolds which his uncle Stan gave him space to plant in the tiny back garden, actually a yard with a bomb shelter and roughly surfaced paving stones, with a narrow border for flowers on one side and at the top. This home, this enclosing world that was gradually, imperceptibly falling away. One day he tripped on the pavement as he walked down the road and instead of slapping his other foot down to stop himself from falling, he broke into a little run, just a few recovering steps.

He noted immediately that he had never done this before, that he had done something that adults did. He felt neither pleasure nor sadness at this recognition. Sometimes he and his brother would try to stay awake all night, convinced that in doing this something would be disclosed, that something so far withheld would appear. One night, his brother asleep quite soon, he managed to stay awake until dawn, until he saw cold, insentient light washing over houses and the sounds of human stirring and he felt that he had seen something terrible and pitiable. The revelation, it seemed to him later, was of the arbitrariness and frailty of the ways in which human beings organised time and imposed it upon themselves, but then, at that time, the growing sound of brutal morning traffic seemed to him a horrifying violence, something being torn apart and clumsily stitched together, an enormous—it seemed to him, desperate—effort involved in heaving an implacable, mad order into place, in keeping it in place, so that he felt sad and wished to return to the protection and comfort of the established regularity he had sought to defy. There were stone fights between different streets and one day there was a stand-off between the boys from Morant's street and boys from Thornhill Road way and a boy called Terry, shouting come on everyone let's charge them, suddenly ran ten yards or so at the other faction before realising that no one had followed him. Morant, not involved in this skirmish, had watched the episode from the steps of his house, knowing that Terry, an excitable and blustering individual who was given to tearfulness and who was now stranded in no-man's land and being pelted with stones, would not be supported because he was not the sort of boy that others would follow. Above all, there were run-outs when one group would be given a couple of minutes to scatter to the more remote corners of their neighbourhood before the other group sought to catch them, the game only ending when the last man had been captured. In this way they came to know their streets and their place within those streets, to know how vast the world was and what pleasures it offered in the way of becoming lost and being found, of becoming unknown and new. Later there were more purposeful explorations and one day, walking east with a friend, he came to a road as busy as the Cally but which, astonishingly, had another name. Not everyone had a Cally. His family lived three doors up from a disused church on the corner of his road and a side road. The church, which was now used as a factory, had steep steps on either side of its frontage but only the ones nearest his house were used for the factory's business and one day he and two other boys were sitting at the top of the far steps dropping cap bombs over the side onto the pavement. Caps came in thin strips which contained, arranged at equal intervals along their length, tiny amounts of powder which would detonate loudly when struck, emitting smoke and a pleasingly military smell. Usually caps were fitted into toy pistols but on this day Morant and his friends were inserting them into the heads of small cast-iron bombs the size of a man's thumb. They began by placing single caps into the devices but then experimented with loading two or more caps at a time to see if this would increase the size and sound of the explosion. The results were disappointing until one of his friends put four caps into the bomb and produced a much more impressive effect. That, his friend said, had been an American bomb. Morant was instantly annoyed. He did not see why America was always deferred to in this way, why English people seemed so happy to accept their inferiority to America and its achievements. He, this boy who was a devout lover of the Wild West and an eager consumer of American comic books, used to be irritated when he heard uncles or friends of his parents talking about emigrating to America or when populations swooned over the latest American singer. He hated the way that their boxers used to regularly defeat British fighters and had cried when he and his father listened on the radio to Marciano brutally beating up Don Cockell. Inside him there was a little English patriot who had a vague sense of past glories and faded triumphs and, encouraged by his father, for a time in early childhood he was excited by Britain's military achievements across its disappearing empire. The first disturbance of this simple jingoism came in his first year at grammar school when his English teacher, one of the few teachers he found interesting at school, started a debate about the Suez invasion and it became plain that Mr Redpath was not sympathetic to the venture. Morant told his teacher that his father had said that Hugh Gaitskell, the opposition Labour leader, should be shot for his criticism of the enterprise, for not supporting our troops in a time of war. Mr Redpath said something like your father thinks that, does he, and Morant immediately recognised this as a kind of condemnation of his father's views. But his irritation at America worship was fuelled more by what he saw as an acceptance from his friends and many of the adults who surrounded him that they lived in a second-rate country whose pleasures would have to be taken second-hand from somewhere else where lives were lived more urgently, excitingly, and were burnished with a glamour that was unavailable on their own grey and uninteresting island. It was here, he later saw, in resentment of American cultural imperialism, that the sixties began, but although he knew that something, some eruption of creativity and joy must happen he had no sense of what it would be like when it arrived, until, one New Year's Eve at his friend Brian's house, during an evening when Brian had told him what he already knew, that he was homosexual and, what he didn't know, that he met men in public toilets, the record player deposited a 45 disc onto the playing surface and a song, a sound, like no other he had ever heard, was played. It was a kind of blues but wasn't seeking to reproduce some preformed style; it was entirely and confidently of itself, and although it was about love it was pleasingly sinister and dangerous, a call to transgression and pleasure. He asked Brian what the track was called and his friend said Love Me Do. This was always, for Morant, where it began, the moment when he knew that the new thing was beginning. At that moment and through early adulthood it seemed to him that everything was about to change. The way things were, the accounts society gave of itself, seemed thin and unconvincing. All around him there was a blathering about what was important and true, a story about reality that was constantly contradicted by events, but with which people, it appeared to him, largely colluded. If you worked hard you would be rewarded; science was about to solve all our problems; we were progressing towards a more open and just society; the royal family was what made Britain great; the western democracies were the fully evolved form of government and their intentions benign; the British were a fair-minded and tolerant people; affluence was the goal of life; the class system was dying; consensus was good and dissent bad. He did not at first think this coming world in any detail but knew that it would entail the overthrow of authorities, that desire would be unleashed, that envy, fear and guilt would give way to an unbounded pleasure, that life would be organised and lived for fulfilment of one's being and not in thrall to poverty or out of fear of opinion. Once he left school one thing he knew precisely was that there had to be an end to work. He was appalled by people's readiness to entomb themselves in occupation that could have no meaning for them, that was apart from anything they might truly value and wish for, occupation that offered a provisional security, a barrier against destitution, in return for diligent acquiescence in routines and procedures which required the individual to deny, amputate or pervert all creative energy, all curiosity and playfulness. Once during the several years between leaving school and going to college he had witnessed something cruel. He had been working in a warehouse loading boxes containing packets of potato crisps. He and his co-worker, a young Scottish man, Alan, had little to do most of the time; occasionally a lorry would arrive and they would have half an hour's activity but this tended to occur at the start of the day and after lunch; the rest of the time there was nothing to do except scrunch up one of the giant packets to see how, in truth, so very few potatoes had gone into the making of the crisps. Morant had found a book lying around that explained the workings of the internal combustion engine and, because he felt he had neglected finding out about such matters, he spent a couple of days reading it and was eventually pleased that he did indeed now understand how such motors worked, although this knowledge did not stay with him for long. Alan had travelled around the far east and was getting money together to go to South America later in the year. One morning they were sitting outside the loading bay, Morant enjoying the sunshine and Alan reading a book, when one of the firm's regular workers, a man of about sixty wearing blue overalls, asked them why they weren't working and they explained that they had nothing to do, that they'd got everything ready for loading onto the lorries after lunch and that was it really. The man, who conveyed no threat because it was immediately obvious that he was an individual of no power or consequence in the organisation which employed him, suddenly became very angry and accused them of not knowing the meaning of work and said that the country was going down the drain because of people like them, students who didn't like work. Alan said that they weren't students. The man ignored this and said you could always find something to do. Alan had said what, like sweeping up. When the man was their age he was proud of doing a good job, of keeping busy. They didn't know the meaning of the word work. By way of an attempt at being friendly and to calm the man's evident upset, Morant asked him what he did and he said it was his job to clean the company's vehicles, the lorries, the company vans and cars and he never had a minute. It emerged that he was on his way to pick up a consignment of cigarettes, Benson and Hedges, from a wholesale tobacconist at the top of Pentonville Road, near the Angel. These were intended for the use of the company's directors. Morant tried to be friendly and asked him how long he'd been working here and the man said that he'd worked in this job, man and boy, for forty-three years. Alan put his head in his hands and said no, no, no, why, why. Morant had hated the way the old man looked, puzzled but much worse than puzzled; he clearly understood something of the judgement that had been made on his life. For a moment there was a shift, a collapse in the man's understanding of the world and his place in it. Whatever discountenanced meant, Morant saw it in this man and he wanted him quickly to retrieve his certainties. When Morant left school he had gone from job to job, working in factories and offices, on building sites and for local councils as an unskilled labourer. He had learnt how to stack pallets and window frames, insert some part, whose name and function he had forgotten, into a transistor radio, to file documents, place an order with a business in Sheffield or Leeds for a particular kind of steel, drive a dumper truck, dig a trench, lay pipes, use a pneumatic drill and a hydraulic jack, wheel gas cylinders on and off lorries, mix concrete, but never to adopt the appropriate telephone manner for use if a delivery was late to the factory. None of what he'd learnt stayed with him, apart from using a spade. He remembered two things clearly. One was his fellow workers' inventiveness in avoiding work. In offices they would find it necessary from time to time to leave their desks to make an inquiry in another part of the building and this would lead to extended discussions that had nothing to do with the original inquiry. He recalled a young man in a sales office, who turned out to be a weightlifter, who told him that he had a game in which he would leave the building and walk around the local area, sitting on a bench in a leafy square, browsing the local street market, buying a newspaper, to see how long he could be away from his desk—so far thirty-five minutes was his record. Morant recalled working for a water board as a student, and hours of leisure in the sunlight watching swallows skim the water of reservoirs whose fence posts he, as part of a gang, had been conveyed by lorry to repair; in a clothing factory workers would hide in the deep lofts of warehouses and some would even sleep there. At a more elevated level, he noticed, in an office of an international drugs company, that the chief buyer, the brother of a bishop, would take time to pray several times a day, during which period his secretary would protect him from intrusion; in the same office it was common for the other managers to return from a long lunch and sleep for the first hour of their afternoon, one of them snoring shamelessly. The other memory was of the baffling seriousness with which some employees took their work. This went beyond the palpable career ambition of the few or the even fewer who, creepily, seemed to have imported into their beings the values, goals and ethos of their employers, so that their identities, their interiorities, were furnished by, composed of, the threadbare tat and shoddy of whatever occupational imaginary they had landed in. They seemed really to care whether orders for the electric blankets, the chemicals or the garment interlinings they manufactured had been processed in time or whether others were pulling their weight or why two young men were sitting idly by a loading bay. In one buying office his boss, a middle-aged Yorkshireman called Billy Sorenson, had a manic commitment to securing steel at the best prices and with the speediest supply and would regularly hurl prodigious rage down the telephone at individuals whose companies had failed to make a delivery, often tearing the telephone from his bullied assistant Tommy Dobbins—a young, too carefully dressed mod who was coming to terms with the fact that he and his wife had recently had a child—in order to administer breathtaking anger and abuse. Some workers in the office referred to Billy and Tommy as Ratman and Dobbins. In truth, the reason that most workers cared a little and attempted to do their jobs reasonably dutifully was not even because they feared losing those jobs, but because otherwise they would have had to face the empty horror of what they were involved in—the manufacture and circulation of goods or the maintenance of utilities which only a very deluded person could feel a personal and emotional investment in; the trading off of their freedom, their creative energies, for a wage that might meet some of their already properly diminished dreams. Even Billy Sorensen's devotion to his firm's interests, Morant suspected, was only a performance, a role he had manufactured that got him through the days and which perhaps, cleverly, enabled him to release the pent rage he felt at the frustrations and denials he had accepted into his life; sometimes Morant would imagine what these might be—perhaps the severely inhibiting expectations of the parents he could not please and of whose love he had never been sure, the wife whom perhaps he had never loved, the son of whose success as a trader in the city he was proud but who nevertheless puzzled him and the daughter whose every sentiment seemed to amount to a critique of what he had made of himself; and perhaps the work he despised. Later, in the eighties, working as a teacher in a pit village in South Yorkshire Morant saw the consequences of unemployment, as a government and its heroised leader, in ecstatic thrall to an idea of freedom unleashed and unbound by a liberated capitalism, laid waste to the coal and other industries of the north and judged as a tolerable bargain, a manageable consequence, the impoverishment and immiseration of the towns, villages and cities in which hundreds of thousands of their fellow citizens lived. It would be too much to say that the ministers of this government anticipated the poverty, the blighted idleness, the newly meaningless communities, the collapse of social and moral structures, the ensuing criminality and drug abuse, the wreckage of individual and family life that went with the destruction of industries and unions, the subsequent decades of degradation and silted anomic drift. It would be too much because like all such people they lacked the necessary intelligence, were incapable of seeing beyond or around their own millenarian fantasies; like all those gripped by hot religion they were angry with history and too loftily impatient to reckon social consequence. In short, he thought, they were morally inept. But the whole vicious and squalid enterprise was, if such people were moved to justification, worthwhile if markets could be freed and people allowed to buy the houses they rented from their local councils. (In those mortifying years the country had been led by a cartoon figure, a humourless woman of limited but precisely focused understanding, a person of uncontained, ferocious conviction, who combined jingoism, a simple-minded conflation of freedom and capitalism and an authoritarianism that channelled an infantile sexual theatre of control and punishment. Broadsheet newspapers reported gossip about the sexual charge felt by her ministers in her presence—or indeed in her absence when their imaginations were unconstrained by the physical facts that she appeared no differently to many other conventionally groomed, middle-class and middle-aged women. Morant could see that the ex-public school boys who surrounded her in government and who had been boarded at schools where a matron's strictness stood in for the love of parents, would have harboured certain susceptibilities, but he could never quite see how this particular female caricature had found lodging in the wider sexual imaginary. The embarrassing fact was, though, that his country had been represented in those years by a figure which recirculated a stale, enfeebled English sexuality of glimpsed stocking tops and suspenders, male impotence and sadomasochism reduced to some sort of nursery naughtiness. It had been represented by characters from a Carry On film). This, it seemed to him, was how capitalism arranged matters. It offered you—in fact, prescribed, because nothing else was on the table—a lifetime of toil that drained the soul and sometimes the body in return for a measure of material comfort and security. Then, if it pleased, it would relieve you of the pointless toil, the meaninglessness, and return you to the meaningfulness of a life without the numbing distraction of work, a life for whose challenges it had, necessarily for its purposes, rendered you incapable of meeting. By the middle of the eighties Morant had to admit that everything he had hoped for and assumed would happen had not come to be.

On a November day in 2008 that had begun with a shopping trip to Sheffield, Liz looking for a dress for her daughter's wedding and Morant moving between Waterstones, video stores and wherever Liz happened to be at different times, a day that had taken in a brief visit to an exhibition of watercolour paintings whose distinctiveness lay in the fact that they did not look like watercolours, the paint applied thickly and insistently, at least in the pictures that Morant was interested in, without that lightness of touch that is usually deemed appropriate to the genius of the medium, and continued with lunch in the street, a pedestrian concourse that was staging what was called a continental food market, Liz eating an ostrich burger and Morant some teriyaki vegetable noodles. Afterwards Morant held Liz to the agreement that they would go into the Peak for a short walk. Liz was always suspicious that any visit to the hills with Morant would involve unpleasant exertion, but he held to his promise that the walk would be short, undemanding and would include opportunities for sitting down. They went no further than the lower reaches of the beautiful Derwent reservoir, just up from the Ladybower bridge, and walked on a path along and above the water. The air was utterly still and the hills on the other side of the reservoir, the russets, greens and what seemed to his slightly colour-blind eyes, the faded orange tones of the moors, trees and pastures, were reflected perfectly in its water, or, rather, not perfectly, because the land, the autumnal vegetation in the water, seemed even more bewitching than the real land above it. That November was mild, although the day was overcast and felt, although it did not in fact appear, misty. They walked over a little wooden bridge that had something to do with a small, brick water company building and back onto a higher path that returned them to where they had parked the car. He felt none of the anxiety that he had anticipated, the concern that Liz would not enter into the moment with him, not share it. He had wanted very much that she should feel the same way about this as he did. They sat on a bench that gave a view of the grassy slope beneath them, the colour-steeped lake and the sweep of land that led up to the high Derwent edge. A newly married couple and the best man and his girl, all of them in their twenties perhaps, the bride in a short white, recognisably wedding, dress, the men in suits and ties, arrived and walked down the bank ten or fifteen yards, to take pictures of the bride and groom, of the groom and best man, but not the other woman because her heels would not navigate the soft ground, so that she simply looked on, smiling in a very pleased way. The groom kissed the bride, the best man kissed her, and the groom, laughing, kissed the best man. Were these things the entire wedding celebration, these individuals the entirety of the wedding, or had they gone free on an impulse to visit this spot and memorialise the moment? Morant disliked weddings, not so much the actual ceremony as the dressing up, the tedious conventions of speeches and toasts, the wildly optimistic expectations that people seemed to have concerning the future prospects of the couple. For some reason, however, he was touched by this little group and felt an impulse, which he hardly understood, to give them something, but he had nothing to hand. In any case he was hopeless at gestures of this sort. Liz found the young people amusing, but, thankfully, was not given to sentimentalising these matters. After a while Morant suggested that they should go and when they stood up they kissed and he held her tight, feeling her breasts against his body, stirred just as he had been when they first held each other forty years earlier. If they had stayed together they would have had three children, girls. It was in a way embarrassing that he had fallen in love with a beautiful woman, as if it were a mark of shallowness. But what he had found irresistible in her was her reckless independence, her confidence, her seizure of life. He knew that through all the transmutations most of which he had not been witness to—as she became a mother, as she gave up teaching and tried to make a career as an artist, as a poet, in both these endeavours producing work that, for all its formal limitations, was both disturbing and comforting, absolutely of itself and without calculation, during the long years when she trained as a psychotherapist, throughout the cancer that only friends and family knew about, as she became a grandmother—through all these years what marked her off from anyone else he knew, was something you could call strength, resolve, energy, but which he knew as health, a rightness in relation to life. It was this health, this being good at life, that decided her to hitch-hike across France on her own after Brid chose to stay on in Paris with a Polish boy she had met, taking her to nights on the sand dunes of south-west France and a meeting with— what she would never have described as—a bourgeois French family who invited her to stay with them in their rented house and who encouraged her to befriend their son who looked like Mick Jagger, perhaps hoping that this lovely, charmingly mannered young English girl with her delightfully bad French would liberate him from his shyness and his virginity. Later, Morant would think of this episode as Liz in an Eric Roehmer film. In their early days together he was often taken aback by her volcanic passions for music and poetry and her carelessness of study. She refused or could not see any obstacle that stood between her and what she wanted to do. When they first lived together, in a bedsit in Stoke-on-Trent, she said she was going to cook him a meal, a curry, and when he returned to their room later that day he found her furious because it hadn't worked out. She had put everything, cauliflower, lentils, tomatoes and spices, into a saucepan and boiled it to a mush. She had then no idea how institutions worked. She thought that schools were organised to set teachers free to do what was needed for children to learn and in her brief career as a teacher she was reprimanded for over-stimulating the children, for taking pupils out of the classroom without clearance to visit woods and markets, for not following accepted codes in writing reports, for not following prescribed disciplinary procedures and for lessons that encouraged exuberance and independence in pupils. She failed to see that the primary concern of schools is the government and shaping of behaviour and the instillation of docility and that if you wanted to work against those aims you had best do so by stealth, silently as far as possible, accepting one's alienation, one's position of exile from the environment inhabited, and by the exercise of a restless cunning in the endeavour of doing some good. Later, working in the NHS psychological services of an impoverished northern town she assumed that her department was set up to identify and develop the best and most appropriate treatments for the miseries patients suffered. Consequently, noticing that her job description licensed her to work towards the improvement of the department's practice, she organised discussion groups, training and supervisory sessions, arranged visits from leaders of national initiatives and sought to establish links between therapists and psychiatrists. She imagined that the process of self-critique and development involved in such activity would be welcomed by her superiors and entirely failed to see that the more it was applauded by rank and file practitioners the more it provoked unease amongst the senior management and some colleagues at her own level who saw her activity as a reproach to them and as a pitch for career advancement. The result was that the head of department, with the connivance of a couple of her favoured staff, conspired to have her suspended for not following due procedure in record-keeping. When Liz pointed out that what she had done—keeping patient records in her own filing cabinet and not in one of the centrally located ones— was common practice and that furthermore such accusations were difficult to take from a department that, as she had pointed out two months before, had stored unlocked files in a toilet area used by patients whilst redecoration of the secretaries' office was taking place, her fate was sealed. She was cleared without censure of any sort, but over the next three years two more charges against her were confected and two more suspensions ensued, with the final one achieving partial success for management. Morant had talked with Liz and planned strategies for the endless hearings she was required to attend throughout this period, increasingly involved as her husband became more ill. He knew that she had done nothing wrong and that she was being hounded by fearful and bitter people who envied her energy, knowledge, creativity, goodness and, it had to be said, were unsettled by her beauty. He knew that some of the attacks she had been subjected to by school authorities in her earlier career as a teacher had been in part justified by her prodigious neglect of protocols and administrative procedures, but he knew that she had no such culpability here, her only errors being an unbending dedication to her work and an utter naivety about the self-preservational brutality of management regimes. In their discussions she regularly accused him of cynicism when he told her, over those many months, that departments such as hers were primarily concerned with the appearance of efficiency and cost effectiveness, of identifying a system that would serve the governing rationality of, and prosper within, the regulatory environment it inhabited, and that it would be hostile to any initiative that introduced doubt or complication into its function. It had been claimed by a technocratic imagination and had no interest in thinking too hard about the appropriateness and efficacy of treatments, having committed to ones that could yield calculable, easily understood and, thus, publishable results. Hence six week turnarounds of patients through behavioural therapies and glancing contact with histories, narratives, contexts or dialogue—just a talking therapy that was all talk from the therapist and all listening from the patient, neatly and economically reversing the classical flow in these relationships. Liz saw that this was how things were run, but still found it hard to accept that such sealed regimentation was impermeable to reason and moral argument. Near the end she was dismayed by the revelation that the person she had been communicating with in human resources was clearly unsympathetic to her plight and she expressed astonishment when Morant said that this was unsurprising since human resource departments were put in place to make it easier for management to sack people. All these things took many conversations to say plainly. He wanted her to know the truth that her rightful anger obscured but he didn't want to shake her resolve; he wanted her to know her enemy and that although it would not be defeated she could emerge from this with honour and some sense that she had achieved something. One day near the end as he drove her home after a meeting with her union representative he told her that he thought the tribunal would have made its mind up already and that the outcome would be predetermined. He was about to say that she could, however, make matters difficult for her inquisitors—that although they would sack her she could wring concessions from them—when she started sobbing, the first time she had given in to tears throughout the extended and systematic cruelty to which she had been subjected. He pulled over and, for the first time in twenty years, held her, feeling her hair against his face, the warmth, the strength, even through the coat she was wearing, the scent of that so long desired body and knowing again—a flooding relief, a restitution— the completely remembered moment when she first opened towards him. She lost her case and even though she was advised by her union that if she took it to court she would win and receive substantial damages and compensation she was persuaded by Morant and others that it would be too much to put herself through another year or two of torture, especially when she was having to cope with her husband being so ill, so she agreed to take matters no further in return for compensation of £10,000 on condition that she did not make the settlement public. Characteristically, this was a decision that she soon regretted. Later that year Gerald, the man Morant could not bear to think about and for whom he could dredge up pity but no charity, this impostor, this, as he had decided, nondescript, colourless figure who had become a senior executive in an international breakfast food company (he gathered) and by whom his wife had born two children, died, and perhaps six months later Morant took his rightful place in Liz's bed, or rather she took her place in his bed since for him there could never be any question of sleeping in the bed she had shared for fifteen years with her husband, whose name had been, implausibly, ridiculously, Gerald. On this November day in north Derbyshire, cradled in a small world englobed by high mist, Morant still hoped that one day he and Elizabeth Carey would live together, even when that evening, spellbound as ever by her body, her mind, she said, once more, that this could not yet happen.

At college Morant had had an intense friendship with a P.E. student called John Guzman. Morant had never been best friends with anyone, but John had singled him out for this position. They were to be best friends. John was wild and, apparently, fearless. Much of the time he professed ignorance of the motivations underlying human behaviour or the reasons why people thought and felt as they did. He would ask Morant why some other students had adverse reactions to his more extreme behaviour, like drop-kicking lampshades in the common room, riding a bicycle through the refectory at lunchtime, or shooting crows with an air rifle and then telling people about it. He had once suggested to Morant that fat people should be imprisoned and starved until they reached a normal weight, this on the grounds that they were disgusting. Morant knew that all this was not entirely innocent behaviour but was done to test the limits of what people would find acceptable, what they would put up with and it was done to elicit, to produce for his scrutiny, defences of what he saw as unthinking, reflex conformity with respectable ideas; although it always seemed to Morant that, despite his contempt for anyone comfortably settled in a conventional morality, John was not primarily concerned with scandalising the bourgeoisie so much as trying to understand why such people were so content. He and Morant ran a college film society for a while and once, while they were watching Le Chien Andalou Morant had the thought that his friend was a bit like the main character in that film, except that John felt doubt. They did not last long as projectionists because they sometimes forgot to have a new reel of film ready at change-overs and if John became bored with the film he would experiment with seeing if it could be played at different speeds or he would try projecting a v-sign onto the screen or subliminal messages urging riot or copulation; on a couple of occasions, at Morant's suggestion, they played the reels in the wrong order to see if anyone noticed; a surprising number of the audiences didn't and of those who did, several, rather than being annoyed, were pleased to have spotted the discontinuity and were keen to let them know, as if in so doing they were joining John and Morant in some clandestine, unruly purpose. However, a lot of people were irritated by this behaviour. John's car was equipped with an engine designed for a bigger vehicle and set up for high performance in various ways that Morant had no interest in understanding, and he drove it at all times with incessant aggressiveness, an unrelenting commitment to speed and risk. Once he gave Morant and a girl student, Vicky Gray, a lift back to college just after his car had been subject to another upgrading of its performance, and on the A5, after some tight over-taking to test the car's acceleration, he made two circuits of a huge roundabout at unusual speed and, it seemed to Morant, sideways, in a controlled skid (or was it a slide), in order to test the car's road-holding and Vicky asked from the back if he always drove this fast. John said no, that he was running the new engine in and he couldn't go faster. Later Morant considered whether this was an irritable response to a disapproving question or perhaps a kind of boasting, aimed at him rather than Vicky, but he concluded that the truth was, partly, that John, intent on gauging his car's performance, simply didn't take in Vicky's terror. He had difficulty imagining other people's interiority, although he was aware that these depths existed. He seemed to be unsettled by the existence of so much inwardness, such a diversity and excess of it. He was doing a joint P.E. and English qualification and it seemed to Morant that he understood subjectivities on the page of a novel, where they were set out for him. Years later when Morant had lost contact with John, Morant asked Liz if he might have been a psychopath, but she said no because he was manifestly capable of feeling, although the sorrow or sadness he felt was probably rooted in his own sufferings—he felt mainly sorry for himself. However, Morant thought that perhaps all empathy began in consciousness of one's own sorrow, in pity for oneself. What was remarkable was that John's sympathies were engaged so capriciously, so haphazardly. One day, perhaps in the college bar, perhaps in Morant's car as he drove, John said that a girl in their English group had told him that her mother had had no interest in her and had doted on her older brother and that as a consequence she had never had any confidence, had always doubted her abilities, never believed that anyone would like or value her. He had never spoken to the girl before and this had come out during a journey when he had been taking the girl and John's girlfriend, Anya, to the digs they were to live in during a teaching placement. Morant found it difficult to engage with this girl's plight because, in so far as he had considered her at all, he had found her a bitter person and somehow sly. John asked why people treated others in this way, why such cruelty existed and he started to cry, so much so that Morant had to pull over and park the car or it may have been that they weren't in the car when this happened but drinking in the college bar so that Morant had to take his friend out of the bar and they sat and talked on a low wall some distance from the college building. John was inconsolable, unreachable. Nothing, he said, mattered; everything was meaningless. Sobbing constantly, he asked what hope there was, what could be done about all this shit, this pain, who there was who was doing anything about it, how there was going to be any change. Morant remembered a sociology of education seminar where the group discussed some recent reading about class inequalities in education and the system's failure in relation to working-class children and John had looked appalled as if this was a fact he had never encountered before and he asked the tutor who was doing anything about this. It was all right being presented in session after session with these analyses of what was wrong, but why weren't they being told what to do about it. Morant's recollection was that the tutor said something along the lines that research of the sort they were considering could be polemical but that organising political action wasn't the responsibility of academics. However, the group could discuss implications for their practice as teachers and for educational policy. John would have none of this and said that if all this stuff was true then it was pathetic, a load of students who had no power discussing what they were going to do about it on teaching practice and that academics should be shouting about it from the rooftops. Looking back Morant was surprised on two counts: one was that this had been a time when some academics were emphatically vocal about the kinds of change required to bring about just social change, a time when the conclusions and recommendations of educational research that urged social change influenced government policy, but he could recollect nothing of this in the tutor's response to John; and then his memory was that he, Morant, had himself seemed to accept this separation of learning, of knowledge, and political engagement—he couldn't recall arguing alongside John and this puzzled him. Perhaps it was that his new fascination with scholarship, the pleasure and satisfaction he was deriving from his encounters with theory, held him back from standing alongside his friend. He half remembered thinking at the time that John didn't understand how academic inquiry worked, where it fitted in with the making of social policy. He knew that contrary ideas sit comfortably in most heads and it seemed that at this point, perhaps just at this point in this room, he, Morant, believed both that academic research had an allotted and useful place in the government of things and also that it was complacent about the influence it exerted on decision-making. It would not be long before he would come to the same judgement as John. But he thought what also stopped him from supporting his friend was that there was something shockingly personal about John's anger, that it was not at all a plea for political engagement but rather a cry of rage against a wanton, derelict authority, a bereft howling for something that had not been given in his life. Morant knew that John hated and loved his mother. He knew that his older brother was considered a failure by his family and that, as John told it, he had been bullied at school because, like the rest of the family, he spoke posh, with the consequence that when John went to the same school and a group of boys had approached him to find out if he was as ripe for victimhood as his brother, John had fought the group's leader and won, so that he was left alone thereafter to speak English as he wished and to become, something that was perhaps related to his physical prowess, very popular with girls at the school. Morant had met John's mother and father a few times on visits to his house in the south-western borders of London. He remembered that the first thing Mrs Guzman had said to him was and what do you intend to do with your life, David, and when he had said that he'd try teaching for a bit and see how it went, she said that she couldn't see him working in a school for long. During these visits he observed that she often made slightly unsettling observations of this sort, offering summary judgement on what people said, what they had done, that seemed to be based on too little in the way of evidence or reflection. Later in that first visit she had said to him so do you have a girlfriend, David, and when he said that he was married but separated she had said, yes, that would suit you much better. John appeared to be at ease with his mother, not intimidated by her, confidently challenging her at times, but generally in accord with her views and plans. It was apparent that she had many plans—a residential week she was organising for children at the private school at which she taught, a placement she was hoping to arrange for her older son in a friend's business, planning a concert for some sort of charity, a visit to a retired and invalided colleague in Wales, a holiday she was organising for the family, staying with her husband's relatives in Spain (she hoped John and his girlfriend would join them on this excursion). John's father was a quiet man who was a master craftsman of some sort involving, as far as Morant could recall, plastering and renovation. He did the cooking while Morant was there and Morant, because it was something that interested him, watched, asking questions as Mr Guzman prepared Spanish dishes with devout precision, strictly submitting himself to simple but clearly inviolable procedures which—this thought occurred to Morant—returned him to an earlier, hospitable place and time that offered welcome anchorage in a troubling world. At the first meal he ate at the house—beef chunks and peppers in a tomato sauce with fried potatoes—John's older brother, Francis, visiting unexpectedly, had disagreed with his mother about something to do with where he was living, a brief argument that was, it seemed to Morant, heavy with subdued feeling, and then John had said he might jack in college and when his mother asked why he had said because it's shit, it's all shit. His father had become tearful and said problems, problems, why does it always have to be problems. Afterwards, as he walked with Morant to the railway station,

John apologised for his mother, saying she was a wicked cow. This was a friendship different to any other Morant had had or would have in his life. It wasn't based on shared confidences, jokes or ideas or politics, nor on interests or enthusiasms that they had in common. There were aspects of John's thinking and behaviour that he was uneasy with—his contempt for so many people on the basis of rules that never became very clear to Morant. It was obvious that he was capable of visceral loathing of people because of their appearance, the way they spoke, hopes and ambitions that they might express, the way they presented themselves in seminars—too quiet, too eager to please, too pleased with themselves, too given to making extensive notes. He was obviously acutely sensitive to and suspicious of the ways in which people dressed and how they offered themselves in conversation and social exchange. He seemed to detect the artifices of selfhood and perhaps to despise the fear and weakness, the pathetic desire to be known, that drive and fuel those contrivances. In others this might have produced pity or sympathy; in John it produced, at times, a physical disgust. It was the rules of exclusion and acceptance that Morant failed fully to understand. Some who might have been predicted to be beyond tolerance were approved and others, who seemed to Morant amiable enough, were subject to a kind of loathing. John did not like Morant's more obviously counter-cultural friends, although, presumably in deference to Morant, they were never openly condemned. John, it occurred to Morant, knew that their unconventional dress, their aloofness and studied difference, were aspects of a critique of the way the world was run, but he was perhaps unable to get past the self-advertisement involved, perhaps felt that they were more in love with the idea of dissent and revolution than actively seeking to bring it about. But it was more than this. Morant imagined it like this: that John was repulsed by the subordination of the body to secret dreams, cabalistic scheming, by desire too long held in and gone foetid; these hippies wore too much, were too covered up, didn't get enough exercise and looked unhealthy. But he also disliked Liz. It seemed that exuberance could go too far, especially perhaps in a woman, and Liz's vitality irked him, although Morant never knew if it was this or perhaps that her looks were not sufficiently understated. Perhaps he blamed her as the cause of Morant deserting his wife and child. John's girlfriend, Anya, was the other beautiful girl on the campus, fair-haired with the small, perfect features of certain Scandinavian actresses who appeared in English and American films at the time. She dressed with rigorous, restrained stylishness and offered a calm, composed self to the world that seemed to Morant to involve some tight policing, too much calming. And yet, at the end of his first term at college, before he knew John, he had ended up with her at a Christmas dance and found her warm, open. He couldn't remember if they'd kissed, nor did he know why he hadn't tried to pick up with her when they returned to college the following year, except, of course, that he had been in the midst of his obsession with Brid. Years later, Morant wondered what it was in him that John saw, that caused him to elect him as closest friend. For his own part, Morant was, as he always had been and always would be, drawn to a certain kind of recklessness. John's was not chaotic, rarely the uncontrolled outcome of internal disorder; it was nearly always purposeful. Even when it was malicious, John's wildness was aimed at smashing what was wrong. It seemed to Morant that it was moral; driven by terror, perhaps, but also by unbearable pity and a longing to do good, although his friend did not believe that justice was possible, that goodness could be installed in the world. When they left college the two couples lived near one another in south-west London and one evening John said why didn't Morant come out for a drink with a teacher at his school. They met, on the teacher's recommendation, at a working men's club he frequented in somewhere like Chertsey. Morant had not known that there were working men in Surrey. They drank a lot of beer and played snooker or it might have been pool. Neither Morant nor John were skilled or even enthusiastic snooker players and had only ever played together once before, one summer in a pub in Stoke-on-Trent, where, during a lunchtime break from the building site on which they were working, they had waited their turn on the table as four black teenagers finished their game. To Morant's fascination, throughout the game these young men maintained a stream of abuse and apparently jocular threat, calling each other by a word that Morant had thought they would have detested. This was the first time Morant had come across black people enacting this appropriation of the term. Suddenly the group stopped playing, threw their cues onto the table and left. A few years later in this working men's club—Morant could not remember exactly how it happened—John's colleague, whose name was Cropper, began trying to impress them by saying how radical he was, a nonconformist, a bit of a rebel. His frequenting of this club, its proletarian identity, was offered as a marker of his subversiveness. After a while, leaning across the table as he shaped up to take a shot, John said, so you're a bit of a rebel, are you, Peter, and then, as he focused on addressing the cue ball, I think you're a bit of a wanker, and Morant had said, Cropper, wanker. The next fifteen minutes or so were spent in smashing the snooker balls around and off the table with Cropper scurrying about to retrieve them, pleading with them to stop pissing about and to be careful not to damage the table, which led to them observing how easy it would indeed be to miscue and tear the felt or perhaps accidentally break a cue. They tried to see if there was any danger of striking the ball so that it flew off the table and struck the screen of a television that had been placed in the corner of the room. They examined a number of other dire possibilities, mainly involving the breaking of glass or damage to the table's surface, from drinks spillage to dribbling onto the baize whilst lining up a shot. Morant suggested that they should make the game really radical and subversive by doing away with the uncomfortable business of leaning over the table to make a shot and actually climb on the table to putt the ball like a golfer. All this time John and Morant were repeating the refrain Cropper, wanker, as if it were a football chant or a street-seller's cry, bringing their host, who was terrified that an official or other club members would walk in, close to tears. At some point they left Cropper and the club, to go where and do what Morant could never remember, getting into Morant's car, a red Ford Anglia van which had been bought on John's advice and looked like a post office van. After the purchase John had said that the car should have a name and Morant had suggested something like the Red Raider but John had said that Dobbin would be more suitable. In the van on this warm summer's evening Morant drove off and coming to a series of bends asked John what was the difference between a skid and a slide. He asked how you did the kind of controlled sideways movement through bends that John regularly effected in his car. Following John's instructions, Morant lost control and they ended up with the van turned over on a grassy area at the side of the road. Morant switched the engine off and, checking, was pleased to find that apart from a sore right forearm he was uninjured. John's thumb on his left-hand, however, was twisted somewhat grotesquely and a little later at the hospital it was confirmed that it was broken. Morant's main concerns were, firstly, that he would be prosecuted for drunken or dangerous driving, and, secondly, that the car's recovery and repair or replacement would cost money that neither he nor Liz had. But there was more than that. For a couple of days, until what would happen to the car was sorted out and it became clear that the incident hadn't attracted the attention of the police, before he had successfully resigned himself to the financial implications of the incident and had adjusted to life without a motor vehicle, he felt that things were out of joint, as if his life had slipped out of the frame in which had been held, as if it had lost secure boundaries and could leak away into formlessness. This passed, however, but he remained angry with himself for deepening his and Liz's penury. Yet there had been something exhilarating, something liberating about the event. Morant knew that John was worshipped by his pupils, that he had turned his classroom into a shrine devoted to the work they produced, not just the walls but the ceiling too covered in their writings, designs and drawings, that his room, as far as Morant could make out, had been made into a haven, a warm and nourishing space set against the hostile, persecutory regularities of the rest of the school. John taught in a middle-class area. Morant did not. In his, Morant's, boys' secondary modern school, a corrupt and continuously failing institution, the head teacher was a large, fat Cornishman who had previously been a head of P.E. and before that, it was said, a fairground wrestler. It seemed that he had been appointed to his present post on the grounds that since the school was populated by feral children it required brutal leadership to keep it in order. He was indeed brutal, although in a random way. There were stories of boys being sent to him to receive awards—certificates, perhaps, or just gold stars—whom he would assume to be miscreant and whom he would therefore cane. On one occasion which Morant observed he assaulted a student P.E. teacher in the dinner queue, taking the young man for an inappropriately dressed pupil. Brutality was not, however, his most distinctive characteristic; for this one would have had to choose between stupidity, venality and ineptitude. Every morning the head would walk along a path that passed Morant's classroom, accompanied by the school caretaker— the colleague with whom he worked most closely—on his way to a café on the other side of the main road that ran past the school. On two occasions he interrupted Morant's lessons, once rapping on the widows to inquire why some children were standing on chairs. When it was explained that this was a drama lesson he said all right but don't let them stand on chairs. On another occasion, on a warm summer's day, he leaned into the room through the open windows and said wasn't this an English lesson and if so why were the pupils drawing. Morant informed him that they were storyboarding scripts for films that he intended to make with them. Film, Morant said, was part of the English examination syllabus they were following. This was a lie, although it would be a truth eventually. Years later Morant realised that the term storyboarding was not in currency in education at that time, nor was it a practice that he was aware of being discussed or argued for, although it was to become common some years later. He was to feel unexpectedly pleased—the northern word chuffed best described his feelings—that he had unknowingly anticipated, had indeed independently invented, this progressive technique, as if it were proof of a thoughtfulness, a seriousness that he had forgotten his earlier self possessed, but more than that, it suggested a welcome continuity in his life, an unexpected sign of its coherence. The head never spoke to him apart from on these occasions. His way of opening up a relationship with a new male member of staff was to say that he had a son who would make two of you.

This encounter often occurred, Morant had been told, whilst head and subordinate were standing at the urinal in the men's toilets. His son played in the back row for a west London team which was then nationally known but whose fortunes declined once rugby became more competitively and commercially organised. Morant was, he understood, bigger than the head's son which meant that a relationship never opened between him and the head. This man invited the principal of a local Borstal to speak and hand out awards at the school's annual prize giving. The suspicion that this was not the most astute of decisions was borne out when the principal of the Borstal told the boys and the very few parents who attended the prizegiving that his charges at his school were very much like the kinds of young boys who went to schools like the one in which he was speaking and that indeed they were largely drawn from such schools. Morant was told by an older member of staff that there were no curtains in the school hall because the head had diverted them to his own house where they were hung by the head of P.E., a man who also ran a decorating business. The school streamed its pupils so that in every year there was, in descending order of scholastic aptitude, an A, B, C and a D class. Morant's timetable consisted of one first year C class and the rest D groups, except in the fourth year where he was given the E group, the only E class in the school. 4E had been set up because there were an unusual number of disturbed and illiterate children in that year and the solution to the problems they presented involved gathering them together into the one group. With a few exceptions—a couple of them children whose lives had wounded them so much that they rarely spoke, whose project in life seemed to be to shrink into an invisibility that rendered them beyond the touch of others, and two or three boys who clearly came from extremely impoverished backgrounds—4E were skinheads, first-wave skinheads who wore Crombie overcoats and pork pie or trilby hats. Morant could not remember if they also wore the braces, half-mast trousers and boots that are most popularly associated with the subculture. He remembered them as somehow more dapper. It was almost impossible for him to teach these children. Early on in his time with the group if he turned his back to write on the blackboard a rain of missiles would descend on him, mostly screwed up balls of paper and other classroom debris, but also, on different occasions, ballpens, books, bits of chalk, a used condom, a shoe and a dead mouse. Several of the boys, if he approached to help them with their work, were visibly distressed, shrinking away, their lips curling in defensive anger. Any approach to individual children was accompanied by cries of watch your arse he's a bum boy. They were obsessed with homosexuality, asking him if certain members of staff were poufs and telling him about trips to the common to beat up queers. On a trip to Box Hill with another class a teacher had commented on how beautiful the wooded hills were and a boy had said yes and behind every tree was a bummer bumming someone up the arse. These boys loved ska and one of them said to him that the darkies made good music sir didn't they, although, like the rest of the class he professed hatred of black people. One day he asked a boy, a tall, powerfully built, perpetually grinning boy who had evaded all attempts to educate him and who regularly misspelt his name Davies as Daives, why he disliked black people so much and he said because they weren't like us, they weren't civilised, they weren't intelligent like us. Morant never penetrated the collective defences of this group, although he was aware that eventually they regarded him affectionately and even held him in some sort of esteem, largely because he undertook the training of the school's boxing team for the

Surrey schools championships, an occasion on which all the titles were shared between the only two institutions to enter full teams, his own school and the Borstal, most of whose competitors he noted were black children. Later he was ashamed that he had become involved in this business. None of the competitors had been properly prepared and the bouts were flailing, desperate affairs; in one fight a small boy had cried throughout and was still sobbing when it was announced that he had won his contest. One Monday lunchtime a group of boys in 4E entered his classroom and offered him two bars of chocolate which he accepted with some surprise as a sign of their growing regard for him. He took the next two days off—he couldn't remember if he'd been unwell or had just awarded himself rest from his largely unsuccessful struggles as a teacher. When he returned to school he was met with grins from colleagues and inquiries as to whether special branch had paid him a visit. In his absence the police had visited the school because a number of boys in 4E had stolen confectionery and other items from a store. When questioned by the police they admitted their guilt but added, as if in mitigation, that Mr Morant had had some of the chocolate they'd stolen. That year he was one of only two out of six probationary teachers who began at the school in September to make it through to full qualification in July. The other was an art teacher who worked in a protective environment in a distant part of the school. Morant's classroom was on the ground floor of one of two wings that ran in parallel from the main building towards the road beyond. In his year at the school he seemed to be the only permanent member of staff at work on his corridor. A succession of supply staff taught in these rooms. Morant got to know none of them and was only aware of them as a bellowing presence amidst sounds of crashing furniture and the laughter and screaming of young people. There were two exceptions. One of the rooms on the floor was a music studio which was usually occupied by a man who was perhaps in his early thirties and who belonged to a rock group which was well-known for its mixing of jazz, blues and vaudevillian humour. His lessons were unusually quiet but were occasionally punctuated by noisy and, one guessed, violent outbursts in which conflict would spill out onto the corridor. If Morant was teaching he tried to ignore these episodes as he knew that if he left the room to find out what was going on his class would try to get out of the door to view what was happening, but on one occasion he was preparing a lesson in his room during a free period when there was the familiar eruption two doors away and when he went out the teacher was punching a crouching, protesting boy in the back of the head and upper body. After a few seconds he pushed the pupil back into the room and seeing Morant, said little cunt, I'm not having it. In the staffroom this teacher seemed to be continually enraged by the children he taught. Morant did not remember any music ever coming out of the man's classroom. However, there seemed to be an understanding that he would for periods of time be absent, probably touring with his band, and while he was away his duties would be taken over by an older man, a quiet, smiling individual who played the piano throughout his lessons. He explained that the continuous playing seemed to calm the boys and, in any case, he enjoyed the opportunity to use the piano as he did not have one at home. He was a mild, gentle man who seemed unsurprised by the disorder that surrounded him. Morant judged that he had been privately educated and fallen on hard times, perhaps because he drank too much and perhaps because he had no appetite or flair for the tasks of leadership and self-enterprise set by such a background. Morant and he enjoyed talking about cricket. During the early months of Morant's first year of teaching he became convinced that schooling, like the occupations he had undertaken before going to college, was an empty, hypocritical pursuit that pretended to a meaningfulness that it did not possess. By the end of the year he had pieced together enough understanding of what he was doing and enough satisfying practice to feel that, although he knew next to nothing about what this job involved, perhaps it could be done to some good purpose and that things would have to change for this to happen. He got through the year because he was in love with Liz and everything that they did together seemed infused with an epic charm. His awareness of her beauty invested his life—the drinking with colleagues from both their schools in a local pub, the novel he was writing, their visits to friends in the north, a camping trip to Cornwall at Whitsun, their endless love-making—with heroic significance. Their life together was going to yield something marvellous. Towards the end of that teaching year he was visited by an adviser from the local education authority who observed a lesson and told him afterwards that he had obviously come through a trying experience well. He said that the authority knew what circumstances were at the school and he was sorry for what his first year in teaching must have been like. Afterwards Morant knew he should have asked why no one had offered support during his time at the school. In September he moved to another quieter school nearby and at the end of that year he and Liz moved to Yorkshire because Liz wanted them to buy a house and they couldn't afford one in Surrey. Morant was happy to do this because he missed the hill country and was still in thrall to the north as other and more real than London. John Guzman clearly saw this as a desertion and although he and Morant visited each other a couple of times, always without their partners, the relationship did not survive. Morant remembered this friendship with affection and missed

John's daring, his wild recalcitrance, his drive towards freedom. It seemed to him that he had desperately sought values to hold on to, something worth retaining, something to shore up against the assaults of a world that was bleaker than Morant could imagine. It seemed as if he saw the world's violence without remission.

One morning in the second half of his sixth decade Morant went for a walk. He had intended merely to walk to the newsagents to get his newspaper, something that he always enjoyed as inaugurating the new day, but a couple of places ahead of him in the shop he observed a man wearing the uniform of an office worker, the brutal ugliness of the white shirt and tie, and he became disturbed by what later, after some thought about why this choice of dress had unsettled him, he understood as its sterile, fascist insistence on a blank sameness, its submission to an order based on nothing more than a bewildered fear, becoming hatred, before the unfamiliar or that which was not to be immediately understood, and horror too at the messiness of ordinary, vital life, a panic hatred of all that might disturb the mad peace of not thinking too much. Not that he wanted to be too harsh on this man who did not look at all like your idea of a run of the mill confident young fellow on the up, with his shaven head and face that had that unmistakeable drawn scrapedness, like when you come out of a swimming bath and your face looks scrubbed and pealed of several layers so that it hardly seems ready to present itself to the world, vulnerable yet brutal, a stripping away of a human layer, of personality perhaps, towards an animal, a threatened animal, self, this face, this poor head here in the newsagent's, of someone who had borne too many blows in life, not enough love, a poor, wary, hardly even making working class, man, who perhaps, Morant didn't mean to be patronising, thought that adopting this uniform would hook him into a world that had always seemed impossibly, woundingly beyond, the, as Morant imagined it, severed world in which he lived, a beggared, graceless existence and, of course, he looked all wrong in this uniform, an impostor, reminding Morant of a child dressing up in adult clothing—after this, he became aware, once more, with traffic tearing past him, of the violent wrenching activity of getting what passes for reality, the work of imposing the necessary meaning on nothingness, under way, and so he left the shop without buying a newspaper, needing to take a longer walk. On this bright, breezy morning in mid-March, he passed through the grounds of his village's church, a handsome limestone building that had been built, for the most part, in the twelfth century when the village had obviously enjoyed, as it did now, considerable prosperity. In the spring sunshine his mood lifted and he thought that one could imagine the church's graceful architecture, this reflector and receptacle of light, as in praise of the beauty appearing once more in the natural world. He wondered if he was glimpsing the joy, a promise of full life, that peasants might have felt in the middle ages, the threat and menace of damnation, Christianity's fearsome eschatologies fallen away, so that all that remained was the prospect of bliss. Later on the walk he went along a path lined with young trees that led to the village's mill pond. In the few days since he had passed that way the path's sides had been suddenly filled with mostly low-lying vegetation, amongst which he could identify cow parsley, a few daffodils, celandine, nettles and hogweed, and it was easy to imagine what would be the case in a few weeks' time, the air in that sheltered green space made heavy with the warm, off-sweet scent of hedgerow blossom and drying earth. At the mill-dam, a pond created by the damming of the river—no more than a stream—that worked its way through and around the village, gulls wheeled and swooped above his head against a sky that was full of racing, torn clouds that kept giving way to pools of blue. The water was busy with mallards, moorhen, more gulls and other ducks, some white like the farmyard ones in children's picture books, many of them variously marked (he wondered if these were mongrel progeny) and some larger black and white ducks which he had not seen before and which, on subsequent walks, he observed were the most aggressive and successful at the rape that passed for courtship in the duck world. A young mother had brought her children to feed the ducks with sliced white bread and further along the paved walking area that ran alongside the water he passed some grandparents whose grand-daughter—less, he guessed, than two years old—was pointing at an empty plastic bottle that had washed up in a corner of the pond and saying look, look. She seemed, if not astonished, surprised and, he thought, disapproving of this intruding object. It was familiar but part of somewhere else, not here. Suddenly, he was all at once aware of the warm sun on his face, the willows whose thin tendrils picked up an orangey-green glow from the sunlight, the busy, scudding sky, the brilliant surface of the water and the noisy birds feeding, landing, taking off, squabbling, a whirling life, and these few people, wrapped in something like love and eagerness for life, and his strong body walking in this world, and he felt a rush of joy, an exultation that brought him close to tears, at the loveliness and promise of shining creation. At that moment a little nick of pain told him that the skin on his bottom lip had split, a surface lesion, and when he dabbed it with his finger he saw a thin smear of blood and he knew that it was spring because this always happened when spring came. Like a bud forcing its way painfully into life, bruising through a stem, a vegetable memory aberrantly sealed into this animal body. It had not always been like this. When he had as a young man in his late twenties first lived with Liz he had hated spring because it seemed that life was erupting all around him and here he was in a house with a mortgage, in a job that required him every morning to drive through this unconfined, irresistible fecundity to the kind of imprisonment to which he had thought he would never allow himself to return, and in a relationship which he seemed to have imagined wrongly would be for ever free, improvising, opening onto endlessly new vistas and bound by nothing more than a shared appetite for inexhaustible experience. This had seemed the destiny of their love, the unwavering, inevitable narrative of their life together. He had never thought that Liz, this uncontainable spirit, would want a settled life, stability and what seemed to him something disturbingly like respectability. He would wake early on March, April and May mornings to the cacophony of birdsong coming from the high trees at the back of their house and what he heard was not joy but a brutal shrieking driven by implacable genetic dictates—territorial lust, obliviousness of all otherness, blind violence, fear and a mechanical urge to reproduce. Liz had started to talk of children. He thought of a passage from Updike's Rabbit Run which he had brought to a drama workshop when he was at college and contemplating a fatherhood he dreaded. The tutor, Roger Caldwell, wanted for some reason to create an improvisation around, as far as he could remember, the experience of parenthood and had asked the group to gather poems and bits of prose on this theme. It became clear that Caldwell, the father of several children, intended a celebration of the bringing into being of new life, of the joys of procreation and fruitfulness, of the love, optimism and hope engendered by the miracle of birth, so that it was not well received when Morant offered as his contribution this from John Updike: The fullness ends when we give Nature her ransom, when we make children for her. Then she is through with us, and we become, first inside, and then outside, junk. Flower stalks. But that is what he had felt as a young man and it was why Liz had sensibly decided that he was unfit to be the father of her children, and unlikely ever to be ready to become a father. His unruliness had been extreme in those years and made more so by the signs and manifestations of a settled and subdued life, the opening around him of an enclosed space, a position of acceptance and security in the world. It was some time in his thirties when he had begun to lose the oblivious self-absorption which, it seems, marks youth, that he was struck by how obedient people were or, to put it differently and perhaps more kindly, how willingly they walked onto paths laid out for them. He wasn't sure by whom or by what, although he knew that it was more than society, the prevailing common sense of the times people happened to live in, as unforgiving as those pressures were. What he noticed most had to do with reproduction. He had not before seen fully how tyrannical was the urge to have children and to live as a family. He thought, though, that it wasn't always an urge, a visceral, gut-level drive, so much as the only realistic option. He was sure that for all those of his age who were marrying, having children, one partner at home, wheeling children about in push-chairs, the other working at a job he (of course he) perhaps found an interesting and fulfilling way to spend so much of his time, for all these there were others who grudged every moment spent in work slavery but accepted it as the price to be paid for feeling that you could sustain or at least manage the appearance of a proper life. There must, he had supposed, be couples whose conscious, delirious, purpose in life was to breed and gather children around them, but the impression he had of most people was that you did this—you reproduced and set up a family—because it was what always happened, it was the way you made sense of things, gave shape and value, a solution, to the puzzle of being. It was the young women with prams and push-chairs that really astonished him. Girls he had taught as teenagers, now intelligent, well-qualified young women, had married and become mothers, spending their days wheeling, carrying and walking their children to shops, play areas, play schools and nurseries and to the mill dam to throw bread at the ducks. Presumably they spent a great deal of time in their houses feeding these children, playing with them, reading to them, changing their nappies and dirty clothes, putting them to sleep. He passed them in the village with their buggies, as these push-chairs were later called, chatting to other young mothers, exchanging news about their offspring, admiring and smiling at one another's children. They were clearly reassuring themselves about their children's development, but more than this they were establishing, confirming, the importance and worth of what they had—presumably—chosen to do with their lives. And he knew that what they were doing was important, but he found it astonishing that so many of them, in such numbers, had chosen to do this with their lives. He had not known that human beings were so predictable. And then there were their husbands, young men steadily losing any youthful grace they had, clothing themselves in that mild, understated obesity that young men in their twenties quickly acquire, in their suits and ties, their company cars and behind their desks, toiling at jobs that would disgust them within ten, perhaps twenty years if they had any sense at all, all of them accepting without demur the, as it seemed to Morant, caricature roles they had been prescribed. And he would see them coming into pubs at about 9.30 in their football gear after five-a-side, exchanging banter with one another and any other men they knew, and Morant could not resist the thought that this, the way these young men moved, the noise they made, was no different to the exchanges between primates that he had seen in nature documentaries, the ritual trading of calls and cries, the presentation of bodies in ways that affirmed membership of the group, the clan, unthreatening but not submissive. He had felt annoyance at these young people, their enslavement to reproduction, to family life, their tidy, clean houses, their emphatic lack of imagination, the timidity that he saw in their need for security. He wondered what it would mean for the world if just half of them were to decide that they would not marry and would not have children, that they would not take jobs that satisfied no deeply held desire and that they would look elsewhere to make some chosen sense of their existences. Such, he had thought, need not be a selfish decision and it need not lead to social chaos but to a purposeful, careful re-ordering of the world so as to accommodate this new way of making a life and perhaps that new way would be a better world, less driven, less manic, more open to fuller possibility. In this early life as an adult he was being invited into a regulated, socially approved orderliness, a domestication which he saw that others desired and embraced as a kind of recognition, a confirmation that their lives would from now on have a reassuring trajectory, but which he knew then to be a deadening of the spirit, a closing down, a fearful retreat, a miserable surrender of desire in return for the promise of safety. He had in his early years as a teacher on several occasions been drawn in, at their parents' request, to giving extra lessons to children in the village, and he had been dismayed by the houses he visited, the spotless tidiness of those carpeted rooms, the few pictures—reproductions of paintings depicting plains threatened by approaching storms, usually with horses galloping before, or elephants majestically defying, the tempest, or impossibly pretty scenes of cottage gardens or of Scottish highland landscapes draped in mists or, on one occasion, a painting of a young woman, some nearly but not quite diaphanous material flowing around her body, as she sat on what might have been the edge of a bed, her perfect face blank—and the three piece dralon suites with contrasting satin, or probably satin-effect, cushions arranged with precise calculation on the settee and chairs. He didn't despise what seemed to him the impoverished, tightly circumscribed imaginary of those rooms; they saddened and frightened him. And thus, the fighting, the drunkenness, the constant unreasoning chase after the affirmations of sex and love, the petty refusals of propriety, the professional rebellions that disrupted his career. Later he would see all of this, except for what was involved in the movement from woman to woman, as in part a necessary self-histrionics, a display to himself that he had not submitted entirely to the vast, enveloping project of government that sought to place him usefully in its grids and channels. Liz told him she was leaving him, taking a job in Manchester, and he was enraged, and although he saw her several times over the next couple of years she maintained a careful distance and they did not again make love and all contact finished when she told him she had met this ridiculous-sounding man Gerald and that they were to be married. Again and not for the last time he felt grief and desolation, and he thought it might annihilate him, but not jealousy because he knew that Liz could not possibly love anyone but him, although he felt a violent loathing at the thought of her sleeping with another man. He heard about her through friends over the years, the children, the retraining as a psychotherapist, the house she and her husband owned in Italy, their life in the USA when her husband's firm moved him there, their move to Leeds, her motherliness and eventually her husband's illness and then, twenty-something years after they had parted, a woman friend had told him that Liz would like to talk to him and that he might ring her at this number and at these times. Fearful, full of dread, he did so and afterwards they met in York where, over a meal in a vegetarian restaurant which later moved to London and became popular with Bollywood stars and their Spanish footballer boyfriends she told him that her husband was dying and that she was having a bad time at work. She had heard that he was at the university and asked him to tell her what he did and they exchanged stories about shared friends. He learnt about her children, a girl and a boy, both in their teens. She said that it was stupid that they had lost touch and he said wasn't it something different from losing touch (he was annoyed, as if she were saying that it had been some sort of oversight, no more than a forgetfulness, like a failure to keep contact with an old friend, and he could not have kept contact because if they had he would have been driven mad and she should have been driven mad too; contact had been impossible). It had been a decision, and he stopped himself from saying that he had never ceased thinking about her, dreaming about her, fantasising accidental meetings and reconciliations, wondering as he picked up a telephone that it might be her—he never quite cured himself of the idea that the next post would deliver a letter from her. He didn't tell her that, as he knew would be the case, she was as irresistible as she had always been and that even when he had been a chaotic, insufferable, half-crazed presence in their younger life he had then as now always loved her. She didn't ask him if he was in a relationship at the moment—she would have been told by friends that he wasn't—and it was apparent that what she wanted right now wasn't sex, but she did want intimacy. It seemed that she was seeking re-entry into a remembered closeness. His heart filled at this. At this moment she wanted to talk to him and no one else and he knew with immense relief what that meant. He was careful not to touch her, not to seek her hand at the table or do more than kiss her cheek when they met and parted. He was good at this sort of holding back, a carefulness. Later she told him that from their first meeting at that time she had wanted to hug him, to cling into him, just to immerse herself again in the warmth and—the word she used—completeness they had felt as young people. For months they had chaste meetings when they talked, in cafés, in his car, sitting by the river in York, about her husband's suffering, the decisions she was having to make about his care, her fears for her children, the family's future and what she was going through at work as her psychology department pursued its goal of purging itself of psychoanalytic perspective. He learnt that her husband had been a good and kind man, humorous, and that he loved being a father, that her mother-in-law was kind and helpful but now very old and that she had several good friends who had helped her through this period, one of whom—a woman he did not know—suggested that she talk to him, to Morant. He wondered what conversations, what judgements, had been in play for this suggestion to have been made. He surprised himself at how content he was to talk about these things, to sit near her without touching. Sometimes she asked him about his work, shared friends she'd lost contact with and, once, about his mother whom she had justifiably loathed. A year or two later, sheltering from August rain and drinking tea in a small café in the hills just behind the Dorset coast, he asked her why she had got in touch again, why him. He could see that she needed to talk her way through the awfulness, the anxiety, but why, after all these years, did she think of him. Asking this was a breach of the reserve they had both maintained and he knew it was a capitulation, weakness, a humiliatingly selfish reaching for her regard. He should have kept quiet, waited. She said that it was because she knew that she could trust him and as he heard this a wave of feeling surged through him and she saw that he was moved and reached for his hand. He said that he was sorry for how he'd been, in those years, and she gave a small smile and was quiet. What touched him was that something of him had survived, had found home in her being, had got through all the roaring and mutiny. He said to her that he had been too full of himself. She nodded slightly but again said nothing. Seeking her reassurance, her approval, he said that he had no doubt that he had done good things and he knew that he had been valued, by colleagues, by some of the young people he had taught and also by friends and she interrupted him and said quietly that of course he had, of course he had, it was obvious from what she had been told that he had done good things. He said that this was going to sound pompous but he felt that in his professional life he had been honest and serious and she said that of course he had and that people admired him for it. People clearly thought he had had a career that counted. He said, do they. He knew that he was valued by colleagues, but he wanted to hear her confirm it. She said you must know and he said that he supposed he did. It was just that he had been a bit brutish and she laughed and said that was a funny word, why brutish. Too full on, he said, spilling all over people, crossing a line between exuberance and—he couldn't find the word, so said boorishness. She smiled and said that he had been a bit out of control at times but that brutishness and boorishness were not how she or anyone else thought of him. He said, some people might and then, I swear too much and she said yes, you do. He swore more than anyone else he knew and it could be a bit oppressive. What he would have said if it had been the right moment and if he could have brought himself to say it, was that there were the obvious, big things, the drunkenness and what it brought in train, the brawling, the pursuit of sexual intrigue, although he did not feel bad about most of that, but he was more plagued by smaller shames, by failures to behave as gracefully or as properly as he ought. He had always carefully policed his behaviour as a teacher but he couldn't forget occasions—that they were very few was no consolation—when he'd been excessively ironic or playful in the classroom or seminar group, when the moment had been more about self-display than the encouragement of thought. Then there were times with friends, particularly on the mountain-biking and walking trips they sustained over three decades, when he had suddenly glimpsed what might have been how others saw him and it seemed that what they saw was irritating. He was one of a group of male friends who had known each other for thirty years and who, like many such groups, now and then, briefly and often at the beginning of an evening before its themes had emerged, engaged briefly in a bantering game in which they riffed on caricatured versions of each other, boasting of their own noble qualities and selflessness and subjecting others to absurd insult and derision. The game offered several pleasures. It celebrated the friends' intimacy, the comfortableness they felt in one another's company—only people who knew and liked each other could say these things. There was enjoyment to be taken from the ridiculous, spiralling inventiveness of the bragging and mockery and the very occasional moments of real wit. And there was a delightful precariousness in working a line that bordered genuine criticism and hurtfulness, of approaching actual fears, weaknesses and antipathies, for the caricatures that were alleged or inhabited were always based in some kind of reality, always stemmed from personal attitudes or qualities that had, it was claimed, been revealed in an event or events that had actually taken place. Thus, because Morant had once arrived on a walking trip without money or a bank card and on another occasion had drunk too much of the water he was sharing with his fellow walkers, leading, so it was claimed, to general dehydration, he was always configured as selfish and greedy. Matt said that one of the key sentences in any understanding of Morant's personality, uttered first in a restaurant when the group had been sharing a number of dishes, was oh dear, I seem to have given myself rather a large portion. An additional accusation was that he liked his own way when it came to decisions about where to walk, eat or drink. Then there was an awkwardness to do with women. His friends were long and faithfully married and, although it did not happen often, if the conversation turned to the mysteries of female behaviour or whether it was entirely distasteful for middle-aged men to admit to admiring younger women and whether they still turned to look at women's arses when they walked past and whether this was pathetic or not or if one of them referred to a supply teacher who had been on the staff when they had all worked together and said that had he not been a model of marital rectitude he would have given her one (one friend, Davey, said that if he had she wouldn't have noticed) Morant would feel uneasy and he was aware of his marginal position here and felt, perhaps imagined, that everyone was aware, perhaps curious, perhaps slightly resentful, of his different status and if one of them, say Colin, the youngest of them by some years, had said, when he was a little drunk, that he thought they should consult Morant on these issues because he was an expert on women, there would be a moment's embarrassment which was not relieved so much by Morant's saying that his somewhat chequered, as he put it, experiences with women hardly qualified him as an expert in the field, as by Davey, always keen to head off too much feeling, protesting that it was not a good idea to seek opinions from a pathetic old degenerate. The diminutive stature of one of the group, Peter, provoked some ridicule but it was his inclination to order and tidiness, his secondary modern education and his emphatic opinions that led to his caricature as a sort of Daily Mail reading, petit-bourgeois fascist. On his appointment to the post of head of Art and Technology, Davey and Morant had referred to their new colleague as Dr Bollock and E(a)rnest because they had each, on separate occasions, walked past his classroom when he was wagging his finger at a pupil in admonishment, and at the first staff meeting he attended and every one thereafter he expressed at length very decided views on the running of the school; but the epithet that stuck was the Weasel. On one camping trip Peter had told the group that he had earlier that year attended a parents' evening at his daughter's school, during which he questioned her art teacher about her performance. Afterwards he had been told by someone he knew at the school that the teacher had reported an unpleasant interview with an unnervingly intense parent who had asked persistent, difficult questions about curriculum and pedagogy and who wouldn't let anything go, always coming back at him, a little man who was like a weasel. This was a persona that Peter assumed with glee. Morant's response to his depiction as selfish and overbearing was to deny the caricature at every point and to cite his habitual saintliness in every regard, but, however much he enjoyed the sparring, it irked him that it was the characteristics of a brutish insensitivity that his friends had settled on. He didn't intend it but it seemed that he trailed a certain ponderous maleness. Then there was the time that Matt told him he had received a Christmas card from James, Morant's most regular walking companion, who said that a knee injury had been preventing him from doing any walking, but his incapacity had yielded the unanticipated and welcome bonus of escaping Morant's boasting and gibes. Morant had laughed at James's artfulness, the knowledge that Matt would repeat the line to Morant, and he admired the felicitous phrasing, but later he had thought was this how he seemed to people, that his playfulness had too much swagger to it. He wondered if his friends, as well as liking him, hated him a little. After all, from our earliest moments of consciousness we all resent the existence of others. We are all imposters, required to invent a self that can see us through this life, a necessary protection against the abstract violence, the strangeness of all those other selves and the world that they have made. Some, he thought, do this skilfully or without apparent effort and appear at home, plausibly at one with things, whilst with a few you could see the work they were putting in to make a self that would convince others, that would elicit respect, admiration or, at least, acceptance, recognition that this person belongs, is fit for this world. Sometimes the effort to do this becomes too exhausting and it falters and the individual—and sometimes it is those who appear most secure, most at ease with life— begins to, as they say, let the mask slip, begins to weary of, as they also say, presenting this face to the world, and once he or she allows this to happen he or she glimpses the terrifying truth that this face, this self is not real, is entirely a work of imagination, a more or less oppressive, more or less hateful, mask and begins to doubt that it can be credibly sustained any longer and to see that if this failure should come to be, then he or she will not be recognised, that this world will cease to have the appearance of a home and will be a featureless, desolate place peopled by counterfeit beings whose masks indeed conceal a nothingness, or, at most, an involuntary malevolence. It is at this point, he thought, that people become depressed, unable to cope, go off the rails, as they yet again say, and divert themselves from the gaping vacuity that surrounds them by engaging in the grim compulsions of self-loathing, a steady, intent destruction of self, or they fall apart more spectacularly, like poor, parent-haunted John Capel, who gave himself to the air above a motorway as it passed Luton, or the head of history he knew a little at a school that neighboured his own, an impressively calm and composed man in his thirties who always spoke sensibly and not without humour at meetings they both attended, and who took several weeks off work after his wife left him for another man and during that time became increasingly troubling to friends who visited him, eventually, and horrifyingly, living on some waste ground, sheltering up against the back of a supermarket in the small town where he had lived and taught. These examples were outliers, Morant knew, but they seemed to him indicative of a truth that we ignore, perhaps have to ignore, as we do our best to immerse ourselves, to saturate our lives, in an unthinking meaningfulness. Sometimes Morant remembered people he had known, but not always very well, people who had seemed to have difficulty with life, who had been odd as young men and women, out of joint with things. He would wonder what had become of them, although he knew what had happened to some of them. John Capel had decided that he needed to kill himself and was eventually successful in that enterprise. When he was at his grammar school there was a younger boy who at break times used to walk quickly across the quadrangle and then stop suddenly, putting a finger to his mouth in a mime of thought, before moving off again and repeating the action. He would do this several times and then, with a sudden decisiveness, hurry into one of the school buildings. He had no friends and, although he was never bullied as far as Morant knew, he was viewed with incurious derision by the other boys. On procession to a nearby church where the school was to celebrate and give thanks for something or other, as it did on several occasions during the year, Morant and a couple of others were supervising a younger class when this boy told him that he had spoken to an angel the night before. There was another boy in the year above who appeared to have a thyroid condition in that he was greatly overweight and had black hair growing thinly on cheeks that seemed permanently flushed. He was interesting to other boys because he knew every bus and train timetable in and around London and on buses on the way to the school sports field he would be tested on routes between distant parts of the capital. Buckhurst Hill to Purley, Ongar to Rickmansworth: what seemed incalculable transits would immediately be plotted and offered, with variations, from slightly smiling, moist lips. The boy rarely seemed to move. There seemed to be no self animating this heavy flesh. Instead Morant had an impression of a wary presence sitting behind the boy's eyes, a watchful consciousness that may have been amused or baffled, perhaps alarmed by the wayward volatility—the energy beyond calculation—of the boys who surrounded him on these occasions. He knew of people who made a start to life but could not quite keep things going. At college there was Tom Rawlings, a public school boy who mixed with friends of Morant's. He was an amiable individual who enjoyed conversation. He would listen attentively to what someone had to say and then would join in, displaying familiarity with the topic, an easy, confident knowledge of the subject under discussion. This was done gracefully and without any obvious desire to dominate; he was sensitive to the interventions of others and apparently interested in what they had to say, but it was clearly important to him that he gave an impression of being in the know, in on things. What he did was quite generous, social, in that he attempted to create a group who shared with him particular, special knowledges. What this languid, affable young man wanted was to bring into being a small, knowable world that was hospitable to him, a community within whose borders he might be safe. Morant did not dislike Tom, but he found his presence oppressive. In his memory Tom was always sitting back in a chair, in a bar or someone's room, smoking and drinking incessantly, smiling, pleased at the companionship that had gathered around him, the fellowship that for its brief duration gave him home. He had a face that seemed already middle-aged and it made Morant think that he had reached forward too soon for a place of repose, of comfortable certainty. He heard stories of Tom being rendered insensible on formidable drinking binges in his own room, of vomit-stained collapses in town and he remembered that Tom never did anything; apart from studying foreign languages he had no interests, no cultural or sporting involvements; he just talked and drank and smiled. Morant's friends told him about Tom after he left college; his visits to their homes, his disappearances at mid-day or late at night in search of drink, the time he woke at night and mistook a wardrobe for the lavatory, his incessant importuning for money of a girl with whom he had been briefly involved at college, his work in army intelligence, his dismissal from the service, his death. There was the young head of music at one of Morant's schools, Samuel, who told him as they sat near one another in the staff room that these were the people he wanted to move amongst, showing him a sheet of music, something composed by Peter

Warlock, and when Morant asked him what sort of people he meant he said different, creative people, the avant-garde. He then sketched a picture of a group of artists, writers and composers who seemed to be centred in Soho in the 1940s and 50s and who were scornful of convention, reckless drinkers and creatively impassioned. He seemed to be referring to an avant-garde coterie which Morant recognised and was aware of as being based in Fitzrovia and Soho in that period, but there were odd inclusions from earlier periods like Warlock and Wyndham Lewis. Samuel had been born in a South Yorkshire pit village and was openly ashamed of his parents, although Morant noticed that he visited his widowed mother a great deal. On Friday evenings in those days Morant used to meet friends for a drink, young teachers all of them. The pub was a vast hall furnished, as far as he could remember, with bamboo tables and chairs, or perhaps that was just a brief phase as he also recalled sitting on and around heavier furniture, and it was prowled by a man who must have been in his thirties, a dwarfish figure with a face distorted beyond normality, as if invisible hands were locked on his cheeks and temples, stretching the flesh towards the back of his head, but asymmetrically so that everything on the right side of his face, eye, nostril, lips, was pulled downwards and on the left everything was wrenched upwards. He looked like an animal about to be predated. This was the pot boy, whose job, probably self-appointed, was to collect empty glasses and bottles and return them to the bar, in hope of being rewarded with a drink. These drinking sessions started early at about half past seven and for a few weeks they were disrupted by Samuel arriving at about ten o'clock and saying hello gentlemen I must buy you a drink and then, whatever protestations were offered, however firmly it was impressed upon him that he was not to buy everyone a drink because it would be too expensive and there wasn't enough time for everyone to buy him a drink in return and anyway most people had had enough and some thinking about going home, he would return from the bar with three, four or five pints of beer and whatever any women present were drinking. He would then finish his drink quickly, sometimes in just three or four gulps, go to the bar and return with as many drinks as before. He would drink this pint just as quickly and it would be apparent that he was very drunk, morosely drunk. He would sit with the group staring at the table and after a while would start to swear softly and then to mutter about the people around him, sometimes picking up on someone's comment or story, muttering oddly stilted things like oh a very witty point or he likes to cause a stir, or at other times saying they think they know me or they think I can't see through all this or I can see things they can't. Then he would get up suddenly and leave. He had a brief relationship with an incautious Home Economics teacher in the school and when she broke up with him he returned a one bar electric fire he'd borrowed through the front window of her flat. In his second year at the school he started going on job interviews. He would return and when asked if he had got the job would say that no, he'd been offered it but he'd turned it down because he didn't like the set-up, and on other occasions he might say that the head had begged him to take up the post, saying that only he could turn the department around or that the local authority adviser in on the interview had taken him to one side and said that he'd done well to refuse the job because he should wait for a post that would really exercise his talents, or members of staff had told him that he would be wasted in the role. Eventually, these interviews seemed to involve him spending more time away from school than working in it so that he was summoned by the acting head teacher to be questioned about what had been going on during these unsuccessful excursions and to see if his pursuit of career advancement could be managed in a way that was less disruptive for the school. The absences for interview continued, however, until the acting head rang one of the schools Samuel was visiting and was told that they had had no letter of application from a Samuel Cooke and indeed had no vacancy for a head of music, so that they were not that day or on any other in the foreseeable future interviewing for that post. By this time Morant had left this school and his interest in and awareness of Samuel and his strangeness dwindled to nothingness so that he never discovered what happened with him, although he knew that he was no longer at the school. Normality—it seemed to him a shallow, hypocritical, wilfully ignorant, precarious disguise. He would see on television news that friends and neighbours had been shocked that a man had killed his wife and children and then himself and these neighbours had said that they had been a lovely family, he'd been a nice bloke, no one could have predicted it, they couldn't make sense of it, refused to believe it and there would be newspaper articles exploring the reasons why, how it could be that, an ordinary person could be concealing such terrible depths—pure evil. People were disturbed, shaken, their confidence in normality, reality, undermined, and he, Morant, would be horrified, but never surprised. He would think that if he had known these people he would still not have been surprised. Personhood, the sort that gets you by with other people, seemed often to him like a skin stretched painfully tight across you, a face, a body, a mask, a clingfilm shroud straining to hold in place an interiority that was unbiddable, tumultuous, angry at its containment, and this was not unusual, but to one degree or another the condition of being of everyone. It was nearly always men who did these dreadful things, who burst normality, and it was nearly always men who, in his experience, seemed most obviously labouring to hold the whole deception together, but this did not mean that women were exempt from such performance.

In his sixties he was always saddened if he saw cooling towers. In the late eighties Morant, Matt and a third friend, Davey, went away camping for four days in the Whitsun holiday. Over the next four or five years three other teachers at the school joined them on what became an annual event, even after some had dispersed to schools in other parts of the country. On the first trip, to the Berkshire downs, the only time they went to the south of England, Matt and Morant had walked along the Ridgeway whilst David, who loathed walking, rode a bicycle in adjacent parts of the countryside, at the end of each day collecting the walkers in his car. The following morning he would drop them at the point where they had finished the day before, and so on. These trips accumulated a folklore over the years, beginning in this first year with Morant's forgetting his walking boots and neglecting to equip himself with any eating implements or proper camping equipment, bringing only a bulky duvet and a small plastic dessert bowl. On the first night they camped on the site of what seemed to be a demolished house. It offered no washing or cleaning facilities apart from a tap above a broken sink that was surrounded on three sides by the remains of brick walls. The ruin had no roof or ceiling, and in the morning Morant was discovered by his friends attempting an all over body wash in the small plastic bowl, thus revealing what to them seemed an obsessive concern with cleanliness which perhaps indicated a guilty past. They discovered a toilet bowl which stood, unhoused and curiously elevated, behind a wall in another part of the site, but which, Davey realised after using it, stood in full prospect of a Ridgeway viewing site on a hill above. Matt's subsequent attempt to use it was disrupted by Davey taking photographs of him as he sat on the pedestal. Later that second day, after Davey had left them on his bicycle, Matt and Morant noticed that the route he had described to them took him up Dean's Bottom, a destination that they agreed had been influenced, perhaps unconsciously, by his experiences as a public school boy. The walk provided them with many opportunities for indulging what might be seen as juvenile salaciousness, the countryside seeming to abound in place names that had a sexual suggestiveness, including the first of many Knobs—Scutcher's—which they were to encounter over the years. It was not, in fact, until a few years later when Englishmen other than Morant joined the group that Matt's Welshness was exploited for sheep-related innuendo. Davey was also Welsh but was less obviously so because his parents had sent him to private schools so that he spoke like an Englishman who had been educated at what was, as he liked to point out, a top-drawer public school. At the end of the Ridgeway walk Matt and Morant met Davey at Avebury and when Matt started to talk about what was known of the henge he was quietly appalled, and Morant impressed, by Davey's serene lack of interest in the ancient stones. He was looking for a pub that sold decent beer. Davey was very interested in several things—music, certain kinds of novel, beer, Everton F.C., cycling, the sun, his daughter, friendship— and he liked to grow vegetables. Beyond these he had few interests. More than any other of Morant's friends, he was shaped by the sixties. After university he had lived in what sounded like a chalet above the beach at Aberystwyth, in a kind of commune which Morant knew would have been decidedly unideological and dedicated to good times, while he pursued MA studies of an obscure 19th century novelist. Morant gathered that he had, during this period, made some money driving a grocery van to outlying villages, or perhaps he had been a milkman. At some point at Aberystwyth he had met Frances, who was not a university student but—Morant couldn't recall exactly—was doing something like working in a library or taking a course in English as a foreign language. They married while Davey was at university or perhaps just afterwards. When Frances became pregnant Davey decided he needed to get a proper job, so he did a PGCE in Cambridge at some institution probably not affiliated to the university and secured a post in a comprehensive school in a market town-cum-pit village in the North Midlands. He worked in a department with other young people of his age where, as he later admitted to Morant, he failed to learn anything much about English teaching or, along with most of his colleagues, to become a mature adult. After several enjoyable years at this school he was interviewed for the post of second in English in Morant's department. He got the job because he was the only male to be interviewed and the school felt that another man was needed in a department that was all female apart from Morant. The other two interviewees were clearly superior to Davey and Morant argued furiously with his head and the school governors that one of them should be appointed, eventually having a row with a surprisingly cockney woman governor who said that those two women were all right but were too quiet and would get eaten alive by our kids, a view that Morant described as sexist, an opinion that scandalised the rest of the interview panel. Davey was appointed and the two women departed, one to become, after several quick promotions, a head teacher, and the other to become a head of department, then a deputy head and eventually an HMI. Davey said that he had initially been somewhat daunted by

Morant who seemed at interview an intense, perhaps humourless, person. As a second in department he was dutiful and discharged unfussily and efficiently such responsibilities as Morant asked him to assume. He was entirely lacking in creativity as a teacher, in how he worked in the classroom and in any role that was concerned with curriculum innovation. He was a good, safe teacher who got on well with his pupils and had what was clearly an easy classroom control. He told Morant, some years into their relationship, that he never quite believed in what he was doing, indeed in what education was supposed to do, or, as he said: to put it differently, he didn't really know what he was supposed to be doing. Morant observed that he hadn't mentioned any of this at interview. Morant was aware from early on that Davey was overawed by his seriousness and conviction, his, as it appeared to him, thoroughly worked out understanding of the job, how it should be organised and conducted, and this feeling persisted even after they had settled into an ironising, joshing friendship. Davey was sustained by an antique notion of duty—he would do his best by the school and the pupils. For Morant a sense of duty was fine but he couldn't imagine it without commitment to a set of values that were in the end political, some sort of transformative project in which you felt invested. Davey's duty was the sort that got you through, even or especially when you didn't really believe something was worth doing. Morant always imagined that his friend had picked this up from his schooling, the kind of ethic that was intended to fill the essential hollowness of the social mission of the public school, to fill it with a fine noise. Fortunately it was about all that he had retained from this background. Davey was an English (albeit Welsh) and educated version of a good old boy, and he was politically sound with a proper distaste for the bullshit and hypocrisy of the powerful and for unjust hierarchies. Also, he liked working class culture, the clubbable inclusiveness of pubs, the wheelers he went out with several times a week, the humour and prejudices, the exotic arcana, of people he met and came to know in these contexts, relishing their distinctive knowledges and etiquettes, accumulating a dense learning about cycle mechanics, beer, the protocols of football support and how to behave in a Liverpool pub. He didn't want to be working class but it seemed that he saw something rooted and perhaps authentic in these people from whom his upbringing and education had been designed to separate him. He seemed to admire their capacity for an unreflective exploitation of such opportunities for enjoyment and fulfilment as they were presented with in life, like the Lincoln City supporters he regularly encountered in his local pub who produced detailed, beautifully presented itineraries of away game destinations, itemising pubs—their beers, the standard of food on offer, the levels of friendliness of landlords, staff and clientele—and the public transport options that might guide or determine their choice of venues on the way to or back from the game. He admired and was perhaps cheered by such careful, peaceful attention to the possibilities of pleasure. Davey was very serious about pleasure, bringing the same concern for logistical precision to an evening out with friends as to a cycling holiday through Sri Lanka or southern Italy. On one Whitsun trip, after a day's walking and riding, he dragged the rest of the group after him around Brecon, refusing pub after pub as not offering satisfactory ales, unconcerned by or unaware of the irritation that was building around him. Since the point of an evening out with mates was enjoyment how could one consider compromise on the quality of its central activity. On this point Morant was at one with Davey. An evening spent drinking unpleasant beer was an evening spoilt. However, the incident put on display certain of Davey's fundamental characteristics—his self-centredness, his need for control of the circumstances of his life and, it seemed increasingly to Morant over the years, implicit in that painstaking concern that his life should proceed in an ordered and appropriate way was a certain precariousness, as if he might lose the grip he held on things. Davey's defences were always on show. Only to those who knew him well, though, since to almost everyone else he was the embodiment of geniality. He knew a particular kind of maleness inside out. He wanted to be left to have good times and not have to make too many judgements. He didn't really think that you could change very much about the world but he believed in behaving decently to everyone and, at work, where Morant could not tolerate laziness, cynicism or bullshit in a colleague, Davey could forgive any dereliction if it was accompanied by a certain roguishness. He was scrupulously polite to women, perhaps because he was wary of them. Morant knew of only one occasion where he had let matters slip in this regard. A female deputy head of legendary idleness had interrupted his conversation with a group of male colleagues to ask him if he had optically read some assessment data and he replied that no he hadn't, he'd read it with his arse. He knew immediately that he had behaved unpleasantly and apologised later that day. Wherever he went he made friends and he kept them. After Frances's death and his early retirement from teaching he was more often away than at his house on the edge of a small Nottinghamshire village, visiting friends in various parts of the country and abroad, going on cycling holidays in Crete, France and North Africa with other friends or making new friends on solitary holidays in Turkey, Australia or Kerala, new friends who would, once home, offer new destinations for conviviality. His house was a plain, sturdy structure, presumably Edwardian, that stood alone at the end of a lane leading nowhere out of the village, its orderly rooms filled with heavy, rustic furniture bequeathed him by relatives. Morant understood from Liz that this was fine stuff, although he found it a little ponderous, sitting too heavily in those rooms. There were odd touches that Morant found irritating—bamboo canes instead of proper poles for curtains and curtains that seemed to be made of tablecloth material, pottery bowls filled with bits of wood and dried up burrs and nut shells, the sort of plywood box that might be used during a house removal, now serving as a seat in the hallway next to a telephone. He wondered to Davey whether these represented the remnants of a foraging, make-do hippy aesthetic or were evidence of some sort of peasant race memory and he told him about a television programme he had seen in which several elderly scholars from the Celtic fringes were discussing whether there was an essence of Celticness and one Irish professor was of the opinion that it lay, if it was to be found anywhere, in a tendency to drive motorised farm vehicles erratically and a disposition to fill any gap in a hedge with an old bedstead. Beyond a small vegetable garden at the back of the house was an acre of land which when Frances had been alive had been used to graze a horse. From here you could see the cooling towers of one of the several power stations positioned at intervals of several miles along that stretch of the River Trent. These power stations were heavily picketed during the miners' strike in the early eighties and the strikers' inability to mount an effective blockade was decisive in bringing about the failure of their campaign. When he was at home Davey had frequent house guests but his life was always organised to a strict routine. During the day, unless a gale was blowing, he would cycle across Nottinghamshire and Humberside, often with a wheelers club from the nearby market town, and in the early evening he would drive to a pub in another, smaller, town, an establishment that offered the choice of at least eight real ales. He would drink two pints of beer as he talked to several of the many people he had got to know over the years, then perhaps have the barman fill a four pint take-home, and drive back to a meal he had prepared earlier. If he didn't take beer home he would drink a bottle of red wine during the evening and perhaps watch some TV or make calls to friends or relatives. Mostly, however, it seemed that he listened to music and read. He knew popular music from top to bottom, even the stuff he despised. Morant knew that what he most treasured was from the sixties—above all, perhaps, Velvet Underground, The Grateful Dead, Love, Van Morrison, Nick Drake—and he loved the blues and was persuaded to take country music seriously after listening to Gram Parsons. Once he made a tape for Matt which concluded, to Matt's horror, with some cowboy yodelling. He also knew a great deal about folk music although he refused to listen to English folk which he apparently saw as dismal dirge or hey nonny no and country gardens. He had other aversions which seemed to include almost all women singers and Leonard Cohen, the latter a rejection that was mysterious to Morant but which he sometimes thought might be based not on the singer's alleged gloominess so much as his preoccupation with the trials and pleasures of love, of intimacy. Morant admired the way in which Davey kept listening to music through the decades, developing enthusiasms for new stuff right up to his death in his late fifties, when a song by a group he had come across a month or so before was played at his funeral. Frances contracted breast cancer in her early forties and refused conventional medical therapy and what she saw as its invasive cut, burn and poison approaches, submitting herself instead to a then famous dietary regime which some people believed could cure cancer. Morant could not later recall if she had eventually agreed to surgery or other medical treatments but it seemed that she had survived and seen off the disease. In less than a year secondary cancers appeared and although she consented to radiation treatment and chemotherapy she died within a few months. Morant knew this pretty, fragile-looking woman as a gentle, quiet person who seemed, before her illness, to be making attempts to remedy her lack of education and career by taking night school courses and eventually training as a counsellor. He hardly knew her really, although he had, on the way to the Brecon Beacons with Davey one Whitsun, met her parents in a small bungalow in Herefordshire or Shropshire somewhere. The father had recently broken his leg and his shin and calf were exposed, alarming bolts protruding from the flesh. On arrival Morant had asked Frances's mother what the pleasant-smelling little shrub was by the front door and she gave him a cutting of the lemon balm as he left. He was, because he was good at such things, able to keep it alive during the trip and when he got home he planted it and was never quite able to control its proliferation throughout his garden. He formed an impression of gentility fallen on hard times and in the car later Davey told him, not without contempt, that his father-in-law had squandered what money the family had had—which amounted to what his wife had inherited and what she earned before retirement from her job with the local authority—on ill-informed financial investments. Morant gathered that he had never held any job for long and had given up work early because of what he claimed was ill-health. Like many silly men, Davey said, he was annoyingly full of ideas and opinions. One consequence of his irresponsibility was that his daughter was unable to go to university and had instead to get an office job. During the period of Frances's illness Davey was clearly—visibly—unhappy and struggling to deal with the situation. It was generally assumed that this was anxiety and concern for his wife, the consequence of his love for her. To Morant and one or two other friends it seemed that the strain he was undergoing had just as much to do with a desire to be free of the burden of care and then, perhaps, with guilt or shame that he should have had such treacherous feelings. Frances's funeral was followed by a wake in the meeting room of a local pub. This occasion was informed by a fervent determination not to be gloomy, an almost raucous insistence on celebrating Frances's life rather than mourning her death. Morant found this unsettling; he would always weep or rage at the passing of someone he loved, at all that had left the world, at all—the hopes, the pleasures, the animality and the love—that might have come to be, at never again sitting with those people, lying next to them as they farted in a tent, having them appear unexpectedly at your back window in ridiculous lycra, wheeling a bicycle and demanding lunch, and, in cases, holding them, feeling the warmth of their bodies against yours. Nothing more unexpected to come from them. There were people who, if they died, Morant's only response would be desperate grief. After Frances's death, Davey struggled on for a year or two with his teaching. A job that he had always disliked and which always worried him became more unbearable when Morant was seconded to the local authority to work with schools on literacy and Davey became temporary head of English. He hated the responsibility and had a long period off work with depression, for which he was medicated and briefly counselled, after which he retired on grounds of ill health. Translated to financial independence because the mortgage on the house had, upon Frances's death, been paid off and because a maiden aunt had left her favourite nephew (Morant had thought such things only happened in 19th century novels) most of her estate, Davey spent the next decade and a half travelling the world, often to visit his daughter in the various tropical countries where she worked in some sort of training role for charities and for the World Health Organisation. An early cycling trip down the east coast of Australia had included a detour inland that had taken in a village with a pub where Davey had inquired if they had accommodation. After a drink and a chat the landlord announced to everyone in the bar that they had a Pom in the house and they ought to have a bit of a celebration, so the village was notified and turned out for what Morant liked to think was a barbecue and what was definitely a party. If Morant had arrived at this village he would have had a friendly conversation with the landlord and perhaps one or two locals and then retired to his bed. Davey was personability distilled; his presence promised these people an evening of good cheer and amusement. At home he had a series of relationships with women, usually people he had met earlier in life, all of which foundered upon or were interrupted by anxieties about ensnarement in the responsibilities, the care and the net of promises that attend such relationship, except that in his last attachment he had grown fond of and concerned for the woman's young boy and had told Morant that although the only selfless thing that he had done in his life, the one achievement, was contained in his relationship with his daughter, he felt that he had also acquitted himself well with this boy. Even when he did something good, Morant noted, he doubted himself, whether he had done it for the right reasons, was always afflicted by this sense of failed duty, by an estrangement from the loving things he did, as if he mistrusted the reality of his feelings. And then Davey found a spot, a raised discolouration, high up and at the back of his right arm, which was soon diagnosed as a melanoma. After two operations to remove the tissue surrounding the lump and a number of black-outs he was told that the cancer had moved to his brain. He received some sort of laser treatment which for a while offered what immediately seemed to Morant the forlorn hope that the cancer had been dealt with, but then it returned and he was increasingly heavily sedated and eventually told he had perhaps six weeks to live. He was surprised that he might have that long and Morant saw—and wasn't surprised by this—that Davey was glad to be over with it, with life. An international on-line effort of support and solidarity was co-ordinated by friends in the village, his daughter returned to look after him and a stream of friends from around the country and beyond came to visit him in those last weeks. One Saturday morning a week or two before the end all the Whitsun walkers visited him and Davey was propped up on the sofa in his living room, his face puffy, swollen, and his speech slurred, swearing profusely and smoking again after several years during which he had appeared to have defeated the addiction, surrounded by unopened bottles of beer that visitors had brought, nearly all of which he would never drink because he could manage little in the way of alcohol at this time and because, as he commented, most of it was fucking shit. He had no time for politeness now, giving himself permission to swear and be ungrateful, to speak as he wished. He demanded that his friends one by one hug him and when Morant, because he felt that this urge to tactility contradicted everything that had gone into the relationship between these two fastidious men, said that it wasn't really his sort of thing, Davey said, without anger, well fuck off then, so Morant hugged him. By then he was returning each evening to a nursing home whose tolerant staff had in his first week there allowed him to have a drunken party with some wheeler friends. One night the following week Morant, previously uninvolved in Davey's care, was pleased to drive him back to the home, following a car driven slowly by Davey's university friend Mark who had, with his wife, been stopping at Davey's house. Davey kept urging Morant to drive a little more slowly and Morant, since he wasn't driving fast, wondered whether it was the drugs or the cancer that was producing this perceptual disturbance. He said that Morant should be careful to keep his grandchildren out of the sun and then, after a few seconds of silence, he said mates. His mates were looking after him. At the nursing home Morant watched Mark, with touching patience, undress his friend, put him into his pyjamas and guide his penis with careful precision so that the stream hit the toilet bowl, and then helping him into bed. Two nights later Morant and James visited him at the home. He was unconscious, lying on his back, and they sat in vigil with him and another friend who arrived some time afterwards and whom they did not know. They guessed correctly that he was finally dying and after an hour or so they kissed him on the forehead and left, James tearful. On the way back home they stopped at a Retford pub that Davey had liked to visit occasionally and in an almost empty room each drank a pint of indifferent bitter. Davey's daughter, Alice, asked Morant if he would like to choose a reading for the funeral service and he immediately thought that perhaps it should be something from a Cormac McCarthy novel, probably All the Pretty Horses, but he couldn't find a suitable passage until Matt rang him and suggested one which Morant read at the service. He explained that Davey had loved this novel and that this passage, which begins as the main character hitches a lift on a truck after release from a Mexican jail in which he had been unjustly imprisoned, seemed to suggest something of Davey's warmth and delight in the company of others and his goodwill, the essential decency that made him such a good and lovable man. And so he read how somewhere on the other side of Paredon the truck had picked up five farmworkers who spoke to John Grady with great circumspection and courtesy and how, with light rain falling, in the almost dark he offered them his cigarettes and they accepted thanking him once as they took them and a second time as he lit the cigarettes for them, and one of them, older than the rest, nodded at his cheap new clothes and said that he was going to see his bride and he said it was true. They said that that was good and, McCarthy writes, that after and for a long time to come John Grady would have reason to evoke the recollection of those smiles and to reflect upon the good will which provoked them for it had power to protect and to confer honor and to strengthen resolve and it had power to heal men and to bring them to safety long after all other resources were exhausted. On the journey, Morant read, the rain stopped and the night cleared and the moon that was already risen raced among the high wires by the highway side in the lavish dark, the fields rich from the rain with the smells of the earth, crops and horses, and at midnight they reached Monclova and he shook hands with the workers, thanked the driver and then watched the red tail light recede down the street and out the highway leaving him alone in the darkened town. He did not say that John Grady would not win his bride, nor that the passage made him think of the loneliness and the hope that drove Davey's constant travelling and that would cause him always to seek company in the darkened town. It was difficult to believe that his friend, so full of delight in life, so averse to self-reflection, was dead. James said that for some time afterwards if he was driving and saw someone in full lycra on a road bike he would for an instant wonder if it was Davey. Davey was the only public school graduate Morant had ever befriended. In fact he was one of the very few he had encountered on a regular basis in his life. He and Liz had spent a long weekend at a bed and breakfast pub in a Dorset village and on the second evening found themselves surrounded in the bar by what seemed to be sixth formers, all of them boys, apparently returning after a holiday to the public school that lay just outside the village. They were obviously very pleased to see one another again. He was struck by the rapt attention they gave each other, as they spoke and listened, maintaining eye contact much longer than was usual in a male conversation. As Morant waited at the bar for his drinks to be served a boy approached and was delighted to find, sitting on a bar stool, another boy whom he kept addressing as big man. An habitual politeness, no doubt instilled in him by his working class upbringing, prevented Morant from listening to the details of the boys' conversation but he detected an undertone of pathos as if something had been, or was on the verge of being, lost. The first boy was consoling the big man. There was, it seemed to him, nothing homoerotic in these exchanges but there was love and idealisation of some sort. When he returned to Liz he tried to explore his ideas with Liz, suggesting that these young people perhaps invested more than was usual in their school friendships, a passion that either they had no outlet for at home or that was produced by the long hours they were forced to spend in each others' company. He offered this banal thought tentatively to test the waters for further speculation as he knew that it was easy to annoy Liz on this topic. Sometimes Liz said that he, Morant, was obsessed with class, that his thinking about too many issues was forced through a class grille. He always replied that he was very interested in it, that it fascinated him and he thought that it had become a neglected category of analysis, but that he wasn't motivated by class anger or hatred. He didn't really see himself as having the right or inclination to claim affiliation to any particular class, but he was class-conscious and thought that everyone should be more class-conscious. On this occasion Liz said that she hadn't noticed any unusual intensity at work in the conversations around them. She said, as he knew she would, that it would be no surprise if they inhabited relationships with each other more intensely than was common amongst other social groups since it would be compensatory for the parental neglectfulness, the irresponsible cruelty involved in abandoning care for your child and sending them away to these places. What rejection these children must feel, what bewilderment—they must feel that they were being punished for doing something wrong. If they had spoken about private education in the past she had always emphasised the damage done to the children sent away to boarding schools above what Morant had seen as the poisonous social effects of separating one small group of children from all the others and then developing them as a ruling elite. He said to her that he wasn't sure whether these boys were really deeply absorbed in each other or whether they were acting out attention and care, not out of cynical calculation, not because they were being false, but because they had seen that this was what people did when they were concerned about other people. They adopted the outward forms of empathy and engagement because they had never completely lived through such involvements in their family lives and thus were not sure how to empathise. He had been the recipient of this kind of gaze when he was much younger. As a teenager he had gone to Brighton with his older cousin and his friends. They were curious about the mods and rockers fights that at that time had become a feature of bank holidays at seaside resorts, but their main reason for pitching tents in a wet field outside the town was to meet girls. His cousin and a couple of others did bring some girls back to the camp-site but Morant wasn't sure that they managed to persuade any of them to have sex. One of the girls showed some interest in him and he caressed her breasts, but he didn't find her attractive. Amongst his cousin's friends was an Irish lad who worked as a stagehand in a West End theatre and on the second day a colleague of his arrived at the site. Sid was amiable and obviously keen to mix with everyone, immediately joining the kick-around that several of the group were engaged in. He wasn't very good at football and he was posh. Morant felt ill at ease in his company and when he looked back he knew that it was and wasn't because of class feeling. It wasn't resentment or distrust—the young man was clearly pleasant and well-meaning, a nice person—but there was a disjunction, an awkwardness in communication that he came to think of as deriving from his and Sid's differing social backgrounds. In part this was to do with the almost anthropological curiosity that Sid directed towards the behaviour and views of everyone around him. But this was understandable; Morant would have been similarly interested if he had found himself living with a group of public school boys for a few days, although his curiosity would have had more disguise to it. Morant discovered that Sid had been a boarder at a school in Hertfordshire which played a yearly game of football against Morant's grammar school, apparently because the two schools shared trustees. Morant remembered that he had played in a game at the school and that after they had showered and dressed the team had gone to the refectory—a term he had not encountered before—for a tea served by women in full-length aprons, and a member of the opposing team had asked him and his team-mates if they had had enough food because if they hadn't he would call one of the sluts over to bring some more. Morant, whose mother was then working in a transport café, was not so much angered as surprised at the stupidity, the heedless lack of social awareness implicit in this boy's language. What unnerved him about Sid was the unwavering seriousness of the gaze he directed at him in the two or three conversations they had together, a concentrated focus on Morant's words that seemed disproportionate to the substance of what Morant had to say about what to do if you had a hangover, whether sport could be a force for moral good or whether Lawrence was all he was cracked up to be. Sid seemed to be scrutinising him, trying to read his face, his expressions, for truths and meanings that were not on supply. Morant was uneasily aware that he was trying too hard to explain these things to Liz. It wasn't that Sid was desperate for contact, for a recognition and intimacy that he had never been granted; it felt as if these were merely attempts, clumsy attempts, to understand what, for someone else, an inner life might be. Liz had no time for any of this. These friendships, and their relationships to their schools, were the abiding and significant attachments of their lives, the insufficient compensations—counterfeits—for what they had been deprived of. He supposed that this was true. He had always been struck by the thinness of the public school personality, as if several layers of selfness had been missed out, and this, it seemed to him, led to a fatal simplicity of understanding. From what he'd read, these characteristics were most nakedly on view in the pre-war upper class, a weird social fragment whose knowledge of the world was rigorously limited by their lack of interest in people from any class but their own, whose absolute confidence in their essential superiority sat with a comical naivety about their own emotions and those of others. Unfitted to run anything, they ruled the country, the shrivelled descendants of Nietzsche's aristocratic warrior class, unreflective and beyond good and evil, not because of their unbroken strength of will and desire for power, but because they had become imbecilic. These young people around him were, he guessed, not of that class, but it seemed to him that the schooling that they inherited from a colonial past performed its aboriginal function of separating them from the rest of society and forming them for rule, by ensuring that their passional attachments were to their caste and its destiny. It was just that the reason for rule, the justification for submitting to a leadership formation— the caste destiny—had disappeared with the dying away of empire. All that remained was to huddle together with others who were like you and to preserve a way of life that had lost its foundational meaning. So, that there were schools that turned out young men like Sid and Davey did seem very interesting to him. There was an obvious innocence, a gaucheness even, concerning the world beyond the one in which they had been cloistered, unless, like Davey, they chose to immerse themselves deeply in that different world. Morant had once been eating with James in a restaurant in Sedbergh when they became aware of a group of young men who appeared to be enjoying a school reunion. It was a quiet restaurant and they were speaking too loudly about people they had known at school, about a trip several of them had made to Shanghai and about the positions of career eminence that their acquaintances had already achieved. It became clear that these young men had not attended the public school of the town in which they found themselves but that they were ex-pupils of the most famous of all schools. Then they had begun to talk about teachers and one of them said that such and such a teacher had been absolutely brilliant and they all agreed and another said that you know why he was so good, it was because he had taught for years in a comprehensive school in Middlesbrough and had become really good by working in difficult circumstances with you know kids who weren't intelligent. James, who had been obviously irritated by this group, pushed back his chair and was starting to get up to have a word with them when he was headed off by a woman from another table who asked them to keep their voices down because other people didn't really want to listen to their opinions. What was remarkable was their obliviousness to people beyond their table, to the fact that what they said might be offensive or annoying to other people, that others might be different to them. Or else they didn't care. In the early nineties Liz's daughter had gone to a university in south-west England, one that had a reputation as a refuge for privately educated children who had failed to get into Oxford or Cambridge, and there she had on a couple of occasions gone to rooms lived in by such young people. She had noted with some astonishment the contrast between the luxury and comfort of these places and the house she shared with five other girls, accommodation that straddled the border between shabbiness and squalor. On one visit a group of young men began a complaint about unemployed people, the shiftless, quasi-criminal underclass, the benefit scroungers and single mothers shitting out babies who were dragging the nation into decline, and Sarah said that she had gone to a comprehensive school in an ex-mining village and that they clearly didn't have any idea of the problems that people in these places faced, nor of how they had, through no choice of their own, arrived at these circumstances and one of the young men had said shut the fuck up you commie bitch. It made him love Davey even more that, for all that he was scarred, he had, not fully reasoning why, managed to free himself from this upbringing, that he had sought a fuller being. Morant recalled that just before he was diagnosed with cancer, he, who had always been amused by nationalism and any suggestion that he might return to live in Wales, said in explanation that it was near impossible to get a decent pint of beer, said that actually he had recently felt a certain hiraeth, a longing to return to his own shore.

David Morant wondered why he felt love for the country in which he lived. It was a country that was decadent, vain and not inclined to address the truth about itself and the violences and injustices it had inflicted or was now inflicting on its own and other peoples. In this it resembled most other nations that were or had become powerful and wealthy. It was a country that liked to think of itself as admired across the globe: for its invention of parliamentary democracy, the modern industrial world and every sport in existence except tennis and lacrosse, its campaigning against slavery, its brave and initially lonely resistance to a mad mid-twentieth century eruption of fascist barbarity, its sense of humour and ethic of fair play, its talismanic possession of what was alleged to be, what was, it seemed, universally recognised as, the greatest writer ever to pick up a pen anywhere on earth or beyond apparently, its liberality and tolerance, its manifold and seminal contributions to science and its sturdy common sense. It was, of course, a fact that few of Morant's countrymen were much aware of how parliamentary democracy had come about or how it worked; they knew little about the industrial revolution and had never, at least willingly, attended a performance of a play by Shakespeare; they knew little and cared less about history, although they knew that we had beaten the Germans twice, and they were aware, in a fuzzy sort of way, that their country had once been the major world power and perhaps that an English pirate or sailor of some sort had had to interrupt a game of bowls to go off and sink the Spanish Armada. They seemed somewhat equivocal about liberality and tolerance, particularly with regard to poor and foreign people, although it must be said they sometimes resigned themselves reluctantly to doing the right thing; they were largely unaware of Newton but the minimally educated amongst them appreciated that Darwin had been important. Yet they felt pride in their country—some because, whatever their deficiencies as to detail, they thought that it had done some good things that had shaped the world and it had not been as brutal during and after its conquests as most other countries had been in the government of their colonies; others were proud because their country had indeed been irresistibly brutal during its imperial moment and had also throughout its history displayed a refusal to bend the knee to any other nation, all this stubbornness and belligerence justified because it was done in the best interests of less resourceful and mettlesome peoples who were in need of a benign subjugation if they were to be made free. At times this pride was affronted by the fact that when consulted the people of other nations often seemed to think that the people of this proud nation were hypocritical, arrogant, treacherous, not given to best hygiene or dental practices, cold and unfriendly. These were hurtful and bewildering misunderstandings, ingratitude for the proud country's donations to the world's politics, science, the arts, civilisation generally, industry and let it not be forgotten, the gift of the greatest pop group ever to sing and play their guitars and drums in the world or anywhere else. On the whole Morant was with the foreigners in this matter. But he loved his country, although he wouldn't go so far as to say that he was proud of it. He loved the land, the varied, beautiful countryside that itself told a story of tenderness and care as well as tyranny, brutality and expropriation. As a child travelling with his parents in their car, he would see a velvet sweep of meadow climbing up to woodland and, beyond, glimpses of rolling hills that seemed to him to beckon towards another England like the one in children's nursery rhyme books that he read throughout his life, an England of millers, minstrels, ragged beggars, skinny and half-starved dogs, kings and queens and knaves who rubbed shoulders with peasantry, crows and kites, where a man could leap into a bramble bush and scratch out his eyes and then jump into another bush and scratch them in again, where animals and inanimate objects sometimes spoke or danced and children fished streams, dancing around mulberry bushes, not caring a jot for anyone else, greedy fat boys sticking their fingers in pies and pulling out plums, sleepy girl shepherds with unblemished skin who lost their sheep—an England careless, jolly, anarchic, sunny and free. This seemed a glimpse of a different England that had certainly existed, still existed, but only in rhyme, story, dance and song and in occasional moments of grace. He did not want a return to this world because there was nothing to return to—it was a story, a race memory—and he didn't want to live in a world that was lawless and cheerfully violent. It wasn't even a golden age because it lacked what all golden ages must offer, the reign of justice and a perfected social being. But there was something in it that he yearned for, something unbiddable that spoke in defiance and mockery of all those empires of thought and rule that demanded compliance with, submission to, their versions, their judgements of what could and should be. In later years he came across a writer who had a character in a novel reprise the views of another character about his own country, another erstwhile imperial power, stating that it was economically decrepit, had nothing left but a congenital imbecility and hypocrisy in every conceivable area of administration and policy, was in fact no more than a rummage sale of intellectual and cultural history, an unsold remainder of government merchandise, in which sale the citizen is given only the last bid, the leftovers, a country in which any sign of intellectual energy is instantly transformed into a sign of intellectual weakness. This writer was sometimes criticised for a hysterical loathing of humanity but Morant thought that hysteria had its uses, hysteria was an understandable reaction that was revealing, not just of the hysteric's neuroses, but of the insurmountable corruption and idiocy that produced the hysteria and he thought that he would like to be hysterical at times and that yes this was about right, this writer's catalogue of moral degeneracy was just about right about Morant's own country and its tawdry, peacocking pride in ceremony, in spectacle that was invented to dazzle a population that was then, when this loathsome and absurd pageantry had been invented, and now, held fast in a state of infantilising ignorance, in a state of imbecility, and now this pageantry, this quite recently invented and bogusly historical spectacle, was offered to the world as a sign and display of a grave and rare national seriousness. Here is a country of enduring and admirable substance. But it looked to him like the mad at Bedlam, or the characters in Genet's brothel, dressed up in grotesque parody of rule, a country whoring itself to the world, a powdered and rouged, ancient Restoration decadent, and the world lapped it up, flies round the shit of this desiccated, deadening mummery, a country whose actual history had consisted of the usual, common to all countries, savagery that is licensed by the will to rule, but also by an imperial history of cunning and ruthless exploitation, vast intercontinental theft, blood-soaked repression, torture, the destruction of indigenous economic and social orders and the careless infliction of famine. And a country that had offered itself and its people, more perhaps than any other, to a vicious system of gambling, usury and licensed avarice that produced a population whose individuals had no idea why they were alive or what they should do beyond breeding, shopping, improving their homes and pursuing riotous or furtive pleasures in order to deaden the pointlessness of their existences, a country that was now beyond government because it had been given up to and was now ordered according to the requirements of this system of usury, gambling and avarice which politicians now dared not question, pimping their country, spreading its legs, selling it, to the agents of this system because they could see no other way of survival as a nation except by prostrating their country before these half-witted masters of the universe and, what's more, could imagine no other way of keeping favour with its citizenry, or at least that part that voted in national elections, the decent majority, hard working families, people who played by the rules and other thought-obliteratingly simplistic, sickening, lying characterisations, and which had been schooled to know no other reason for existence than to acquire ever more disposable income. And this country's habits of thought, its customary way of considering the world, of considering it pretty much done and dusted and not much to think about, nothing that common sense or an empirically guided realism can't handle, so that there wasn't really much to understand, no need for much thought, so bad things happened because of evil infecting individuals or descending on whole areas, whole countries—and history didn't count, the past shouldn't be dwelt upon, you couldn't make excuses for educational failure, rioting, poverty on the basis of people's childhoods, however destructive, however bleak, or a class's, a community's, a race's, a faith group's, a country's past ill-treatment, however neglected, however abusive it had been, since not everyone who had suffered neglect, abuse, injustice, poverty and so on, went on to riot, abused children and women, became indolent, unemployed, probably criminal, and lived off the state. It was simple, some individuals couldn't be bothered because they were, by nature, lazy, nasty, given to criminality, couldn't be arsed to play by the rules, lacked decency and so on, really there was no need to think further about this, it was all down to, it could only be, evil. Or genetics, which were real and accounted for a lot, but could be sorted out by science which was baffling, but amazing, our only hope. Science might one day discover how we should live together. A complacent people not much given to or caring for thought. And then there was the world. He had taught himself to ignore analyses that formulated theories of co-ordinated class conspiracy, secret elites, state or corporate cabals that ruled the world, the world being too various, too ramshackle and power not available, too promiscuous, for gathering up into such scheming, but he had been unable to ignore certain facts. It was clear that those who governed and those who owned the media of news and information edited the world to their own ends and Morant remembered the great English judge who spoke, concerning some unjustly accused Irishmen, what seemed to Morant at that time and now, an indiscreet truth, that it was better that innocent men remain in jail than that the integrity of this great country's judicial system be impugned. And then it was manifestly the case that the world was ruled by the rich or at least that it, the world, was ordered to their liking. They did not need to plot, co-ordinate or conspire, although that undoubtedly went on when their leaders and representatives met, because it was unimaginable, to them and everyone else, that things should be arranged differently, arranged in ways that would not be comfortable for them, the rich, not arranged, disposed, according to the values of self-interest, greed, ruthless competition, the maintenance of monstrous inequalities and systems of privilege, ordered according to the necessity of ensuring endless economic growth not just at the expense of social flourishing but also at the cost of despoiling and disfiguring earth, sea and air and all that lived therein—beyond imagination that it might be arranged in other ways, other dispositions made. This was a world that composed itself as it needed to be for its mechanism of wealth creation, its system of gambling, usury, theft and licensed avarice, to function, a world that had to have the rich and the poor, the informed and the ignorant, the satisfied and the discontent and all manner and all conditions of deluded and unhappy people if it was to work. If, as seemed to be the case, all societies, all groupings of people, from the neolithic on had sought control of the world and of its people then this last one, this current order, was simply the most daemonically inventive and exacting, the most dazzlingly magical, yet devised. This order in which he lived, an order that saw itself as based on freedom, on the individual's freedom of thought and action, was the most efficient, the most thorough, right down to the examination and shaping of individual souls, system of control yet devised. It seemed to come down to this. It seemed, from all that he had read and all the sense he could make of his life and this world, that there were two possibilities. Either we are tragic creatures, cursed by consciousness, by the uncanny trick of being able to reflect on our lives, victims of a prolonged infancy which breeds in us inexorably crippling fears, guilts and delusions and victims of the harsh schooling in becoming human that requires us to abandon, to rip ourselves away from our sleeping animal consciousness, so that we become prey to an insatiable, unrelenting longing born of an immemorial rupture, which means that it is a miracle that any of us manage to build sanity and goodness and the best we can hope for is a stoic refusal to bend to the fates and to the sense that something, some fullness, has been lost forever, and through that very trick of self-consciousness, attempt to wrench poise from experience so that we can feel the majesty and the teeming pleasures of this life. Or, we can throw off that enslavement, those chains, because they are only human inventions, a way that the fearful and calculating have evolved for keeping human potential in check and under their rule, and if such conditions were changed—and they can be—human creativity and joy would seed the world, free of the constraints that deform and distort human desire. He tended to the former view. Once he had been reading Nietzsche, a man who had in the end been driven mad by his extreme sanity, a man who, as far as Morant understood it, had striven to imagine a way of being that was free of crippling self-consciousness, a man whose figuring of a form of pre-abrahamic humanity, an aboriginal aristocratic bearing that was untouched by sympathy, guilt or doubt, a being that acted in unreflecting affirmation of its desires, in ways that might be cruel but were never vicious, was, like the world of English nursery rhymes, in the end no more than a figuring of what had been lost but had never really been. At this time Morant had had a dream in which he was dreaming. In this dream he dreamt himself, as he sometimes did when he was awake, as the father of daughters. He lay in bed at about six o'clock in the morning in one of his daughters' houses, slipping in and out of sleep, never quite waking fully. Soon he would have to get up, shower, dress and drive to another daughter's house to get her across London for a hospital appointment and to look after her two children while this took place. In one of the more waking moments in the dream he found himself wondering which earlier historical periods he might choose to live in. He decided that he wouldn't like to live in any earlier society because they were all likely to be more brutal and disease-ridden than the one in which he actually lived. Then he started to dream himself on another journey. He was outside a long, palatial building whose appearance did not become clear in the dream, but which seemed to have a hedge fronting it and behind the hedge, although he couldn't see it, a ditch, almost a moat. He knew that the present he was inhabiting was Roman and that there was to be a violent conflict, a duel, involving a legendary figure who had faced, fought and won many such challenges and a younger warrior. He was aware that the older warrior's victory was almost certain. Then a gladiatorial figure appeared, leaning out from an entrance to the palace at the far end of the hedge. He moved jerkily, warily, almost comically, as if miming alert caution, like a puppet figure. He wore a helmet or perhaps it was a tricorn hat and he held a short sword in his right hand. He spied a figure to Morant's left, a bit further up a grassy bank that rose gently to another hedge. This man, if it was a man, did not move and was hooded and cloaked. The gladiator moved quickly and again with that cartoonish abruptness towards the hooded figure and immediately struck him with the sword. After several blows his opponent was still standing, unmoving, and somehow the gladiator's sword had become stuck in what seemed to be a helmet inside the hood of the other figure. Morant saw the gladiator's face clearly. It was the face of an idiot, young, suid, his open mouth showing a few widely spaced teeth, the face of a man who had experienced little and knew only a few things. He looked puzzled that he should be unable to detach his sword from his antagonist's helmet and that it should have been rendered useless in this way. He was incapable of imagining the annihilation that awaited him. This was grand guignol, a genre Morant had always detested. In the dream he walked quickly towards the entrance from which the younger combatant had emerged, unwilling to witness the savagery that was about to ensue. Inside the house he made his way through a series of long rooms in which people were engaged in desultory orgy, although he could not recall—he believed that in the dream he did not see—any specific acts of debauchery. The rooms were filled with beds, almost like a hospital ward, and were occupied by couples most of whom seemed to be resting from their endeavours. He had an impression of soiled, stale sheets, a tired and played-out sensuality or a sensuality that wearily, unenthusiastically, obeyed some external compulsion, perhaps a customary expectation. In one bed a fat elderly man with pendulous breasts and a horse-faced, ectomorphic woman lay and Morant asked them the way out of the building and they said to keep going in the direction he was taking and that after the last room he would find a corridor leading to an exit. He arrived at what seemed to be a store-room, cluttered and untidy, full of ring-binder files, cardboard boxes of documents and plastic chairs, and this room had a window that would not open and no door to the outside. The corridor itself did not lead to an outside door. This was a variant of a dream that returned, tediously, again and again. He was in a building— his old school, a huge factory, a block of flats—and he did not know the way back to the outside, however much he walked corridors, scaled walls or surveyed things from high windows or rooftops. The difference this time was that whereas he never felt threatened in these dreams on this occasion he was aware that the hooded warrior might, perhaps would, be pursuing him. He had to go back to get better directions and to do this before the faceless nemesis could find him. He began to do this without feeling great fear, simply a necessary urgency. Then he woke up, still dreaming of a journey across London. Merciless violence, Rome, puppetry, a faceless figure, pallid orgy, a labyrinth, a pursuer. What to make of this. It made him think that perhaps the ancient world was not a site of vital affirmation but of a dumb compulsion, a place where flesh did not express itself with joy but with a stale weariness, where violence was not enacted with aristocratic decisiveness, but repetitively, addictively, as a way of compensating for deadness of feeling. Greece and Rome were about death, not life. Tawdry, banal, coarse.

When he was a young man Morant had been bewitched by the glamour of a boxer whom many consider to have been the greatest of all pugilists, Sugar Ray Robinson, who had relinquished the noble name he had been born with, Walker Smith, because, it is said, he did not want his mother to know that he had become a boxer. Morant, after he had renounced interest in boxing, had been reluctantly captivated by the career of another boxer, the Argentinian Carlos Monzón. Robinson was grace and intelligence, his athletic power ordered by extraordinary wit and courage. His boxing, even as it enacted the brutal defeat of his opponents, was a joyful thing, overflowing with delightful invention. Monzón was exceptionally tall for a middleweight and had no immediately obvious brilliance as a boxer, nor was he, at least in terms of the single killer blow, a destructive puncher. The intelligence that informed his fighting was narrow but intense, horribly focused and directed to the diminution of his opponent's strength and his eventual destruction. He was sometimes on the back foot in the early parts of his contests but always throwing punches, never covering up but employing footwork—whose intelligence you could easily miss since it was so economical of movement, so unshowy—to avoid punishment, and gradually his unceasing blows would outnumber those of his opponents, who would often take on a look of bewilderment or despair as if they felt they were in the ring with some inhuman and irresistible force and eventually they would crumple to the canvas or seek refuge in undignified retreat. There was something machine-like about Monzón—neither courageous nor imaginative. Robinson, often described as an artist, revealed, like a bullfighter, the beauty that inheres in destructive struggle; Monzón was an agent of atrophy. Both men came from impoverished backgrounds, the one born into rural poverty before his father, in search of work, moved his family to Detroit—Robinson said that it was a lifelong regret that his father, doing two jobs, worked eighteen hours a day, so that he only really saw him on Sundays—the other, one of twelve siblings, growing up in the dispossession of an Argentine barrio. Both were loved by the people from whom they came, but Robinson, like Monzón a handsome man, could sing and dance almost as well as he boxed and shone with a joyful vitality that enraptured the world. When he stopped boxing Robinson returned to poverty, contracted Alzheimer's disease and died aged 67. Monzón, often as violent outside the ring as in, murdered his second wife by throwing her off the balcony of their apartment and was sent to prison for eleven years before dying in a car crash after, inexplicably, being allowed out of prison on parole for the weekend. He was fifty-two. Morant sometimes worried that he did not find Robinson, whom he had witnessed training near the dying end of his career in a Soho gym in preparation for a fight he would lose to the British champion Terry Downes, the more attractive figure as a boxer, but the truth was that he became increasingly intrigued by the relentless destructive intent of the Argentinian.

One evening he went to bed early to continue reading, for the third time, Sebald's The Rings of Saturn. Liz had gone out for her regular Monday night drink with a friend. He read for twenty minutes or so, immersing himself in the strangely pleasurable verbal textures and the interlapping narratives that seem to come unbidden to the writer, pondering how the book's insistent gloom, the patient recording of histories of failure and decay, of defeated hope and the foetid savagery of power, could produce in him pleasure and something like optimism—a vital energy—when he grew sleepy and so turned off the bedside light and after sitting up to take a couple of co-codamol tablets because that evening the arthritis in his shoulders was particularly discomforting as he lay on his side, he went to sleep. After an hour or so—the clock at the side said it was 11:10—he woke up, saw that there was no one beside him and became worried. He went for a piss in the shower room and became anxious about his brother's whereabouts, why he had not returned home. He knew that his mother was out—that could be explained—but why had his brother not come to bed, not come home. He was aware that he was confused and when he shouted down the stairs he did not call a name but just said hello because by now he was not sure who should be coming home, who he thought might or might not be in the house. Eventually a proper understanding of his situation was restored and he knew that it was Liz who would be coming into the bed alongside him, that his mother was dead and that his brother whom he had not spoken to for nearly two years and had not met for far longer than that, was living on the outskirts of Worthing, almost never leaving his house, still trading collectables online, paring his life, his friendships, his enthusiasms, down to a minimum that would satisfy his needs and limit the exhaustion and threat involved in engagement with others.

For years as children they had shared a double bed, its feather mattress sagging into the middle. He remembered something they used to do if they were not sleepy: they would see if his brother could fit his legs inside Morant's pyjama bottoms, his left leg entering his older brother's right pyjama leg, his right, the left; then they would attempt to do the same with the sleeves of their pyjama jackets, but as far as Morant could recall they often tipped over sideways at some point in this operation, which caused laughter or perhaps led to a renewed attempt to complete the procedure. On one occasion their mother had come in on this and asked what they were doing. They weren't touching one another were they. He could still feel the blush of embarrassment at this suggestion and they told their mother angrily that they certainly were not doing anything. As he grew older his brother had been a popular boy, a good footballer and quite successful with girls, but after he married at a very young age, he began to draw curtains around his life. When Morant went back to bed he had the thought that perhaps his brother had died and that he would receive a telephone call from his sister-in-law or one of her sons to tell him that this had happened. He found this a ridiculous and annoying thought. Two days later he went for a walk with his friend James and once they had climbed up from a river valley to the high moors he became aware that although he could sustain a conversation with James his head was swarming with thoughts over which he had no control. The thoughts in themselves were not alarming but his inability to control them, to raise them to full consciousness or to dismiss them from half-consciousness, was perplexing. Shards of thought, words and perhaps images, kept invading his head, but only briefly, and they were fugitive. The more he tried to hunt them down and give them some sort of meaningful fullness, the more they slid away and were replaced by other equally fragmentary thoughts. They refused to be placed in context. What he wanted to know was when he had thought these things before; because they were recollections, but recollections that refused wholeness. And when had he thought them or said them. Was it a few minutes ago during this walk he was undertaking or had he dreamt these things last night. Were they perhaps new thoughts. Were they thoughts from another life he led but did not know he led. Was this an image and foreshadowing of death or, more properly, dying, the falling away of one's powers, so that life and consciousness ebbed down to the unbidden and senseless repetition of bits of language, like a wireless set randomly tuning in and out across the frequencies, and he remembered years before leaning down behind a television in the corner of his living room to plug in a scart connection and as he struggled to insert the thing he saw a strip of paper attached to one of the leads coming out of the television. He had noticed before this small—he guessed once sticky, once shiny—dust-speckled paper tube wrapped around the flex, but now as he struggled to find the correct socket for the scart his face was close to the paper and he read, several times and more or less involuntarily, the letters ILGC and the number 3000495, and later it occurred to him that as he died instead of a sweet image of a place or a loved face or a precious voice accompanying the last pulses of consciousness he would see or keep thinking of, as if in a fever, an image of a thin soiled ribbon of paper, down behind an old-fashioned television set, on which was written the faded and meaningless information ILGC3000495. After a while he realised that this condition had disappeared and he tried to explain to James, as they negotiated the puzzles set by the sodden terrain, what he had experienced, but he wasn't sure that he had made his friend understand what it had been like. A few days later he was reading in bed when he became aware that his head was once more racing with random thoughts and he wondered if this was the beginning of some sort of dementia. The following day he realised that what linked these episodes was consumption of co-codamol tablets so he stopped taking them and these experiences ceased. Around the time of his sixty-eighth birthday it was borne in upon Morant that he was becoming old. This was an uncomfortable recognition. He detested the infirmities that were beginning to infiltrate his body, limiting what he could do, and almost every day he thought about the closeness of death. Curiously the one physical difficulty that had been with him most of his adult life had troubled him less in recent years. Since his late twenties he had suffered from pain in his knees and on three occasions he had undergone physiotherapy for medial ligament damage which, for quite lengthy periods, prevented any but the gentlest kinds of walking. But he had learnt how to manage this fragility and when he went into the hills he used a walking pole and bound his creaking, clicking knees in neoprene supports. In recent years, however, he had been visited by a series of ailments which confronted him with the fact that the scope of his physical capacity was to become increasingly contracted in what remained of his life. He had been walking along a canal footpath when he flung to one side, with his left hand, the long stem of grass he had plucked from the canal side earlier in the walk. A sickening pain had flared in his shoulder, so intense that he had had to stop walking and the world, the footpath that was quilted with leaves, the rooks he had just observed sitting, intensely still, in a tree across a field on the other side of the canal, the water by his side, unperturbed by any wind, easing its way serenely towards the little stone bridge a hundred yards ahead of him, all this collapsed into the tearing pain in his shoulder and upper arm. A month afterwards, the pain now an ever-present ache, an orthopaedic surgeon at his local hospital offered him shoulder joint replacement surgery and six months after that offered him the same procedure for his right shoulder. After establishing, over a number of visits to review his situation, that the two operations would take at least six months out of his life and that their main benefit would be pain relief, with his range of movement probably more limited than at present, he decided to put up with the discomfort, a decision which the consultant, an Asian man with a London accent and a casual but honest manner who had amused Morant on his first visit by ignoring him for a couple of minutes while he appeared to be checking his text messages, agreed was probably the most sensible option, saying that it was actually a procedure that was most popular with what he referred to as old ladies in their late seventies who were just delighted to be free of pain. One day, whilst he was shopping at a supermarket a few miles outside the village in which he lived he became aware of a disturbance in his vision. On one side there was a rippling effect and on the other, the right-side, a blind spot. He had had something like this as a child when he had had too much sun, but then he had felt sick and now he didn't. He could see well enough to finish his shopping and to drive home. He was interested to note how it was possible to manage driving even with impaired vision and he was unexpectedly comforted by the experience, recalling him to those irresponsible times in his early life when he had driven a car when he shouldn't have. When he arrived home he was feeling tired and went to bed for an hour and when he awoke his sight was back to normal. However, over a couple of years he had less severe recurrences of the disturbances and was referred by his G.P. to the hospital's ophthalmology department. After several months and a number of tests, an

X-ray and an ultrasound scan he was told that his problem was not a visual one and he was referred to a ward in General Medicine which he discovered on arrival was the stroke clinic. He kept this information from Liz as she was already alarmed about his condition. After an ECG test which the nurse said revealed no problems he was taken to see a doctor who touched the point of some sort of pin against various parts of his body and conducted other tests which Morant assumed were to determine whether his neural pathways were functioning properly. He was told that in the doctor's view the disturbances he had experienced either brief strokes or migrainous episodes. He was then referred to another hospital for an MRI scan. Liz, who was now acquainted with the full story concerning these visits, accompanied him on a bleak winter Saturday when the hospital seemed to be closed down except for the people attending the medical imaging department, and after a brief wait he was inserted into the mouth of a giant machine as if for cremation and his body's magnetic field subjected to a reordering he didn't understand. In the machine he had in his line of sight a reflected image of the two members of staff who were operating the scanner and periodically he would look at them to see if they were reading results as they were disclosed, but for the most part they seemed simply to be chatting. He was intrigued by the variations of percussive noise produced by the machine and at one point started to laugh because it seemed to be repeating the words bugger off. In the reception area afterwards he was saddened to see that the two other patients awaiting scans were young children accompanied by their parents whose kindly but inexpressive faces disguised what must have been their fear and anguish. He saw the doctor two weeks later and was told that the scan had indicated no significant problems and that the likelihood was that he had experienced mild migraines. However, the doctor said, the MRI had revealed evidence of minor damage, probably as a result of a very slight thickening in the wall of the carotid artery causing a reduction in the oxygen supply to the brain. He was then shown an image of what he supposed, probably wrongly, was the cerebral cortex which was dotted with a few tiny white points. This was no more than the wear and tear that was common in someone of his age he was told, but blood tests had revealed that his cholesterol levels were a little high, as was his blood pressure. These results were not something to be terribly worried about but as a precautionary measure, to guard against the possibility of more serious harm being inflicted, the doctor suggested a prescription of statins and low-dose aspirin, a tablet of each to be taken once a day. Morant was concerned more than anything at the time that his cholesterol and blood pressure levels were elevated. The last time they'd been checked, quite recently, they were at unremarkable levels, and he made a mental note to raise this with his doctor. Then, a few months afterwards, a pain developed over a period of a few weeks in his lower back slightly to the right, at times acute at its epicentre below the top of the pelvis but above the buttocks, and spreading as a more generalised ache around his hip and into his right groin. His right testicle was painful as well. He told his doctor that ibuprofen did not seem to reduce the pain and he was prescribed amitryptilene and referred to the hospital for an X-ray. A week later his doctor rang to say that the X-ray appeared to indicate that the problem was caused by a degenerative disease in the lower lumbar region resulting in compression of a nerve. He had osteoarthritis in the lower back. Morant had been hoping that the problem might be muscular and susceptible to physiotherapy. However, it was a relief not be offered the diagnosis he had most feared which was that his hip joint had gone the way of his shoulders and would require replacement. His doctor told him that there was no need for him to stop hill-walking and that the condition might not get any worse. They would have to wait and see. But Morant hated all this. The physical ailments in themselves were dispiriting but what was worse was the feeling of becoming hedged around by the signs of entry into elderliness, of being herded towards an enclosure where you were expected to accept your status as frail, vulnerable and in need of protection. He worried that his life was beginning to be organised according to a regime of pill-taking: in the morning a capsule he had been taking for at least ten years, what he had seen described as a proton-pump inhibitor, designed to reduce acid reflux in his oesophagus; after his main meal he was instructed to swallow a 75mg aspirin tablet and at night a statin and the amitryptilene pain-killer, which he had been disturbed to see was mainly used as an anti-depressant and to treat children who wet the bed but which now, he was assured, was mainly prescribed in low doses for the relief of lower back pain. He had seen how this went with his mother. One of his tasks had been to load her pill organiser, sequencing her intake of drugs over a week, although neither she nor the carers who visited at different times in the day seemed able, in her case willing, to keep to this routine. He saw now that the cause of the rage that had overtaken her at this time, as much as her weakness and dependency, was that this hounding regimentation was an imprisonment; it told her that it might keep her alive but it would require her living in a cage. He could see all this coming when early one January morning he passed the G.P. surgery and saw outside it half a dozen or so people, all, he guessed, of his age, some a bit younger, some older, waiting for the surgery's doors to open. These, it seemed to him, and no doubt he was being unfair to them as individuals, were people who had accepted the judgement that they needed help to be kept alive, who felt depleted, who had relinquished control of their lives and trusted its direction to others, who had resigned themselves to entry into that half-life that began with a wait outside a medical practice for a lengthening drugs prescription or a consultation from which they hoped to wring some reassurance, all this to end with immobility, spoon-feeding, colostomy bags, incontinence products and carers calling you sweetheart in a nursing home that could never quite rid itself of the scent of piss and shit. Up until his mid-sixties he believed that he had prepared himself for physical decline and death. He had steadily conceded powers and freedoms to time. He had given up running in his late thirties because he risked pulling muscles, tearing ligaments and straining tendons if he ran more than a few hundred yards. Throughout his thirties and forties he had gone through a process of accepting and accommodating to this reduction of his capacities. He began then a long process that led to him now abstaining from any rigorous exercise, except walking. Press-ups and sit-ups were the last thing to go once his osteoarthritis sank deep. He seemed also to have convinced himself that it was inappropriate for a man of his age to pursue an interest in women and the truth was that since he and Liz had lived together it had not occurred to him to seek a relationship with another woman. He had, happily, avoided lust for young flesh, that peculiar pain and indignity that can visit an ageing man. He was unsure to what extent this forbearance was the result of satisfaction with his present circumstances, a triumph of self-shaping, or a lessening of sexual desire. In his forties he had managed to rid himself of career ambition and with it any desire to impress with his achievements, not that that desire had ever been very exacting. He had never really wanted power or position because in his experience those who achieved them in his field were rarely able to do much to change things for the better—for the worse, yes. But now, quite suddenly, he realised that he had not prepared himself at all well for decline. This withering away of his strength and vigour was dismaying and, he felt, shaming, and he was obstinately regretful that never again would his body command the confidence and arrogance he had once delighted in; but what occupied him above all was anger at the limited time left to him. After his mother had moved into a nursing home he had returned again and again to the trail of piss that ran between her bed and along the hallway to her bathroom, attempting to scrub the stink out of the carpets, but there was one patch next to her bed that refused to give way to cleansing, lingering as a reminder of his mother's fury and panic at her body's treason. It was the seasons that got to him, coming and going so quickly. If it was winter he would as always look forward to spring and summer, warm skin, light clothing, eating outside, swimming in the sea, the engulfment of the earth by vegetable life, screeching hordes of swifts swooping over the garden just before dusk, a long view down from a high point in some southern hills across a green landscape laid out by the sun, down to a flat, blue sea. Now he thought that he should not wish the winter away since he had so few years, so little time left, perhaps ten of these summers, these glistening years, and a weakening body coming between him and life. He felt rage that soon it would be over for him, all the splendour of this life, his place amidst it. He had no wish for an after-life, just a lot more of this one. No male member of his family, on either side, had lived beyond seventy-six years. His friend Matt, three years younger, had walked the Simien mountains in Ethiopia the year before and this year was trekking in the Himalayas. There was perhaps a certain desperation in this or at least a defiant determination to make the most of what was left and Morant would have joined him if he thought his legs would stand up to thirteen successive days slogging away in the mountains. Instead he was going to go with James on a shorter walk through mountains in Turkey, that was if James recovered in time from the knee injury that had crippled him on Helvellyn at the end of August the year before when he had been fine going up but in agony going down so that Morant had been required to halt every thirty or so yards to let him catch up. While he waited he was passed, amongst others, by a series of middle-aged ladies who told him how brave his friend was—to his amusement but also slight irritation because he was fed up hanging about and he knew how James would be loving the attention. Morant had observed James's delight if he had the opportunity to fall into conversation with well-mannered women of his age or, even better, younger by a decade or two. And then at the bottom of the mountain, James being unable to complete a loop through a forest track back to where Morant's car was parked, Morant, to save time, walked back the two miles along the pedestrian-pathless main road to the car park, on several occasions drivers gesticulating that he shouldn't be walking there and one, in an ancient mini, even making to drive at him. Fuck you, he thought. He remembered his first fight. For about a week before he had been unable to think about much else. On the day itself he was unwilling to engage with anyone at any level except the functional. At the time he was working in the buying office of a drugs company and he negotiated the day without any of the usual social interactions, the moments of humour and personal exchange that eased you through the tedium of the work. The show was to take place in, as far as he could remember, some sort of galleried municipal hall and as he approached the building the thought brushed his mind that perhaps he and everyone else involved in the contests of that evening would be overtaken by a larger violence because in those few days Kennedy and Khrushchev were squaring up over Cuba. Inside the building he located the changing room where he found his trainer and other fighters from his gym and after changing into his gear he was weighed and for the first time met his opponent. Then he waited to be called for his bout. His trainer bandaged his hands and afterwards Morant sat leaning against a wall with his legs stretched along low bench seating. He felt drowsy and withdrew entirely inside himself, wanting no communication with anybody and without effort freeing himself of any focused thought. He felt at peace. It was like this with every one of his fights. There are two kinds of fear that might afflict a boxer. One is the fear of physical injury, but Morant suspected that this must be very rare since most sane people who feared pain or harm would steer clear of boxing. The other is the fear of humiliation, an emotion that every fighter must face and work to control, except, perhaps, for certain veteran journeymen professionals, the sort who are engaged to test the progress of a young, upcoming boxer on the undercard of the main bout, men who have long ago resigned themselves to defeat, accepted defeat as their necessary occupation, have learnt to live without the prospect of victory. All such fear left Morant in these moments before the fight and once inside the roped-off square they called a ring he was only conscious of a need for circumspection, that victory was never given. When he was called for his contest he was aware of a crowd and the ring all lit-up and now from his corner he took in his opponent, a boy, a young man, of about his own age, slightly shorter than Morant and more thick-set with short, wiry fair hair. He looked like young men he had played football against on the Hackney marshes, young men who were loud and comfortable inside a masculinity that expressed itself as knowing, confident, as having sorted out the world and what it was about, a knowledge and organisation that depended upon and revolved around clear, carefully limited certainties. Morant knew instantly that most of those who were to watch this fight would assume that his opponent would emerge as the winner because he looked more of a lad than Morant, tougher, and Morant was then, aged seventeen, quite skinny and he didn't have a boxer's face. The young man looked as if he expected to win, but Morant knew that he wouldn't. He took in a nervousness in his opponent, which was probably based more on a generalised fear of defeat than any personal apprehension about him, Morant, and Morant saw too stiffness, an inflexibility in his body and legs that would not serve him well in the boxing ring. Once the bell had rung he saw in the first couple of exchanges that his opponent had lost all confidence in his chances. He threw a number of easily evaded punches and then started bouncing around the ring, presumably in imitation of, as he was then known, Cassius Clay. This stopped when Morant landed his left lead for the first time and his opponent went into a kind of crouch, throwing punches without really looking where they were going. Then Morant crossed a right that caught him high on the head and the young man charged forward blindly and held Morant in a clinch in order not to be hit again. The referee separated them and then the bell went. These were only two minute novice rounds. In the second round the other fighter had clearly decided to go for survival and kept trying to grab hold of Morant and wrestle. Morant side-stepped one of these forays and caught his opponent with a left-hand on the back of the head, more of a push than a punch, causing him to stumble and fall to the canvas, and the referee called them together and admonished them both to make more of a fight of it. Then his opponent stood off and it was as if he was accepting his fate. Morant was filled with a sense of power emptying itself from his opponent and flowing into him. There was no pleasure at the prospect of the pain or the humiliation that he was about to inflict on his opponent, but there was pleasure in exerting his dominance and feeling that as he quartered the ring he was steadily, purposefully, cutting down the other fighter's possibilities of escape. He caught him with two jabs and then a right cross full on the jaw, knocking him down. He tried to get up but the referee ended the contest there. Morant felt elation and relief and once his adversary was on his feet, performed the gesture, the ritual of the victor in a boxing match, of going across and paying his respects to the opposite corner. After he had showered and changed he went back into the hall and was approached by a middle-aged man who congratulated him on his win and said that if he was interested he could come the following Monday to the Tottenham and Enterprise where he was working with two professional fighters. He said that Morant was raw but he could sort that out. He could teach him how to box. He said that Morant liked dishing it out but that he was careful not to take it, and that wasn't necessarily a bad thing. One of Alfred Biggins's professional fighters was a Jamaican, Derek Brooks, who, when he occasionally gave Morant and his cousin George a lift home after training, played dirge-like, sentimental songs on his car's sound system. Morant recalled these as examples of lover's soul, although he could much later find no reference to that term as a musical genre. He remembered that Derek and another Jamaican boxer, Anthony, a good-natured middle-weight, used to tease a young Antiguan boy, younger even than Morant, into a state of fury by claiming that on Antigua they ate monkey. In his sixties Morant googled Brooks under his ring name of Al Brooks and found details of his fight record. Derek had been a very good boxer who won a tournament at Wembley Stadium aimed at finding a new British heavyweight contender. Unfortunately the tournament's organisers had been hoping for a new white fighter to emerge as the victor. At that time black boxers were not considered good box office, which is to say they were discriminated against. There was no market for a great black hope and Derek was not promoted, his career not managed in such a way that he might prosper, and the fight record showed a gradual at first and then a rapid decline, ending with a series of TKOs. Morant guessed that by that stage Derek was no longer under the guidance of Alfred, a kindly, interesting and knowledgeable man. Morant also found a hosted blog in the name of Al Brooks which had only one post, a poem about the writer's love for a woman who although they sometimes quarrelled, shared his sorrows and his joys and made him feel like a somebody when he was a nobody. Morant had never seen Derek as someone who would write in this way, but whether it was him or not, rightly or wrongly, he found this unutterably sad. The fight record said that his home town was Tottenham and that seemed wrong too. Sometimes Morant drove through a nearby village, past two pubs that for decades had faced each other across the road. Then one day he saw that one of them was boarded up and within a remarkably short time it became a ruin, the rendering of its walls peeling off, windows cracked and broken and the whole somehow faded as if it was gradually disappearing from the world. It was smaller. It had dwindled. He had never visited this pub, although he had many years before occasionally drunk at the other across the road, the Blacksmith's, during a time when he was briefly friendly with someone who lived in this village, a head of English at a school neighbouring Morant's, a man several years older than him. Richard was divorced, his wife despairing of her partner's recurring infidelities, on one occasion, as Richard told it, emptying the contents of his wardrobe and a chest of drawers out of the bedroom window into the front garden. Eventually Richard rented a small house—dingy, bleak—in the village and continued to drink almost every evening in the Blacksmith's where he was always surrounded by—occasionally Morant thought it was as if he had surrounded himself with, had himself assembled—a companionable group, some of them teachers from his school, but others who perhaps might be builders, businessmen or farm workers. In fact, Richard knew everyone in the pub, any of whom might have been gathered into his evenings. Richard ran a good department and with Morant set up the local English teachers' association and years earlier Liz had briefly taught alongside him in a legendarily progressive school in London. Morant came to see that it was as if Richard hardly allowed the world to touch him, that everything that might weigh upon him—a comfortable home, a marriage, intimacy and love—was as nothing to him. It was enough that he had the regularity of evenings spent in the company of people he knew and who knew him but not too well, in conversation eased by alcohol, and that from time to time he would couple with some woman or other who found in him an inscrutability and controlled waywardness that for her own reasons she found attractive. Or so all this seemed to Morant. Later Richard bought a bigger, no less dingy or bleak house in another village, where almost every evening he drank in one of the two village pubs, surrounded again by a diverse company of people, and then he became an English adviser in Manchester and after a few years died too young of a heart attack. It was difficult to see if Richard had ever loved anyone. He had a son—a teenager and apparently a gifted athlete— who had moved away with his mother after the divorce. He spoke about him as if he were someone of interest and someone in whom he felt a little pride but who did not seem to be an object of his love. It was not that he was avoiding intimacy but, as it seemed to Morant, that it did not occur to him as a need. Occasionally, during the time that Morant had known him, Richard and his group would fall out with the Blacksmith's landlord, over something like the landlord asking them what they wanted to drink when he well knew what they drank and was just being awkward, and they would decamp for a time to the pub opposite. Now if Morant drove past this pub, which as far as he knew had always been busy, he was a little disturbed by its emptiness, its fading away, all that had once been vibrantly present come to a void. What remained was increasingly meaningless brick, peeling plaster and wood, and what had gone was all that had been imagined by men and women, all that had held it together.

He wondered if the love he'd felt for certain things all his life was the same love as he'd felt when he'd first loved them. For example, he'd loved evening sunlight throughout adulthood. When he had lived in London as a young man he had been touched by the beauty of the sun falling across the red brick of St Pancras station as he viewed it from high up on the Pentonville Road. Sometimes on a fine evening he would go slightly out of his way to see, lit by the low sun, the towers and walls of that exotic building which, as one of his teachers had remarked, looked like a fort or palace transported from the Raj. Or it might just be the quality of light on such evenings so that it was as if the air had become liquid as it bathed the London brick on Upper Street in a faded gold and the Angel and the whole world seemed warmer and more intimate. These late afternoon, early summer evenings were full of promise and you felt that you were moving effortlessly in an element that warmed and buoyed so that fulfilment, this evening and perhaps beyond, would arrive irresistibly. There was a panoramic view he had known, or perhaps imagined, across North London as it descended to the Thames, which made him think, perhaps then but certainly later, of the novels of H.G. Wells which he had read in his teens and which were set in an Edwardian world that was brimming with human energies, fertile and dying—in Tono-Bungay, perhaps, a view across London into Kent, a pulsating life, a human landscape, held forever in amber. Then there was the light filtering through the west-facing windows of the flat he had lived in with his young wife on a beautiful Islington square that had not yet in those middle years of the sixties become gentrified, a blackbird always singing outside. There were other instances that came to him: the sunlight sliding through low windows into the pub that he and Simon Greaves would stop at high up on a country lane on their way back to Simon's house having finished work for the day on a Staffordshire farm; that same light at the ends of long walks in the Lakes, North Wales or the Pennines, coming down with friends from the bare peaks and fells, through woods and by streams, trees and hillsides; a pub garden in Hackney one hot summer evening, near water, perhaps the River Lea, Brian telling him about his feelings for their shared friend Tommy, Da Do Ron Ron on the jukebox, the beer 1/5d a pint; more recently mid-August with Matt walking a ridge that ended above Corfe Castle— half of Dorset, it seemed, into Hampshire and Wiltshire, laid out to the north and west—and ahead of them, warmed by the last of the sun, the beautifully ruined castle and the roofs of the village, the village in which they would soon eat and drink. Above all, where and when he had first become self-consciously aware of this light, the slanting sun across the North Staffordshire countryside and into the coach that ran students from one college campus to another. It was as if the world had been wrapped like a present to be opened later; here was something that was more than a promise; here was a gift, the evening ahead, friendship, laughter, intrigue, perhaps a woman. Now, though, the late sunlight of summer afternoons, still lovely, carried all those memories, the weight of all that had been, had passed, would not be again, and if, for example, he lay on a beach on the south-east coast of Crete, alongside Liz, the softened light and now gentle warmth washing over them as the sun approached the hills to the west, he felt a reluctance to leave, to shower, dress and get the evening, so enticing in itself, under way, a desire to hold the moment, not to let it slip away, to use all of it up, not to waste anything, and that impulse was filled with all those other late afternoons, early evenings, all that joy that had passed and was irrecoverable, so that the feeling of loveliness, of loving, he persuaded himself, was not just tinged with loss, but, strangely transfigured, deformed yet intensified.

PREVIOSULY PUBLISHED AT ERRATUM PRESS

Last Days of Pompeii. Vol.1
Steve Hanson

bone bite snare
Michael Mc Aloran

PUBLISHED BY ERRATUM REPRINTS

The Scourge of Villanie
John Marston

Civilisation Its Cause and Cure
Edward Carpenter

www.ingramcontent.com/pod-product-compliance
Lightning Source LLC
Chambersburg PA
CBHW061616190726
48288CB00007B/2339